USA TODAY BESTSELLI

DALE MAYER

Poison
in the
Pansies

Lovely Lethal Gardens 16

POISON IN THE PANSIES: LOVELY LETHAL GARDENS,
BOOK 16
Dale Mayer
Valley Publishing

Copyright © 2021

This is a work of fiction. Names, characters, places, brands, media, and incidents are either the product of the author's imagination or are used fictitiously. Any resemblance to actual events, locales, or persons, living or dead, is entirely coincidental.

ISBN-13: 978-1-773365-08-4
Print Edition

Books in This Series

About This Book

A new cozy mystery series from *USA Today* best-selling author Dale Mayer. Follow gardener and amateur sleuth Doreen Montgomery—and her amusing and mostly lovable cat, dog, and parrot—as they catch murderers and solve crimes in lovely Kelowna, British Columbia.

Riches to rags ... Chaos has calmed ... At least while out on the lake ... Until poison is found, blowing up the peace again ...

Enjoying a beautiful day on the lake, while Doreen tries her hand at paddleboarding, ends up on an odd note after finding poison in a bed of pansies. She garners a tidbit of information out of her BFF, Corporal Mack Moreau, about a man who'd recently walked into the emergency room, complaining he'd been poisoned.

Only on a threat of good behavior (surely it doesn't count if given under duress), Doreen agrees to stay out of his case. But, as it happens, the mention of poison to her beloved Nan brings up another recent death and an old woman who'd been saying someone was poisoning her for months. Only no one listened. Now she is dead.

When Doreen's case and Mack's collide, she's delighted, and so is he. NOT. But, when Nan decides to join in the sleuthing, with her pal, Richie, it's Doreen's turn to worry—and with good reason!

Sign up to be notified of all Dale's releases here!

http://smarturl.it/dmnewsletter

Prologue

A Full Week Later, … Very Early August

SEVEN DAYS LATER Doreen tried once again—slowly—to stand up on the paddleboard and again promptly wiped out. As she splashed into the water, she heard Mack's laughter ringing beside her. She stood in the shallow water and glared at him, then flipped her hair off her face. "I thought this was supposed to be fun."

"It is fun," he said gently, "Just relax, you're doing great. Besides we needed to get you out and away from all that chaos."

"You've got a point there," she muttered, "but I don't know about *this* kind of chaos."

He stood beside her on his board, with Mugs comfortably slouched on the front end of it. She, on the other hand, was spending more time in the water than atop it. Even Thaddeus was on Mack's shoulder to avoid getting dunked.

"This is unbelievable," she muttered. Goliath had elected to stay on the beach. She felt bad about leaving him there, but, until she could control her board, no point in even thinking that he should come out in the water with her. He'd looked at her in horror when she'd invited him and had promptly stalked off to the side, where he'd sprawled in the sand and had remained, tail twitching the whole time.

"Try again," Mack said. "Now remember. It's all about balance. You need to relax."

"Relax?" she murmured. "I'll relax you."

He grinned. "Keep up that fighting spirit. It's good to see."

She brushed her hair off her forehead and slowly clambered onto the paddleboard. The water was warm; the sky was blue. The sun was shining, and it was a gorgeous day. She managed to stand steady on the board and, with a triumphant turn, she spun to look at Mack. "I did it," she crowed. And immediately wiped out again.

When she came back up, sputtering this time, she just stood in the shallow water, her arms resting on the board. "I think it's coffee time."

He grinned. "In your world it's always coffee time."

"Always."

"That's fine," he said, "but you have to get back up on the board, so we can paddle you to the shore."

She turned to stare at the beach, her gaze easily picking up Goliath. He hadn't moved. "Ugh, you know that'll take an hour. So maybe only half that but still…"

"Don't be discouraged. Next time you'll do that much better. I promise," he said. "You will."

"I didn't realize I was so uncoordinated," she muttered.

"I don't even know that it's about coordination," he said. "Most of it's balance."

"And yet you seem to be doing fine. And you said you'd never done this before."

"I hadn't."

She glared. "You know that it's really not fair that you

should take to something like this so easily, while I'm an obvious failure."

"You're hardly a failure," he said. "And, speaking of which—"

She glared at him. "There is no topic where that is a suitable intro. Nobody wants to think of being a failure."

"I was just wondering," he said gently, "if you'd heard from my brother."

"Several times, but mostly because I'm the one hassling him."

He grinned. "I like the fact that you're pushing to have that divorce taken care of."

"I don't want anything to do with my ex, soon-to-be ex," she said, "and the sooner this is done, the less stress for me."

"Oh, I agree," he said. "I just wasn't sure how you felt about it."

"You were just afraid that I would go back to him," she teased as she attempted to get on her board. When there was a long silence, she glared up at him.

He shrugged, but she could see the color mounting high in his cheekbones. She stopped and stared. "And I told you very clearly that I wouldn't."

"I know you did." His lips quirked. "But, in my job, I've heard a lot of women say otherwise."

"No, they say the same thing, but then they change their mind. I get it," she said. "I'm not really into changing my mind right now."

"Good," he said. "So can we get moving?"

"I hope so." She managed to get back up on the board, and, kneeling, she slowly paddled her way back to the shore. "I can kneel just fine." She slid off on the other side at the beach.

Mack slowly paddled toward her, standing calm and graceful on his board. She looked at him in admiration. "I should really hate you for this," she said, "but you look just great up there. I mean it. It's a totally natural thing for you."

"And it will become that way for you as well."

She didn't want to say that she doubted it, but, well, she doubted it.

He shook his head. "Nope, none of that," he said. "Give it time."

"Time is something I do happen to have."

"Yeah, until you get a job anyway."

She winced. "Did you really have to go there?"

He chuckled. "Hey, you've had a couple callbacks at least."

"Yeah, but all they wanted to do was ask me questions," she wailed, "about all the different cases I've been involved in."

"Of course," he said, "that does make sense."

"Yet there are more cold cases. They matter too. How come there isn't more curiosity about those?"

"They do matter, but everyone wants juicy details," he said. "Remember, you're the one who went down this pathway even though I warned you. You wanted a quiet life out of the public eye. How did that work out for you?" At least his tone was cheeky, not arrogant.

Still she glared at him. "Of course I went down this pathway," she muttered. "Besides, I'm doing a lot of good."

"You are," he said, "and, even though I wasn't terribly happy to find out about Gloria's past, I still think we're all better off having it out in open."

"What about Elle?"

"That's a different story," he said. "The lawyers are still

fussing over that one."

"Can we prove that she killed Gloria?"

"No, I don't think so. They'll probably end up with some plea deal."

"Whatever works," she said. "And is it true that she's not getting anything from Gloria's estate?"

"That is true," he said. "It'll all go to charity. Which means, sadly the place will get sold."

"Yes, and what about dingbat?" she asked, his name escaping her mind for a moment.

He looked at her. "You mean, Stranden?"

"Yes," she said, "Stranden."

"That's another problem. He was cleared over the car accident many years ago. But for aiding and abetting a murder? Well, that's another thing for the DA to sort out."

"It's been a lot of years."

"It has, indeed, but again it's a murder case."

"Right," she muttered. "No statute of limitations. No closing those."

"We want to close them," he corrected her. "They just stay open until they're solved."

"Right." She pushed the paddleboard to the sand, and at that point, watched as Goliath sauntered toward her. "Do you think he'd ever get used to being on a board?"

"I won't say never." Mack hopped down lightly beside the cat, with Thaddeus still sitting nicely on his shoulder, and Mugs now happily paddling around on the shoreline. "Goliath has done more than I would have ever thought possible for a cat."

"He has been pretty amenable to many things." She pulled the paddleboard up on the sand. "Now what?"

"We have a picnic. Remember?"

5

"Oh yes," she said. "Did you bring a thermos of coffee?"

"I did." He looked around the beach. "There's a spot over by the gardens." Mugs raced up, shaking water everywhere.

"That sounds perfect."

She lifted her inflatable paddleboard, carried it off to the side, and put it down on the grass. Then she pulled out her towel from the bags that they had brought and Mack had kept on his board, spread it out, and threw herself down. As soon as she was stretched out, she gave a big happy sigh.

"You doing okay?" he asked.

"I am," she said. "It's a beautiful day. Thank you for this."

"Hey, I borrowed the equipment, so all I really put together was the picnic," he said. "We both needed to get out for a bit."

"Absolutely," she said. "And this is lovely." As she relaxed, she added, "How come I'm the only one who's wet?"

"That's because you spent more time in the water than out." And so much laughter was in his voice that she rolled over and grinned at him.

"It was fun though."

"Good," he said, with a big smile. "I'm glad to hear that. We'll do it again."

"Maybe I should try your board next time."

"You think my board is the magical answer?" he teased.

"Maybe," she said. "Mine certainly didn't work worth a darn."

"I don't think the board had anything to do with it."

She glared at him but no real heat was in her gaze. She rolled over and took a look around. "Didn't you say there was coffee?"

"There is." He pulled out the thermos from the other bag and handed it to her. She sat up and filled the cap, looking around. "I wasn't really expecting so many beaches here."

"There are a lot of them," he said. "This is Sarsons Beach. It's got a nice little lawn. The beach itself is rocky though. Several of the others are sandy. But not this one."

She studied the footwear that he had told her to get for this venture. "And I guess it's a good thing I wore these. Otherwise it might be hard to walk."

"It can be, here."

"Still, it's good," she said, "and it's a perfect day." She pulled her legs up and sat cross-legged, sipping her coffee, as she stared out around her. It was one of the few times she had put on a bathing suit all year. As it was, she felt good. She'd gained a little bit more weight, so she didn't look quite so gaunt, and, although she was skinnier than she was used to, she still felt healthy and vibrant. And that was worth a lot.

She let out a heavy sigh, and he looked at her quizzically. She shrugged. "Just, uh, …decompressing."

He nodded. "Glad to hear that. You've been through a lot lately."

She nodded. "You don't even realize how much it all adds up, until it all adds up." Then she let out another heavy sigh, and they just kept coming after that. As if she really needed this. After her coffee was gone, when she laid down and nodded off, he let her.

When she rolled over not long afterward, she lifted her head to see Mugs stretched beside her, Goliath stretched along her side, and Thaddeus was at her throat muttering softly. "Wow, I think I was out there for a bit."

He smiled. "You were tired."

"Yeah, I sure was." She blinked several times then yawned. A moment later, she said, "But I'm feeling better now."

"Good," he said. "Ready for some food?"

She laughed. "Have you ever known me *not* to be ready for food?" She slowly sat up. "I'll use the washroom first though." She hopped up, walked over to the public bathroom, and, when she was done, she returned, this time walking through the gardens. "They're really pretty. Too bad I didn't put more effort into getting a city contract for the gardens."

Mack watched her as she strolled looking at the flowers. "Something will break for you soon," he said confidently. "With them moving the Welcome to Kelowna sign to a new spot, they will probably open a new bid."

"Yeah." Maybe, but she wasn't holding out hope. "How about the will? Any update on that?"

"For your lawyer?"

"Yes, Robin."

"Well, you know that it's good to go. But all that lawyerly stuff has to happen."

Meaning I don't get anything until after probate?"

"Yes," he said, "so it'll be a few months yet. Well a lot of months. I think it's nine months."

She snorted. "You'd think they could give me something."

"Have you asked the estate lawyer?"

She frowned. "No, I didn't want to let him know how broke I really was."

He chuckled. "In that case you might want to reconsider. Maybe he can give you an advance for expenses or something. I'm not sure how that works."

"He said it was all about the probate and due process and that he would let me know as soon as he could. Also he hasn't given me any figures, as the property needs to be sold, and there are outstanding bills to be paid by her estate first."

"It's still worth checking to see if he might give you something up front to help out."

She shrugged. "I mean, if I have to keep going without," she said, "it will be fine for a few more months, I guess."

"What about Wendy?"

"I have to wait another week, I think, to get the next consignment check," she said, "They are coming, although not as big as the first one. Still, hopefully they'll be enough to keep me going for a few more months." She shook her head. "After that, well, I don't know."

"Don't worry about it," he said, "because a lot can happen in those weeks."

"I know," she said. "It's just become more of a habit to worry than not."

"And I get it," he said, "but you're doing okay, honestly?"

"I guess so." She looked at the huge bunches of yellow and purple pansies nearby and walked closer. "These are really pretty." A big pile of dead ones was in the center though. She frowned. "Except for these guys. They need some care. Is this a city park?"

"Yes, so the city gardeners look after it. When they can…"

She nodded, then walked closer to where the dead plants were and noted powdery stuff all around the base of it. "It looks like something was dumped here, something toxic—to the plants anyway."

"Don't touch the stuff then."

She stepped back, looked down at her feet, then winced. "I better go rinse off." She headed to the water, swooshed her feet around a little to clean them off, and then she came back out. "You know, Mack. If families come here, you might want to get that cleaned up."

He looked at the flowers. "Do you think it's bad news?"

She shrugged. "It killed the pansies. I know we haven't had any rain lately, but the rest of the flowers look okay. It's just that one spot. And it's not doing much for the plants. I'd hate to see a kid or some pets get into it. It gave me a tingly feeling on my toes."

At that, he frowned, then hopped up and walked over to take a closer look. "A partially buried box is in the sand here." He took a closer look at it and frowned. "Rat poison."

She looked up at him. "Why would somebody put that here?"

He shook his head. "It doesn't matter why they put it here. They shouldn't have. This is a public site." He made a quick phone call. "We should get this cleaned up in no time."

She nodded. "So please tell me there haven't been any current deaths by poisoning." He stared at her, so she shrugged. "I mean, if you ran here, and you had a murder weapon in your hand," she said, "what better place than to toss it into a garden, where nobody will see it?"

He looked at her, then at the flower bed. "Crap."

She stared at him. "What?"

"We've been keeping it under wraps," he said, "but two days ago we had a man walk into the hospital, saying he'd been poisoned. He was admitted immediately, but he didn't make it."

She stared at Mack. "Poisoned … in the pansies?"

He squeezed his eyes shut, then glared at her. "No! And again it's not a cold case, so you stay out of it."

She frowned, but inside she was like, *Poisoned in the Pansies.* Perfect. And she grinned at him. "Of course I'll stay out of your case."

He glared at her, while she just beamed. "At least until I can't."

And then she burst out laughing.

Chapter 1

Next Day, Monday Afternoon, Early August

D OREEN MONTGOMERY KEPT looking at her watch,
knowing that Corporal Mack Moreau would show up
any moment. Her mind buzzed with questions. They'd spent
most of Sunday together, until their plans had been completely kiboshed when he got another call in. Curious, and
yet determined to find out, she'd asked him about that call
several times, when they had talked throughout the day, but
he wouldn't give her any answers.

Of course he wouldn't, which meant it was a current
case. Of course it was. He didn't deal with cold cases, unless
she dumped them in his lap.

She almost laughed at that because dumping things in
his lap was something she had become pretty good at. And,
so far, he'd been absolutely great at picking up the ball and
helping her out. But she also knew that his hands were tied
more often than not, and he just couldn't do some things.
Which is also when she tended to jump in without him to
get done what she needed. But, at this point in time, she
wanted to know if his current case was connected to what
they had found at Sarsons Beach Park.

She had driven back early this morning, but the box of poison was gone. Now she was relieved, but, at the same time, she wanted an update. She looked down at Mugs, who sat ever-so-attentively at her side, staring at her lunch. "It's a salad. I'm getting better in the kitchen, but I'm surely not to that point where I'm cooking your meals, buddy."

Mugs woofed at her.

She laughed, walked over to the cupboard, and found the dog treats. As soon as she pulled out the bag, Goliath sauntered forward, and Thaddeus—who'd been sleeping on the roost nearby in the living room—immediately opened his eyes. "Thaddeus is here. Thaddeus is here."

She laughed and added affectionately, "You're all here, *idjit*."

He cocked his head at her, opened one eye, and just gave her that gimlet stare. He'd been doing that more often, especially whenever she gave him a term that he didn't particularly like.

"Fine, okay." She rolled her eyes. "I apologize for calling you an *idjit*." Not sure he understood the apology part. He still glared at her. She shook her head and chuckled. "I don't know if I've told you lately, guys, but you have certainly enriched my life."

At that, Mugs woofed again.

Doreen stood here, staring at them, a questioning look on her face. Meanwhile, Mugs nudged her hand, waiting for the treats there. "Oh, right." She laughed at the situation. She was calling them idiots, when she was one too, it seemed.

At least she could laugh about it and now knew, with her growing self-confidence, to acknowledge that she was smart enough when needed. She bent down and gave Mugs a treat and then walked over and pulled out treats for Goliath. After she gave him one, Mugs raced over and barked, looking for another treat.

"No." She shook her head. "You just got your treat. And you know that Goliath and Thaddeus also get treats of their own, right?"

Mugs just gave her the most mournful look, with those huge brown eyes of his, and she felt her heart starting to melt. But she shook her head. "No. I know Mack is coming, and he's likely to give you treats too." She sighed. "We have to consider our budget and must also keep that waistline of yours somewhat in check."

Of course that just reminded her that they hadn't been for much of a W—*walk*—today. And she'd gotten to the point of saying W these days, even in her mind, because not only did Mugs understand the word but Goliath did also, and so did Thaddeus now. Sometimes she thought Thaddeus could read her mind because, even now, he hopped up and looked at her. "Walk, walk, walk."

And that started Mugs off in a cacophony of barking.

She glared at Thaddeus. "Why? Why do you have to go ruin the peace and quiet?"

Instead of giving her a well-thought-out answer, he looked at her, bent over, and bobbed his head up and down. "*He-he-he-he.*"

She glared at him. "You know that you're becoming a real pain, right?"

He stopped and looked at her and blinked.

And once again she felt like a heel. "Fine," she muttered. "While we should wait for Mack, let's go down to the creek." She opened the back door, letting Mugs lead the way, as he raced out into the backyard, barking, but at nothing. She shook her head at that, looked down at Goliath. He remained stretched out on the kitchen floor, eyeing the open door.

"Do you want to come, buddy?"

Goliath sniffed the air, as if to say, *Hah, you finally invited me.* And, with that royal attitude, he sauntered out the door, even as Thaddeus hopped onto the railing out on the deck—a deck that she absolutely adored—and then onto her shoulder, as she walked past. She looked over at him. "You could walk, you know."

And he curled his head against her shoulder and whispered in a low voice, "Thaddeus loves Nan."

"Yeah, I'm not Nan."

He'd started doing that a couple times a day too. Doreen wasn't sure if it was just about seeing Nan or if this was Thaddeus's way of telling Doreen that he needed more attention. He lifted his head and looked at her with that stare. "Nan, Nan, Nan."

Thaddeus was doing his best to convince Doreen to walk down to Nan's. She groaned. "It'll be dinnertime at Rosemoor soon. We'd have to come right back. We don't want to interrupt Nan's dinner or not be here for Mack, now do we?"

Almost immediately she got a text on her phone. It was from Mack.

I'll be an hour late for dinner.

She stared down at it, even as Thaddeus peered at her phone too. On her shoulder, he repeated, "*He-he-he-he.*"

Wow, he can read my mind and my phone too? Doreen shook her head, giving in. "Okay, fine. We'll walk down to Rosemoor, have a quick visit with Nan, and then we'll come back to meet Mack." She headed along the river and quickly pulled out her phone and dialed Nan.

"Hi," Nan cried out. "You coming for a visit?"

"Well, I was thinking of coming for a short one. Mack will be a little late for dinner."

"Ah," Nan noted, with that wealth of innuendo in her tone.

Doreen glared at her phone. "But I'm only coming if you don't bug me about Mack."

At that, Nan laughed out loud. "Oh my, it's that serious, *huh?*"

"It's not *that serious* at all," Doreen argued, her tone turned stiff.

"Come on down, child," Nan replied. "It'd be absolutely lovely to see you. I've missed you. I was hoping to see you this past weekend."

Doreen winced. "I know. I'm sorry. I'll explain when I get there."

She put away her phone, and, with the others in tow, she walked along the river, amazed at how much lower it was now. Mugs could walk into the river bed several feet away from the bank now, without getting wet at all. With the three of them tagging along at various speeds, they finally made it to Nan's.

As Doreen walked across the grass, not on the stepping stones, she still winced. If Rosemoor's old gardener had witnessed her doing this, he would have been on her case terribly. She made her way across the grass to find Nan on her little patio, waiting for them.

Nan smiled up at Doreen, then bent to greet Mugs and Goliath, who absolutely adored her. When she straightened, she smiled at Thaddeus on Doreen's shoulder and then studied her granddaughter and noted, "You look lovely."

Doreen raised an eyebrow. "I look the same as always."

"Nope, not quite. You've put on a little bit of weight, and you look like you're …" Nan paused. "*Settled.*"

At that, Doreen frowned. "That doesn't sound too nice."

"Oh, doesn't it?" Nan asked. "I thought it was a lovely word. Let's just say that you don't look like you're on the edge all the time anymore. You've taken a step back from the cliff."

"What cliff?" Doreen asked, confused. She pointed at the little patio table and chairs. Then sat herself.

"The one called *life*," Nan noted gently. "You don't look like you're starving or worried about where your next paycheck's coming from."

"Well, I should be," Doreen muttered. She watched as Nan sat down and poured tea for them both. "Apparently everything'll still be a while."

"Some of these things take time," Nan agreed. "But you will let me know if you run into serious trouble, right?"

Doreen laughed. "You know perfectly well I would try very hard to *not* have to ask you for any more help. You've been so generous already."

"Generous, my foot." Nan shrugged. "You're my grand-daughter. I'm entitled to spoil you."

"And believe me. I greatly appreciate it. Mugs and I would be homeless without you. And I have so much pending money in progress, but nothing's come to fruition yet."

"What about Robin's will?" Nan asked, referring to Doreen's former divorce lawyer, who'd been murdered, but even stranger, somehow in a bit of clarity—maybe even anticipating her untimely death—had left everything to Doreen.

"It's in probate, and they've still got to sell the house and her other physical holdings," Doreen explained. "Plus, somewhere along the line, whenever that's all taken care of, I'll get an idea of what kind of money is involved and when I'll get it."

"Well, she owned property in Vancouver." Nan beamed at the thought. "We know what the property prices there are like."

"We do." Doreen shook her head and threw up her hands in frustration. "But that doesn't mean I'll get much for it. Besides, I don't even know what all she owned, much less what she might owe to everybody."

"No, I suppose not," Nan agreed. "The lawyers will definitely take a pile off the top, won't they?"

"I expect so," she murmured. "So far my experience with lawyers has not been that great."

"What about Nick? Mack's brother should be a good one."

"I keep bugging him. I'm wondering if he's ignoring me."

"Maybe." Nan had a sip of tea and then laughed. "But don't stop. You know how I feel about the squeaky wheel."

"I do, indeed." She smiled. "And I don't think he's deliberately trying to ignore me. I think my ex is trying to ignore him on the whole divorce settlement issue, so I guess Nick has nothing to tell me yet."

"Of course your husband—"

"Soon-to-be ex-husband," Doreen corrected.

"Yes, dear. But technically and legally still your horrid husband. Anyway, I wouldn't be at all surprised if he tries to argue against your bequeathment from the will."

Doreen stared at Nan in shock. "Robin's will?"

At that, Nan nodded. She lowered her voice, leaned forward. "I mean, after all, they were having an affair. I'm sure he had expectations of getting something from her."

"*Great*," Doreen muttered, "that'll send everything backward in terms of getting things settled."

"Doesn't mean he has a leg to stand on in that department of course," Nan added.

"No. But just the thought of it is enough to make the hairs go up on the back of my neck. He'll just delay what is already a very slow process. I just want to totally be rid of him. Is that too much to ask?" She shuddered. "I am getting a check from Wendy here pretty soon, so I have that coming in." She nodded. "That will help tide me over."

"Good," Nan replied. "And you still haven't heard anything regarding the antiques yet?"

"No. Scott did say that a catalog with all your items has been mailed to me though." She added, "That'll be pretty exciting to see how well the restoration went on everything."

"It will. You know that to do these things right, it'll take time."

"I know." She sighed. "But *taking time* is a whole different story than taking *this much* time."

"It's antiques, and they are very high-end antiques," Nan stated. "You could have an awful lot of money there to deal with eventually."

"Well, I'd be happy to have that problem." Doreen smiled. "I don't mind helping out with all these cold cases. Yet if I could make a living at it? Well, that would make my life easier."

"Would it? What about when you have all that money?"

"You keep talking about *all that money*. I don't know how much that money totals, and I don't know how much or what one would do with that money because I don't have any figures yet. Are we talking millions? Are we talking hundreds of thousands? Are we talking enough to pay the house taxes and the utilities before winter? Or are we talking like I have enough to smile about, but, hey, I need a nine-to-five day job?"

"Well, I would hope we're talking millions," Nan replied quietly. "I spent a lot of money on those antiques back in the day, and, with inflation, everything has just gotten that much more expensive."

She stared at her. "Well, millions would be lovely," she noted cautiously. "But because we don't have any actual figures, I don't want to count on anything."

"And then there's Robin's will of course."

"And again, that's not necessarily anything I can count on." Doreen thought about it for a moment and then added reluctantly, "Mack did suggest that maybe I contact Robin's estate lawyer to see if there was any way to get any of the money now, so that I could pay some bills."

Nan leaned forward. "Oh dear, are you that broke?"

"No, no. Not broke exactly but probate's supposed to take about nine months."

At that, Nan nodded. "And you don't have enough money for nine months, do you?"

"I don't know what I have enough money for," she replied. "It seems like, every time I turn around, I find expenses that I wasn't considering."

"And of course you now have Mack to consider."

Doreen stared at her grandmother, confused. "And what do I have to consider about Mack?" she asked in astonishment. "If anything, he pays for so much more than I do. At least when it comes to food, he won't let me pay."

"Well, there is that, but you know his birthday is coming up. It's not for another month or so though. Still, time to think about what you want to do."

At that, Doreen sat back and stared at her, nonplussed. Mugs leaned his head against her leg in solidarity, as she mindlessly dropped a hand to scratch behind his ears.

Nan chuckled. "You didn't know, did you?"

She slowly shook her head. "No, I didn't know. Now I'll just worry all that much more."

"Worry, why?"

"Well, what will I get him?" she asked in astonishment. "Even if money were not an issue—but it is—what could I possibly give him that he probably already has or doesn't want or need? I mean, the man does everything for me. There's hardly anything I can do that is nice enough for him."

"Well, you do a lot of nice things for him now," Nan noted quietly.

"I don't," she argued. "For instance, he's coming for dinner tonight, but he's cooking the main meal, bringing the groceries too. I made a salad." She raised both palms. "Like, whoopie-do."

Nan chuckled. "But you're also spending a lot of time with him," she added, with emphasis.

She stared at Nan suspiciously. "And?"

"You know that he wants a lot more."

"Well, I'm not giving it to him," Doreen replied. Then blushed.

Nan burst out laughing. "And that's absolutely right. You should hold out and make sure what you have is for real."

"What are you talking about?"

"Oh, dear. I can see that husband of yours really did a number on you. Mack is a good man. Just remember that. He's nothing like your husband, soon-to-be *ex*-husband."

"Thank heavens," Doreen whispered. "One was enough."

"And you are away from that evil man. I'm so thankful for that."

"Me too," Doreen added. "And that I had you to go to."

Nan nodded. "Exactly. You need healthy relationships in your life. And I'm talking about two issues here. One is your growing romantic relationship with Mack, which you should address when you are ready and not a moment sooner. Two is that you already give Mack some pretty priceless gifts, even now, just with your friendship."

"But what do I give Mack?" Doreen asked, obviously confused and growing a little bit perturbed. "I know I'm not stupid, at least not as stupid as my ex made me out to be, but this conversation is making me feel stupid, Nan."

Nan patted her granddaughter's hand. "I'm just saying that you give Mack an awful lot of things that money can't buy, like spending time with him, giving him a pleasant home away from home—or even a home away from the office. I've seen the two of you banter back and forth. In his position, I doubt too many people speak up to him like you do, who dare to tell him the truth. He's got to admire you and to respect you for that, … even if you do get pushy about your cold cases."

"Hey, I'm not pushy," Doreen argued.

"Okay. You're curious. Is that better?" Her grandmother smirked.

"Fine." Doreen huffed and leaned back into her chair.

"Anyway, back to my original point here. You don't

know what an oasis you probably are to that man."

Doreen frowned. "Oasis?"

Nan nodded. "A safe place where he's accepted for who he is. Everybody needs that in life. To belong. To feel appreciated for just being themselves."

"That's true," Doreen murmured. "That's what I want as well."

"Exactly," Nan crowed. "So don't sell yourself short. You are measuring everything by money, which is easy to do when you are as broke as you are, but remember. There are other measurements, like kindness, generosity, being true to self, allowing others to be true to themselves. So you have plenty you could, and you already do give Mack, and it's not always about money. Now, that said, how long will you make the poor man wait?"

Doreen snorted. "You just told me that I should wait until I'm ready."

"You should wait until you're sure that's what you want," she replied carefully. "But that's a different story than making him wait." Doreen stared at her grandmother in complete confusion. Nan tilted her head, smiled, and continued. "You know that words would go a long way for him."

"So would a lot of other things." She gave Nan an eye roll. "I'm not ready for that either."

"And you don't have to be," Nan agreed. "But you know where you're heading."

"I know where we're heading," she noted cautiously. "At the moment, that doesn't mean that I am ready to be heading anywhere faster."

"Has he pushed you?"

"No, of course not." Then she sighed. "He's actually

been very patient."

"And there's a reason for that."

Doreen stared at Nan, frowning.

"Because he cares," she stated gently.

At that, Doreen slowly nodded. "It would *appear* so."

"And you're still being so cautious about it." Nan chuckled. "We're talking about Mack here, not Jack the Ripper."

Doreen shrugged. "I'm not divorced yet. And that marriage was enough to scare me off of relationships completely."

"That doesn't surprise me." Nan shook her head, her grimace evident. "Your ex was quite a pain in the butt."

"Yeah, and he still is," she muttered.

"Have you heard from him recently?"

"No, thank heavens," she blurted out. "But that doesn't mean he isn't out there, waiting for an opportunity to get back into my life."

At that, Nan stared at her, her jaw dropping. "You wouldn't let him, would you?"

"No, no, *no*. Of course not," she stated and frowned. "But that doesn't mean that I don't feel like he's hounding me somewhat."

"Well, that's scary," Nan admitted. "Even hearing that is very disconcerting. He's not a nice man."

"Ya think? No, I absolutely am not letting him back in my life," she muttered. "But that doesn't mean that he won't try something." Doreen sighed, frowned, then faced her grandmother. "After all, you just said he might stop me from getting anything from Robin's will. And, since we know how he is about money and not wanting to let it go, if he loses that fight, then he might think a proper plan B would be to hook up with me to live off Robin's money. ... Or worse."

"Don't go there. I know you deal with too many cold cases to not have it color your thinking too." Nan sat back, studying her granddaughter. "Sounds like you need to have a talk with Mack about bigger issues than just your relationship."

"And what am I supposed to say?" she asked. "I mean, Mack already looks after me in many, many ways. He's overly protective now. If I talk to him about this, these concerns about my ex—and they are just suspicions, not facts, not evidence, and you know how Mack feels about that—yet he could truly go overboard, sleeping in his truck outside my house, just to catch my ex in the act of stalking or whatever."

"Sure." Nan reached over and poured tea into Doreen's still half-full cup that she'd forgotten about that. "I do worry about him though."

"About my ex?" Doreen asked.

Nan rolled her eyes. "No, of course not. He can go take a long walk off a short bridge, and the sooner, the better, as far as I'm concerned." She snorted. "I mean, Robin was bad news, but she tried to do the right thing at the end. Now if your not-yet-ex-husband would kick the bucket, it would make a lot of things really nice right now."

"I won't say it wouldn't because it would certainly make my life a lot easier in terms of getting a divorce," Doreen agreed, "but you also know that, just because it could make my life easier, doesn't mean I'll sit here and hold my breath that something untoward would happen to him."

"He does have a lot of nasty people in his world. Maybe one of them will do you a favor."

She chuckled. "Good thing nobody can hear us because, if he drops dead, and somebody heard this conversation, you know everybody would point the finger at me."

"Sweetheart," Nan drawled and gave her granddaughter a droll look, "you're the double-crossed and betrayed spouse. The public would blame you anyway." And, with that eye-opening thought, Nan picked up her tea and asked, "Now, what's your latest case?"

"I don't have one," she replied.

Nan looked at her over the edge of her teacup. "Really? Why don't I believe you?"

"No, really I don't," she confirmed, "but Mack does, and that's what I'm hoping he'll talk to me about when he gets back."

"Tell me more."

She nodded. "Well, it's partly why I didn't see you over the weekend." She explained about their beach outing.

"Oh, I once went skinny-dipping at Sarsons."

"Nan!"

"I was young too, dear. So tell me more."

"Mack gave me a paddleboarding session. I'm not athletic at all." And then she continued with the embarrassing details, Nan laughing quietly at her antics. Doreen grinned. "Honestly, I was terrible out there."

"You might have been terrible out there, my dear," she grinned, patting Doreen's hand, "but you went out there, and you tried something new, and that is worth so much."

"You're a great cheerleader," Doreen noted. "Honestly, it was pretty sad."

Nan laughed. "I bet it would have been a hugely fun time with Mack regardless. And I'm so happy you went out to enjoy the beach. It's a beautiful area of town."

"It is, indeed," Doreen muttered. "Anyway, we found this half-buried carton of rat poison in one of the gardens at that park," she explained. "And I don't know if it had any effect on the pansies, but something had killed the pansies around the box. I called Mack over because of the pansies, not even seeing the box, but I did note the white powder scattered about. While Mack was looking closer at the bed, he found the box. He called someone at the office to make sure that somebody came and got it."

Doreen stared off in the distance. "But you know what? I went there this morning to check to make sure the box was gone. And it was, although I don't know who picked it up." She frowned thoughtfully. "Something else to ask Mack."

"And what difference does it make?" Nan asked curiously.

"What if the wrong person picked up the poison?"

"How would discarded rat poison possibly play into a case?"

"I'm not sure," Doreen replied, "but he did mention something to me." And she lowered her voice, leaned forward. "You can't tell anybody."

Nan crossed her heart with a finger in the childish movement that was as old as time. "I promise." Doreen gave her grandmother a stern look, and Nan nodded. "I know. There are times when I can talk, and there are times when I can't. This is one where I can't." And then she grinned. "Tell me more."

So Doreen filled her in about the man who had gone to the cops, saying that he'd been poisoned. And that he'd died not too long afterward.

Nan opened her mouth, stared at her, and then slowly closed it. "Oh my. Did Mack have anything else to add?"

Doreen gave her a wry look. "Yeah, that it was a current case, not a cold case, and for me to butt out."

At that, Nan burst out laughing. "Oh, I do love to hear that."

Doreen looked at her. "Why?" she asked.

"Because of course you'll ignore him." And then she gave her that gimlet look that reminded her of Thaddeus and asked, "Right?"

Chapter 2

M ACK DID ARRIVE an hour and a half later for their
dinner date, but she was home, waiting with the
animals. When he pulled up into the driveway, Mugs raced
to the front door, barking and wagging his tail, his whole
body squirming and wiggling, like something was seriously
wrong with him. Doreen laughed at his antics, as she opened
up the door to let Mack in.

"Hey," he greeted her.

She heard such fatigue in his voice that she felt bad.
"Hey. Long day, *huh?*"

He nodded. "Seriously long day." But he bent to greet
Mugs. "Yet I have to tell you, having a welcome like this?
Well, it makes an awful lot of pretty ugly things go away."

"I hear you there."

He managed to finally get the front door closed and to
get Mugs calmed down just enough for Thaddeus to hop up
on Mugs first and then onto Mack's arm and rubbed his
head against Mack's shoulder.

"Not sure what's wrong with the animals right now," she
noted, "but apparently they missed you."

"Right. I was just here yesterday."

"But you left early." She laughed. "It's almost like they know that they got cheated out of that time."

"Of course." He grinned, as he patted Goliath, who was sitting at the top of the cat tree, his tail twitching in disdain. "Except for this guy, I never get quite the same welcome outta him."

"Are you kidding? He's sitting there, letting you touch him," she joked. "That *is* a welcome."

He laughed. "You know what? That's probably quite true."

As they all walked into the kitchen, he said, "I am hungry too."

"Well, I've made a salad," she noted, "and we have steaks marinating, and I did prep some veggies."

He looked at what she'd done and then smiled. "You know something? You've come a long way."

"Just not long enough," she replied. "You're tired. I've done nothing all day, so, by rights, I should have this well and truly cooked for you, but it involves the gas barbecue pit."

He walked out onto the deck, propping open the back door. "We do need the barbecue, so I'll light it right now." And, with that, he quickly turned it on.

She watched while it ignited. "That's the part I don't like," she murmured.

He looked over at her, as they both returned to the kitchen. "What part?"

"The gas part," she replied.

"It's pretty safe."

"*Pretty safe*, yes," she muttered. "But *pretty safe* isn't the same thing as *safe*."

"And *being safe* isn't the same thing as *totally safe*?"

POISON IN THE PANSIES

"Okay, putting it that way, I guess it's foolish." But she shrugged. "It's just one more of those little quirks that I have to deal with."

"Nobody said you had to deal with them all right now," he noted quietly.

She laughed. "You're always so quick to let me off the hook."

"Hey, is that wrong?"

"I don't know," she murmured. "I wouldn't want you to make excuses for me."

"A lot of people don't like barbecues for exactly the same reason you gave," he stated.

She looked over at him. "Really?"

"Absolutely. So, no, I'm not giving you an excuse. I'm explaining to you that this is just life."

"Okay," she agreed, "I don't feel quite so bad then."

"Why would you feel bad anyway?" he asked. "Besides, it gives me a reason to come over."

At that, she slid him a sideways look. "You need a reason?" she asked quietly.

"Nope," he replied, with a cheeky grin. "Besides, I mean, if you had your way, you would have chased me out of here a long time ago."

"Would I have now?" she asked, the corner of her lips twitching. "You do spend a lot of time here."

"I do, indeed," he agreed. "I absolutely love it here." And, with that, he snagged the plate of steaks and the veggies and stepped out onto the deck.

She wasn't sure what to make of his comment. Was it just the location? Was it the company? She didn't know. She traipsed out behind him. "Even when I hound you all the time about your cases?"

"Yeah, and wouldn't it be nice if you didn't?" He sighed. "Yet it's part of your charm."

"Oh, at least I have charm," she muttered.

He looked over at her. "Rough day?"

"I don't know." She gave him a lazy one-arm shrug. "Kind of an off day. Didn't know what I should be doing really. So I did some cleaning."

Mack chuckled. "That's like everything to do with applying on the internet nowadays," he noted. "It's almost anonymous, and you put in all these applications, like deep-sixing it into the garbage can."

"I get it," she agreed. "I just … it's so different from when I was a teenager, applying for work."

"You have been going in person to places though, haven't you?"

"I have," she replied. "And I even asked at the Chinese food place, when I was there a few days ago. I went and treated myself to one dish," she shared. "And I asked him if he was looking for help. He gave me such a horrified look that I realized he didn't think I would be good for business."

When no answer came from Mack, she looked over to see his face working hard, as he tried to hold back his laughter. When she'd caught him, and he knew he had been caught, he burst out laughing.

"I didn't consider that I would be bad for business." She raised her hands in surrender. "I just thought I could help out."

"And you could," he agreed. "But he's right too. I mean, people might just come because you're an oddity. People might just come to get your autograph or to see the animals. However, I doubt you could bring your pets to work every day," he noted. "I'm not sure that having you working there will make anybody come to get more Chinese."

"What if they just came to get Chinese food and not more than Chinese food?" she asked in a confused voice. "Surely that would be okay."

"Maybe, maybe not. I hate to say it, but a lot of people are very superstitious. And you're dealing with a lot of murders. Maybe they think being around you will just invite more bad news to come in their direction. People make illogical links all the time. They could link you with sending them to jail because you do that, as you close these murder cases."

She stared at him. "But that's not fair," she cried out. "How can people hold that against me?"

"I don't know. Maybe because you keep getting involved in all these murder cases."

She glared at him. "That would still be very narrow-minded thinking on their part."

He wrapped an arm around her shoulders, pulled her close, and gave her a big hug. "See? This is why I like coming over here." He grinned. "Don't ever change."

She leaned back, looked up at him. "I don't even know how to change."

He dropped a kiss on her temple. "I have to get the veggies on." And, with that, he headed to the deck again and quickly popped all the veggies onto the barbecue.

She watched with interest, still standing pretty close to him, wondering at the camaraderie and that connection that always seemed to exist between them. She sighed. "Nan says we're getting really close."

He looked over at her. "Of course Nan would say that. Has she put bets on our love life yet?"

She stared at him, nonplussed. "She wouldn't …"

His eyebrows went up, questioning her.

"At least I would hope not," she replied in dire tones. And then she stopped, looked at him, and asked, "She wouldn't, would she?"

"Yes, she would," he stated, his voice firm. "Nothing you and I can say will change that."

She sat down on one of the nearby deck chairs and stared glumly out at the river. "She's really got a problem, doesn't she?"

"It's a problem, yes, but it's a good-hearted problem and not one that any of us will go after her for," he noted gently. "As long as she keeps it friendly and is not getting people in trouble, then we're willing to overlook a certain amount of this bookie stuff that she's got going on."

At that, Doreen sighed. "I hope she doesn't do anything like that to me. It would feel very much like a betrayal."

Surprised, he sat down beside her. "Why would you say that?" he asked. "You know that she loves you."

"Sure, but she also knows that I don't like being talked about or being the center of attention." At that, his lips twitched again. "*Hey.*" She crossed her arms and frowned at him. "Okay, fine. So nothing I've done involving the cold cases makes it seem like that's how I feel. But I do."

"Maybe you should tell her that."

"I have," she replied. "Well, at least I've told her that I would be very unhappy if she did do something like that with my love life."

"It will be interesting to see," he noted.

"We won't know anyway. They'll keep it to themselves."

"Of course they will," he agreed, "and, even if she isn't betting on us, you might want to consider the fact that somebody else there will, and that person won't care about your feelings anywhere near as much as Nan will."

She stared at him. "But that just means—" And then she stopped, her voice dropping away.

"It just means that you should let Nan run with it because, otherwise, somebody else will," he noted, "and Nan at least will do it in such a way as to honor your feelings."

Doreen groaned at that. "No, you're right." She paused. "Dang. I didn't think of that."

"No, it's easy *not* to think about," he replied. "And I don't think it's a big issue right now anyway."

She nodded. "That's because I don't have a love life." At the silence beside her, she looked over and then winced. "I guess that didn't come out quite the right way, did it?"

He stood at the barbecue pit, watching the veggies so they didn't burn, and didn't say anything, but his back was unnaturally stiff.

And she realized that she'd hurt him. "You see? That's why I don't have a love life. I always put my foot in it," she explained. "Since leaving my ex and being able to say things on my own, it's like I have to learn all over again what to say and what not to say and how it impacts people."

He looked over at her.

She shrugged. "Before," she noted carefully, trying to explain how she felt, "he controlled everything, so I didn't get to say things a lot of the time. Any natural ability I might have had to say the right thing at the right time from before I married him just became locked down into this really hard *say nothing more* rule, so I didn't piss him off," And then she frowned. "That's not making any sense."

"No, it doesn't. You might want to try again." He stared at her.

"Okay. You know when I was growing up …" She

shook her head, stopped for a moment to gather her thoughts. "I mean, obviously you learn to say things, and you try hard not to hurt people, *blah-blah-blah.* But when I got married, I couldn't say anything. It was that, you know, I was fed the lines I was supposed to say, and these are the things that I had to do, and these are the married people I had to meet, so I didn't really get a chance to joke around and actually be me.

"And now that that ruling influence is gone, it's like I'm a teenager again, trying to figure out what to say, what not to say, and how not to hurt people's feelings. And I keep messing up." She turned to face Mack. "So I'm sorry."

He looked at her. "And what are you sorry for?" he asked quietly.

And she knew this was momentous. "Because I think I just hurt you."

His eyebrows shot up, and she realized that the *think* part was the problem.

"So I *know* I just hurt you, and I didn't mean to." She felt the tears gathering in the back of her eyes. "And even now I feel like I'm messing up." She brushed away the moisture from the corner of her eyes. She stared out at the river, shook her head. "This is why I don't do relationships."

"Why would you say that?" he asked. "You have to learn to walk before you learn to run."

She stopped, spun around, looked at him. "Is that what it is?"

"I don't know. You tell me," he stated quietly. "I mean, you've just made it pretty clear that we don't have a relation-ship, and I'm not sure if that's what you're trying to say or not."

"No, I was saying that I didn't have a romance." And

then she frowned. "Is a romance a relationship?" He sighed. She was making things worse. "See? See? I don't even know what I'm saying."

"I guess the question really is," he added, "whether you feel like we're on a relationship path."

"Of course we are." She watched as relief crossed his face.

"And are you okay with that?" he asked, but he studiously kept looking down at the barbecue.

"I'm here, aren't I?" she replied equally quietly.

He looked up, searched her face, and then a grin split his hugely handsome face in half. "You are, indeed, but that could be just because you live here and because you're hungry."

She walked over, wrapped her arms around him in a hug. "I'm sorry." She mumbled against his chest. "I feel so socially awkward. I feel like a gauche teenager again, but I would not want to hurt you."

"And I'm glad to hear that." He wrapped his arms around her shoulders, pulling her up close against his broad chest. "I would not want to hurt you either," he agreed quietly. "So, whether your grandmother or somebody else at the old folks' home puts bets on our love life, you'll ignore them because nobody gets to control who and what we feel about us—except us."

She leaned back, looked up at him. "You're so much wiser than I am."

"No." He shook his head at that. "Honestly, you say some things that make me realize that our experiences in life have just been so very different." He shrugged. "You need a little more practice in some areas, and I need a lot more practice in others."

And just then she sniffed the air, and he returned to the grill and snagged the steaks. He took one look. "*Whew*, okay, that was a close one. Now it's time to eat."

"Good, because that's definitely one area I need more practice at."

"Oh, I don't think so." He laughed out loud. "I think you're doing just fine on the eating part. Now the cooking part …?"

She beamed, as she sat down to a plate of barbecued veggies, a large salad, and a grilled steak.

"And shopping," she added. "I still struggle. I don't quite understand how anybody is supposed to live on this little bit of money that I make. I know that people have a lot more money than I do, but, wow, groceries are so expensive. By the time I pay for dog food, cat food, and bird food, it's really hard to come up with enough money to feed myself for the rest of the week."

He looked over at her. "And have you considered that maybe the dog food, cat food, and bird food should come after your groceries?"

She stared at him. "No." Her tone was stiff. "My responsibility, my joy, is to look after them. I'm blessed to have them in my life. And, therefore, they get what they need."

"Even if you don't get what you need?" he asked, his lips twitching.

"I can go back to peanut butter and bread if I have to," she replied calmly. "But I don't want them to suffer."

He didn't say anything for a long moment.

She stared at him suspiciously and then realized that, for him, the topic was already over. He had asked; she'd answered, and he was good with that. "So, how was your day?"

He looked over at her. "It was long but good, and, no, I'm not telling you about the case."

She looked at him with an injured air. "That's not very nice of you."

"What? That I won't tell you?"

"No, that you jumped to assuming that I would ask you."

He burst out laughing. "It's a given that you'll ask. And it's a given that I'll say, *I'm not telling you anything.*"

"Well, now that we've got that out of the way"—she grinned—"how about a cold case for me to work on?"

"Don't you have enough around here for you to fuss with?" He pointed at her backyard garden, which she had worked on in starts and fits, depending on what else was going on in her life.

"Sure, but they aren't *Poison in the Pansies.*" She waggled her eyebrows.

"Current case," he stated sternly, "not for you."

"What if I found another case that might have had poison in it?" she asked. "I could slide that into being connected."

He glared at her. "I don't think so. We don't get very many poisonings in town."

"Well, that's good," she replied, "because, honest to goodness, you know that Nan kept telling me about what a beautiful place this was to live, but, so far, I'm just seeing an awful lot of crime."

He smiled. "Some of it's crime, not always though. One of your cold cases involved flooding."

"No, that's true," she agreed. "And, of course, in some cases, I've been really helpful too."

"You were really helpful in closing out some of the cold

cases. You've done a lot of good for a lot of people, and whether everybody is particularly happy about it isn't the issue," he murmured. "What's the issue is that you went ahead and helped them anyway."

She smiled. "I don't think too many people think that what I was doing was actually helping."

"No. But you know, once you start finding bodies buried for a long time, and you realize how long some of these people have been at their evil antics," he noted, "well, you know it doesn't matter if people like it or not. We're finding justice for the victims."

"And that's the part that really bothers me," she stated. "All these people who got away with murder for so long, and now I just want to make sure they all pay."

"Making them pay is one thing," he replied. "Finding justice is something completely different, so maybe don't confuse the two."

She frowned at that. "I guess I hadn't looked at it from that point of view."

"Well, you do have some reasons to want revenge on certain people," he agreed. "And I'm thinking of your ex and of course Robin."

"And yet …" she answered quietly, "Robin's dead, hoisted by her own petard—or whatever that saying is." She waved her fork at him. "So it's hard to want revenge. I mean, she's paid the ultimate price."

"True," he murmured. "And that's one of the good things about you. You know when you can walk away. Now your ex? That's a different story."

"I know," she agreed. "And I did send your brother another email."

Mack nodded. "I connected with him today."

POISON IN THE PANSIES

"How's he doing?"

"He's getting ready to give you a call. So you can expect to hear from him in the next couple days."

"Or he just told you that to get me to stop texting and emailing him." She laughed.

"No, I think your ex is causing trouble."

"Gee, what a surprise," she muttered. "Is that why you had to connect with Nick?"

"No. Nick had asked me some questions earlier, and I had to get some answers for him."

She nodded. "It's nice that the two of you can work so well together."

"It would also be nice if he moved back to Kelowna," he noted quietly. "I know that's something that he's considering."

She stared at him in joy. "I really like your brother. That would be a good idea."

He looked over at her from the corner of his eye.

"I like him as your brother." She grinned. "I don't like him instead of you."

"Good," he replied, "because otherwise I'd kick his body back to Vancouver again."

She burst out laughing, and he just smiled at her. She nodded. "We're very comfortable together."

"Yep, like an old shoe." When she stared at him, frowning, he chuckled. "And that's just another old saying."

"I don't get all these old sayings," she said, with an eye roll. "What could possibly be comfortable about an old shoe? There's no support anymore. They're broken. Probably really smelly too."

He looked at her, shook his head. "Let's move on from this one. Obviously we'll be at odds over it."

"And how can you be at odds over it?" she muttered. "It's a stupid saying."

He groaned. "So can we move on from it?"

"Sure, we can go right back to the *Poison in the Pansies* case."

"Nope, we can't. Next."

She sighed. "Fine, I'll start in on the Bob Small stuff."

He stopped chewing and looked over at her.

She shrugged. "I need something to look at, and I know that's a really big case, and it's probably more than I can really handle, and, if I do ever solve anything to do with it," she explained, "I was hoping you guys would get the backlog of these cases caught up so I could give a hand with it."

He slowly put down his knife and fork. "That one could be very ugly. Bob Small is considered a serial killer. We've discussed this."

"We have, and I know you're worried about it," she noted. "I can tell you right now that, so far, I haven't a clue where to go with it and what to do on it. All I can tell you is that I got started at some earlier time, and then everything came to a dead stop."

"*Un-huh*," he muttered. "And that *dead stop*, is it about to stay stopped or ..."

"I don't know," she replied. "I'd have to find all my notes and get back into it again. And that file was big. So I'm not exactly sure."

"Right," he agreed, "it was suspected to be a big serial killer case, wasn't it?"

"Lots and lots of connected cases."

"Suspected cases." He nodded. "I don't even remember the details."

"No, I don't either. So, I mean, an easier one would be

poison cases."

"I don't think I have any cold case files with poisons in them," he noted.

"Well, how about from the city of Vernon or from, I don't know, Merritt? It's not that far away. Penticton, Summerland? How about any of those places? I mean, surely somebody in Okanagan Falls might have killed somebody with poison, right?" She looked at him hopefully. He stared at her. "Okay, fine. Too gruesome?"

"Too ghoulish," he corrected.

She raised both hands, then sighed. "And speaking of things not happening yet, I still haven't got that catalog from Scott that he promised me."

"The one with all your repaired furniture?" She nodded. "Yeah. Maybe tomorrow. And that should bring you a ton of money, right?"

"I don't know." She shook her head. Then she thought about it. "Nan seems to think it will, but I'm not so sure. And I can't count on anything, not until it's actually in hand."

"Good, that's wise." He nodded. "Because then you won't be disappointed if it ends up being much less."

"Exactly," she agreed. "That's what I was trying to explain to Nan, but she didn't see it from my point of view."

"But she's got a different vested interest in this, doesn't she?" he asked. "I mean, after all, she bought the antiques as an investment for you. So, in theory, she wants to make sure that you get the highest amount of compensation for them."

"Of course, and yet what she thinks it's worth doesn't necessarily mean that's what it is worth at present," she added, with a smile. "She more or less told me that today."

"Exactly. I'm glad you went down to see her," he noted.

"I thought you would have yesterday."

"Well, we were spending the day together, and then, when you got up and left so quickly like that," she added, "I got into a bit of a funk. Just stayed around home and cleaned some. Thought about what else I want to do in the yard, attacked some of the weeds, you know? I just puttered. Maybe that was good. Maybe that was bad. I don't know. Just doesn't feel like I'm accomplishing much. But then when you said you would be late today, we went down and had a cup of tea with Nan."

"Good. Nan's a special person."

"She is, indeed." Doreen laughed. "And what about your mom?"

"She's doing pretty well," he replied. "And, yes, she does want you to continue in her garden."

"Yeah, but you're paying the bills," she noted quietly. "How do you feel about it?"

He looked over at her, smiled. "I got my brother to help pay now too, so we're doing good."

"He's okay that it's me?"

Mack nodded. "He's absolutely okay that it's you."

"Okay, good. Maybe I'll take a walk over there one day soon and take a look and see what needs to be done again. I've been doing the regular maintenance, but it could use a bit more," she admitted.

"Like how much more?" he asked warily.

She burst out laughing. "I don't know. How big is your bank account?"

He rolled his eyes at that. "Not very big. And it doesn't lend itself to steak dinners all the time."

"I know," she noted, "and this is fabulous."

"I'm glad you enjoyed it." He put down his knife and

fork and finished the last bite in his mouth. He looked around. "You know that we'll have to start doing something about desserts."

"Desserts?" she asked doubtfully. "When I was married, I was never even allowed to have desserts."

"Wow, what a total control freak he was, but you're not with that loser anymore," he stated. "And you could use a few extra pounds."

She protested. "Hey, I already gained a few extra pounds," she replied. "Now I have to watch that I don't gain too many more pounds."

He snorted at that. "A little bit of fresh fruit or something nice to end the day wouldn't be a bad thing."

At the mention of fruit, she stared at him. "You know what? I might have a little bit of fruit." She got up and walked into the kitchen and pulled out two peaches. "I was hoarding these."

He shook his head. "You can't hoard fresh fruit. It'll go bad pretty fast."

She stared at him, looked down at the fruit, and then asked in a worried tone, "Are they bad?"

He took them from her, sniffed them. "When they're ripe like this, you have to keep them in the fridge to stop them from getting too ripe. Yet it really cuts back on the aroma." He turned and inspected them. "They look perfect."

"Good," she replied. "One for you and one for me." He looked down at them, then at her. She raised an eyebrow. "What?"

"So did you buy one for me, or are you just willing to share?"

She stared at him. "I think I bought one for you. I was thinking that two peaches would be perfect for either an afternoon snack or for after one meal together. But I wasn't thinking of it as a dessert."

"Well, I'm thrilled. It's not that I need you to buy meals or food for me," he explained, "but it is nice to know that you thought of me."

"So you could return this favor," she teased, chuckling. "How about you tell me about the *Poison in the Pansies* case."

"And how about not?" He held up his peach and took a big bite. Juice ran down his chin everywhere. He snatched a napkin from the table and wiped his chin. "These are perfect."

She ate hers much more delicately, using her knife to cut it. And by the time they were both done, she added, "You're right. That was perfect."

He looked down at his watch, groaned. "And I have to go."

"Seriously?" She looked over at him, crestfallen.

He smiled. "Well, I'll take it to heart that you'll miss me."

"Where are you going?" she asked.

"Somewhere." He grinned. And, with that, he added, "I hate to eat and run."

She waved a hand. "Go ahead. I'll look after the dishes. You cooked."

And, with that, he gave each of the animals a cuddle, and then he was gone.

She sat here for a long moment, pondering why he would run back to work at such a late hour. Maybe something about another poisoning? And, boy, did Doreen know who she could ask.

She picked up the phone, called Nan. "Mack's back out to another meeting, job, crime scene, I don't know what..

Have you heard anything about a poisoning down there?"

Nan's voice was super-excited as she replied, "Oh my. After you left," she cried out, "I went to Richie, and Richie went over to Annie, and Annie went over to Laura. And, boy, oh boy, we have somebody who knows the man who died."

She bolted upright. So, yes, she should be upset that Nan couldn't keep a secret, as asked. Yet Doreen wanted to know what Nan had found out. "Tell me. Tell me."

Nan replied in a smug voice, "Nope. It'll have to wait until morning."

"Why?" Doreen cried out.

"Because I'm heading off to my salsa lesson."

Doreen stopped and stared down at her phone. "What?"

"We'll talk in the morning, dear." And, with that, Nan hung up.

Chapter 3

Tuesday Morning

THE NEXT MORNING, Doreen, coffee at her side, was on the internet, looking for any information about the poisoning in town. When her phone rang, she smiled at her Caller ID screen and answered, "Hey, Nan. How are you?"

"I'm fine, a little tired. That salsa last night was deadly."

"I can't believe that you're taking dancing lessons."

"Why not?" she asked. "It's good exercise, and it's lots of fun. The men are seriously active here." She laughed. "At least this way I have fun."

Doreen didn't even want to think about what her grandmother had just said. "So now are you prepared to tell me about the information you found out last night?" she asked, with exaggerated patience.

"*Uh-oh*," Nan replied. "And I guess that one upset you. Did it?"

"Well, of course. I've been sitting here the whole night, trying to figure out just what it was that you'd found out," she whined. "There's nothing like not knowing."

"Why don't you come down and have breakfast?" Nan offered. "I've got fresh croissants here."

Doreen's stomach rumbled.

Nan laughed. "I heard that. Even over the phone. Come on down." And, with that, she hung up.

Doreen stared down at her phone. So many people were hanging up on her these days. She almost expected it now. She tossed back the last of her coffee and turned to the animals gathered in the kitchen. "Let's go down to Nan's, guys."

Immediately Thaddeus woke up from the living room roost and cried out, "Nan's, Nan's, Nan's."

Mugs was already dancing at the back door and even Goliath regally stood there, waiting for her. She opened the door, let them all out, and then followed behind them, as they walked toward the river. Mugs raced ahead, and she called him back with a warning. "Stay close," she said.

But he wasn't having anything to do with it. They were heading to see Nan, and Mugs knew exactly where they were going. Doreen was hard-pressed to keep up. Even Goliath appeared to be in a hurry. Doreen groaned. "It's almost like you guys know that we have a new case."

At that, Mugs woofed several times, and Thaddeus cried out, from his perch on her shoulder, "Off to Nan's. Off to Nan's."

Wow. He'd strung those words together all on his own. She twisted her head to look at him. "Hey, buddy," she asked, "how are you so adept at talking now?"

Thaddeus chuckled at her shoulder. Not only was he adept but getting better at talking on a regular basis too. Which she found pretty amazing, considering the limited number of people that her animals interacted with.

Before she realized it, they were already turning the corner and heading toward Nan's patio. Mugs picked up the pace, with Goliath at his side, as they both raced toward Nan, who stood on her patio, looking for them. She clapped her hands and cried out in joy. And Mugs ran right toward her.

Doreen reached them, breathing hard, and coming in second in this impromptu race. "They were just insane this morning," she told Nan. "It's almost as if they know you've got information."

"Of course they know," she replied comfortably, as she cuddled Goliath and Mugs. And Thaddeus, not to be outdone, hopped onto the table and walked over toward her, right up her arm and onto her shoulder, where he snuggled against her neck.

At that, Doreen smiled. "It does my heart good to see how much they love you."

"It does my heart good too." Nan had tears in her eyes as she cuddled Thaddeus. "They've always been very special, but they're certainly having a better life with you."

"Maybe," she said. "It's just so hard to know what they want sometimes."

"Nope, they want you, that's all." Nan laughed. "And so they should. You guys have a great life."

"I think so," she muttered. "Sometimes I worry that I'm not giving them enough."

Nan looked at her. "Enough what?" she asked. "These guys are completely spoiled."

"Are they though?" she asked. "I'm not sure about that."

But then Mugs woofed at her and sat down and looked up at the croissants. "But they're certainly working on getting more spoiled," Doreen noted, with an eye roll. "He really wants part of that croissant."

"And he can have a part," Nan agreed. "The tea's ready."

They poured tea and proceeded to dig into a plateful of fresh croissants.

"Where did you get the croissants from?"

"Here, in the kitchen."

Doreen stopped and looked at her grandmother. "So, since I'm not a resident of Rosemoor, I'm not supposed to have any of these, am I?"

"Sure you are. I took four. I'm allowed four," she replied. "Besides, who'll say anything?"

At that, Doreen wasn't so sure. Somebody was always around to say something about whatever. Still, right now, Doreen saw no point in wasting the croissants before her, and she dug in quite nicely. By the time she'd had two, Nan had only eaten one.

Nan pushed her second one toward Doreen. "You know that I only eat one."

She eyed her suspiciously. "Lots of times you eat two."

"Not today," she replied. "I'm too tired."

And, sure enough, Nan did look tired. "Too much sal-sa*ing*?"

At that, Nan laughed. "Not even sure that's a word, my dear, but the dancing was definitely fun."

"I'm glad to hear that," she replied warmly. "I always thought old age would be, you know, sitting in a wheelchair, broken down, waiting for life to end."

"Oh, I don't think so." Nan shook her head. "At least not for most of us at the center. A few sticks-in-the-mud are just waiting for life to end for them," she noted, "but I never did see the sense of that. There's so much still to live for."

Doreen smiled. "So now will you tell me about this new information of yours?"

"I already told you where the information came from,"

she noted. "But Laura's granddaughter works at the little grocery store up in Rutland. And that's where Alan lived. And he worked there too."

"Alan?"

"He's the guy who died," she clarified. "And apparently the day before he died, he wasn't feeling very good and so people were trying to send him home, but they were short-staffed so he refused to go."

"Okay."

"And then as the day went on, he started to get a little crazier, a little more stomach pain, quite bad. And then somebody made a comment about something, and she didn't know what the comments were, but he got quite agitated. And then he started telling people that he thought he'd been poisoned."

"So you think somebody put the suggestion in his mind?"

"Maybe. I don't know."

"So you know I'll have to go talk to these people?"

"I know." She nodded. "That's why I brought you up here, so I could give you the details of what we do know and what we don't know and who you can talk to."

"Have the cops talked to them?"

"No." She shook her head. "Because nobody knows any-thing about it, as far as I know."

Doreen groaned. "And that just means I'll have to talk to Mack."

"Yep." Nan smiled. "You will. But, once you talk to Mack, then you'll get kicked off the case."

She sighed. "I know. But, if it's an active case and if he needs this information …"

"Which is why I wanted you to come, so we could talk

to you about it."

"*We?*" Then she heard a voice at the doorway. And there was Richie. "Hi, Richie." Doreen jumped up. "Did you want to sit down?"

He took the seat, with a nod. "Normally I'd let a beautiful lady have the seat," he explained. "But I am a little shaky today."

"No problem," Doreen said, grabbing a kitchen chair to add to the patio set.

Richie looked over at Nan, a twinkle in his eye. "We danced too much last night."

Nan nodded. "My legs are shaky too." She chuckled. "I was just telling Doreen what we know."

Richie nodded. "I would call my grandson, but he gave me a lecture last week." Richie sniffed. "So I don't really feel like talking to him today."

Doreen laughed at that. "I'll contact Mack then," she muttered. "You guys don't happen to know any old cases around town that involved poisoning?"

The two shared a glance, then looked at her and asked, "Why?"

"Well, if there's a cold case," she explained, "I could get involved in it, and I could work it without having Mack getting upset at me."

"Right, right." Nan nodded, as she turned to Richie. "Richie, what do you think? Do we know anyone who may have been poisoned to death?"

"Well, there was Chrissy, who died recently, who swore to everybody who would listen that she was being poisoned," he snorted. "But I don't know that we believed her."

"Where is she? I should talk to her," Doreen noted.

"Well, she died." Richie frowned at Doreen. "I just said

that, didn't I?"

Doreen frowned too. "Okay, so if she died, why wouldn't there have been an investigation already?"

"Because she was old for one," he noted. "And I know the family didn't want an autopsy."

"Which would also have been maybe suspicious."

"Not at our age," Nan replied. "You have to remember that when it comes to being old already, there's no budget money. I mean, there has to be a reason for that expenditure. We're all ready to die anyway."

Doreen frowned at Nan. "I don't want to hear that talk from you, from either of you." She stared at both and got noncommittal nods. "But did she not tell anybody that she was being poisoned?"

"I just said she did." Richie frowned. "Are you feeling all right, dear?"

She stared at Richie, nonplussed. "I'm feeling fine." She then faced Nan. "Did she tell anybody in law enforcement?" she asked.

"Ah," Richie replied. "No, I don't know if she did or not. She'd been spouting off about being poisoned for a long time, so I'm not sure anybody would have cared."

"When did she die?" she asked.

"I think it was this year, maybe January?" He turned to Nan. She just nodded.

"I don't know how old a case has to be in order to be considered a cold case," she muttered.

"Well, it wouldn't be a cold case anyway," Nan replied logically. "Her death was deemed to be by natural causes."

"Right, so in which case, it's not a cold case. It would just be a *no case*." That even confused her. She sighed. "But, of course, if that were the case, then Mack couldn't get upset

57

with me, could he?"

"Nope, sure couldn't." Richie rubbed his hands together. "So how do we start?"

Chapter 4

DOREEN WALKED BACK inside her home through the kitchen door and dropped her notepad on the kitchen table, feeling the surge of excitement that kept her feet racing all the way home. Getting Richie and Nan to understand that they couldn't get too involved but could dig for any information that they could from people in the know was one thing, but she couldn't afford to have them on the same case.

Only as she sat here, replaying those words, did she realize just how much she sounded like Mack. She winced. "Sorry, guys. It's too dangerous."

And, of course, Mack would have immediately said that same thing to her. And he was right to a certain extent, but not in any way that she wanted to listen to or to abide by. Which was exactly what Nan and Richie would say too. She sighed and looked down at Mugs and Goliath. "How about we go out exploring?"

Goliath wove between her legs, as Mugs jumped up and down on his back legs, almost like a dancing bear.

She laughed at his antics. "I'll take that as a yes." She studied the names on her notepad that she had in front of her. She really should do some of the work on the internet first. It would help to get the lay of the land and to see what the general area looked like, from the perspective of the Rutland grocery store, where this guy worked, the one who had died recently.

The woman who had died at Rosemoor earlier this year, now that was an entirely different story. Doreen knew she could rely on Nan and Richie to get that information or at least to get a start on it. Doreen would do the rest as soon as she got home again. And, with that action planned, she and her animals walked out to her car, hopped into the seat, securing all the animals, and then reversed down her driveway. She would much rather have a place where she could turn around without coming down the driveway, but the cul-de-sac here was a pretty empty area as far as traffic went, so, in theory, it was all good.

As she drove past her neighbor Richard's place, she thought she saw the curtain twitch. She honked the horn just in case. That would be enough to probably drive Richard crazy, but, hey, just something about him was odd and made her want to poke at him. Which wasn't very nice of her, she admitted. Yet, at the same time, something was off with Richard.

She didn't know whether he lived with a partner in that house or had murdered her and was keeping a social security check or some other godforsaken thing. It was hard to know. She'd certainly heard a weird voice every once in a while, which could be the supposed partner, yet Richard seemed to be a little bit friendlier now. Well, no, not really, not since their street ended up on the Japanese tour bus route. She had to admit that was pretty funny at the time, but now it was just irritating.

Having solved yet another case, Doreen's notoriety was getting to be pretty silly. And hiding wasn't the priority in her world. Some people would have said that she should have just moved, and then nobody could find her, but this was her home. This was Nan's home. This was the home that Doreen had been given to start all over again, and she couldn't just walk away from it.

And the river was absolutely special. She loved being here in Kelowna, with her totally different lifestyle living here. Just so many good things could be said about her move here.

She pulled into traffic and headed toward Springfield Road and then on toward Rutland. As she got up to the little mall, where the grocery store was, she parked, got out, looked at the animals, and froze. Not too brilliant to bring them with her here.

If she had left them at home, she could have gone into the store and could have taken her time talking to the employees and the customers. Now that she had them with her, and she couldn't take them inside, so she was relegated to just walking around the area outside. With Mugs on a leash—even Goliath with a leash on again, something he was giving her a lot of dirty looks over—Doreen decided to just wander the area and to get a feel for the place. Not that that would help necessarily, but it seemed like the thing to do since she was here already. Or rather it was the thing nudging at her to do this now.

Maybe there was something to this thing called instinct. She didn't know. It felt like an odd scenario, but, hey, she was working with it. With the animals on leashes and Thaddeus on her shoulder, she wandered around the small parking lot, looking into the grocery store, and then headed up and around several blocks. By the time she slowly meandered her way back to the mall parking lot, she hadn't seen anything suspicious or anything to make her eyes go wide in any way.

Some of the streets had interesting names. Some of the names were odd, but that's okay. She was interested in all of them. Apparently the river wasn't very far away. If she looked on her map, Peck Road led to the Greenway, which was one of the big walking paths that went up and down Mission Creek. Other roads in that area didn't make a whole lot of sense, like Hollywood Road North and Hollywood Road South.

She shrugged at that. Why wouldn't you just have Hollywood for one and go with something else for the other? But, in her world, city planners never seemed to make a whole lot of sense. The fact that these guys got paid to name stuff just blew her away. She figured something else had to be involved in their job—there had to be because they did such a terrible job at the naming part.

This city had actual streets that were one name on one side of an intersection and a different name on another side. How confusing was that? Had they really not expected the city to grow? Would new streets need a new name, when really just the continuation of an existing street? It just didn't make any sense to her.

But as she stood here and looked around at the parking lot, an old lady walked up to her. "Oh my, isn't that a beautiful dog?" Then she looked at the cat, and her eyes widened. "Oh my," she cried out, "you have a cat on a leash too."

"This is Goliath," Doreen said, with a smile. "He likes to come out for walks, and this way I don't have to worry about losing him."

The old lady asked, "May I pet him?" She bent a hand down to Mugs, who acted up for his adoring audience. The old lady was seriously charmed. She looked over at Doreen. "Do you live here, dearie?"

"No, I just came up to visit." Doreen smiled. "I've never been to Rutland. I'm relatively new to the area, so I'm still trying to get my bearings on places and what happens in each place."

"*Ah*, not a whole lot happens up here—well, at least nothing nice. It's one of the lesser fun places to live," she explained. "I always wanted to live down by the beach."

"I think that would be lovely too. My grandmother's got a house on the river," she hedged. "And that's pretty nice."

"The water would be lovely," she agreed, "but I'd always be afraid of flooding there."

"I suppose," she muttered. "I heard some guy up here died just a few days ago."

The old lady nodded. "Oh, yes, that was so sad. And he was well loved. Had a great sense of humor and so kind. He will be missed."

Doreen looked at her. "Oh my, the poor family. They must be devastated. Was he married?"

"Right. I mean, it's hard enough to find anybody in this world but then to turn around and lose him like that? That's just terrible. He was divorced. Married quite a while ago. I used to tease him about being single all the time."

"I'm so sorry. Somebody said something about him working at one of the stores here."

"Yes, he worked at the grocery store," she replied, "but not anymore."

There was such a sadness to her telling Doreen about

him that it was hard not to say something. "Did you know him well?"

"Certainly well enough to talk to him, as I went to the store all the time. But he was that kind of a person who was just really friendly and jovial, you know? One of the nice people in the world."

"Yeah, we need more of those," Doreen agreed.

"Oh my dear, we so do. It's such a sad world out there. You'd think that people would learn to be nicer, but it seems like that's a hardship for anybody."

"I wonder about that too." Doreen smiled and nodded knowingly. "You'd like to think that they could get along in life and could help their fellow man, but too often it takes them down with them."

"That is sadly very true," she agreed. She patted Mugs once again. "I've got to head home now. You have a good day." And, with that, the older lady wandered off.

Doreen watched as the older woman headed to the other side of the little mall where the grocery store was and up to what looked like an apartment building on the other side. It was always good to know where people lived, although Doreen had absolutely no reason for keeping track of this woman. Nothing in their conversation triggered Doreen's alarms in any way. It was sad that the man who had died was only in his forties or so, per her new acquaintance.

That was one of those shocks that you were never really prepared for. You expected to get married and have a happy-ever-after, and, when that didn't work out so well, it was a blow. It was an ending to deal with. Just like Doreen. She'd married with full expectations of sun, stars, and moon. Too bad she ended up getting a thunderstorm and lightning and then just that eerie calm before a storm.

Even if the storm never hit again, it was always there, that tension, that pressure, that ugliness—all that let you know that the storm could erupt again at any time, and, when it did, it would have devastating consequences. She thought about the earlier painful conversation she had had with Mack, as she just wandered up and down the streets, and how she'd been trying to explain to him about her loose tongue now that she had her freedom. Doreen wasn't really sure how to say things the way she wanted them to come out.

With a headshake, she wandered back to the car, put the animals inside, and decided to go into the store to get a jug of milk. If she was fast, the animals would be just fine. And it would give her a chance to take a look inside. With them all locked up, she raced inside, grabbed a jug of milk, and headed to the checkout lanes. There she saw two of the cashiers, talking together in low voices. She didn't want to disturb them, but she didn't want to leave the animals much longer either.

When she cleared her throat, one of the women looked up. "Oh, sorry." She came over.

"That's all right," Doreen replied. "I heard you guys talking about the poor man who just died."

The woman looked at her. "Do you know him?"

She shook her head. "I didn't know him, but I did hear he had passed away, and, of course, that's just terrible. I was told that he was a nice young man."

"He was lovely," the woman replied sadly. "One of the nice guys in the world, and it's not fair. It seems like the jerks always survive, and the nice guys always die."

"I know. I have had that same thought myself a couple times." And the trouble was, Doreen really had. Seemed like guys like her husband thrived, but then the nice guys, like this Alan, who had just passed away, didn't. "I'm sure it was an accident, wasn't it?" she asked.

"They don't know." And the woman hesitated and leaned forward. "There's a chance he was murdered."

"No," Doreen gasped. "Really?"

At that, the woman nodded. "He kept telling people he was being poisoned."

"Oh no, oh no. Why didn't he get help then?"

The woman shrugged. "I don't know, but toward the end there, he wasn't very clear about what he said he would do. We kept telling him, if he thought he was being poisoned, then to go tell the police."

"And definitely go to the hospital."

"He said something about having been to the cops, but they needed more details."

At that, Doreen stared at her. "They couldn't do more? That is terrible."

"I know. I know." The woman quickly rang up her milk and waited while Doreen paid. Thankfully her card went through with a tap. She wasn't sure whether she should run out of there skipping and dancing for joy or just run and get out of the parking lot, just in case the machine decided to double-check her bank account. Because she wasn't sure if there was very much room left for more gallons of milk or if that was just about it at this point in time. With a quick smile at the woman, she thanked her and headed back outside again.

When she got to her car, she got in, put the grocery bag on the floorboard, and checked that all the animals were doing okay. "Okay, guys, let's go home."

And, with that, she drove toward the exit, only to see an

old guy standing at the side, watching her. She frowned at that, and he frowned right back.

Not sure why, she pulled up beside him, opened her window, and asked, "Are you okay? Do you need a hand?"

He looked at her and glared. "Do I look like I need a hand?"

She nodded. "Actually, you do. It looked to me like you were calling for help."

He stared at her. "No, obviously I wasn't," he replied in exasperation.

"Oh." She explained, "Looked to me like that frown was telling me to come over and help."

"You think that's what people are looking for when frowning at you?" he asked in astonishment, and then he shook his head. "Lord, you really are crazy, aren't you?"

She stared at him. "Do you know me?"

"Who in town doesn't?" he asked. "Those animals are a dead giveaway."

"But the animals were in my car," she noted. "I just went in to grab a gallon of milk."

"Yeah, well, it was pretty hard not to see them," he snorted. "I mean, the bird just storms back and forth on the headrest, and the dog sits up half the time, looking out the window."

She nodded. "Yeah, they're pretty active in my world, but I don't understand why that would bother you."

"It's not the animals that bother me." He glared at her. "You do."

She tried not to take offense, but it was hard. "I don't even know you, so I'm not sure why you would feel that way. I haven't done anything to hurt you, have I?"

"No, not getting a chance either," he replied in a

grumpy voice. "You're nothing but one of those nosy-bodies, sticking your nose into everything."

"Well, hardly," she argued. "Unless of course you're one of those people who are always in trouble and needed to be put away for something that you did wrong."

"Oh, I'm too old to deal with that nonsense anymore," he snapped. "Besides, it's got nothing to do with who I am."

"No, sure doesn't," she replied cheerfully. On that note, she closed her window and then cried out to him, "Have a nice day."

He just glared at her and opened his mouth.

She didn't give him a chance to say something nasty. Instead she gunned it and pulled back into traffic and got out of there. She didn't know why people would have that reaction to her, but Mack would likely say it had to do with the cases that she'd solved and the perspective that a lot of people had that she was interfering.

Maybe she was. She'd certainly upset a few apple carts in the process, but it still wasn't something that she terribly understood because she had been helping other people.

Back home again, she grabbed her milk and the animals and headed back inside. Just as she walked in her house, her phone rang. "Hey, Mack," she said. "Have you decided to fill me in on the *Poison in the Pansies* case?"

"No," he replied. "What were you doing in Rutland?"

She frowned. "And how did you know I was in Rutland?"

"Because somebody phoned in to report that animals had been left in a car. Including a dog, a cat, and a parrot."

She stopped, shaking her head. "Yeah, I did. I left all three of them in the car, while I ran in and got a gallon of milk."

"You drove to Rutland to get a gallon of milk, *huh*?" he asked, his tone neutral.

"Did I do something wrong?" she asked.

"Well, we never like to see people leaving animals in a car," he explained. "But it certainly wasn't a hot day, and you weren't gone for very long, so it's not like it's something that anybody needs to check out."

As she thought about it, she asked, "It was that old goat, wasn't it?"

He laughed. "What old goat?"

"There was this old guy, and he was glaring at me, so, maybe out of perverseness, I don't know," she explained, "I stopped and asked him if I could help him because obviously he needed help."

"You said what?"

"Well, he was glaring at me, so obviously he was cranky and miserable and needed something," she replied by way of her defense. "It seemed to really upset him that I took that frown of his that way though." She snickered.

"Ya think?" he asked. Then he sighed. "And what did he want?"

"Nothing, I think he just realized who I was and said that I was an interfering busybody and that I should leave well enough alone."

"And I suppose you told him that you weren't, right?"

"Well, I'm not," she argued.

"Not in your eyes, no," he replied, "but you know a lot of people don't take it that way."

"Well, he certainly didn't. He was just grumpy. Anyway, I told him to have a nice day, and I left. So I wonder if he called before our conversation or afterward."

"Don't know, probably before, if you left the animals in

the car."

"Right," she muttered. "Anyway, yeah, went up to check out the area," she added cheerfully. "And of course I have a cold case now to work on."

At that, silence came from the other end. "You have a what?"

"That's all right. I'm not stepping on your toes. You guys don't even consider it to be a case." She smiled broadly. "So it's none of your business."

"Anything you do is my business," he noted, his tone grim.

"Nope, nope, nope, nope. I'm not in any danger on this one," she argued. "I won't be any trouble to you. I promise I'll stay out of your world."

At that, he snorted, the sound loud and clear to the point that even Thaddeus looked at her phone and cried out, "Thaddeus is here. Thaddeus is here."

"Wow, Thaddeus is on a rampage."

"He heard you through the phone, so thanks for upsetting my animals."

"Me?" he asked in outrage.

"Yeah, you," she replied, "and your brother never called me."

"Yeah, he's probably avoiding you." Mack laughed.

"Why? What did you tell him about me this time?" she asked in an ominous tone.

"I said that you were on a rampage, looking for money."

"Oh, great." She sighed.

"Well, you might not be on a rampage, but you definitely need money."

"Yeah, but it's not Robin's money that I need," she explained. "I need a way to be self-sufficient, without having to depend on people dying to get it."

There was a moment of silence on the other end, and then, with a splutter, he added, "Well, that's really good to hear. Then I won't have to worry about you trying to knock off people to get money."

"Oh my, can you imagine?"

"I don't want to," he replied. "That is not anything I even want to contemplate."

"No, of course not," she stated. And then she laughed. "But you know a lot of people would blame me for it, right?"

"A lot of people would blame you for a lot of things," he stated quietly, "which is why I try so hard to keep you out of trouble."

"Yeah, it's not working though, is it?"

"No," he roared. "But you could try." And, on that note, he hung up the phone.

She put on the teakettle, took off the leashes, hung them up, and fed everybody a little treat. When the tea was ready, she took her laptop and her tea outside onto the deck. As she sat here, smiling at her beautiful deck, researching the names that Nan had given her, Doreen started her Google search with the one case that Mack was working on because Doreen had been up there looking in Rutland and everybody had said how nice Alan was.

Doreen found a small notice in the newspaper about him involved in some volunteer work. In that article he was surrounded by a group of people and had his arm around a woman at his side, as if they were close. If she was still in his life, she'd be going through a tough time. Doreen's heart immediately went out to the poor woman.

"I'm so sorry," she whispered. "It's tough enough being with someone, but, in your case, if you were happy, then a loss like this is brutal."

Absolutely no point in talking to this woman's picture on the internet, but, hey, Doreen was probably seen as getting crazy about some cases these days. She quickly checked for more information and found it suspiciously silent on any actual helpful forensic data. But then, of course, the authorities may not know anything yet regarding Alan's death. The police were just dealing with this case right now, so they probably didn't have a whole lot to bring to the table yet. Now, if only Mack would let her help, that would be a different story.

On that note, she returned to the information she had found on Chrissy, who had died earlier this year. She'd also been talking about people poisoning her, apparently. And again, it was pretty hard to find anything, but there was an obit with a mention that she'd died peacefully in her sleep.

"Died peacefully in her sleep," she muttered. "So how is that being poisoned?"

But of course no answers were to be found. As she sat here, pondering the lack of information, Nan called her. "Hi, Nan," she greeted her grandmother.

"Oh my dear, we've discussed it here at the home."

"*Uh-oh,*" she replied. "What have all you lovelies at Rosemoor decided?"

"We've decided that we'll help you."

"Nan, I told you when I was there last that I couldn't get you involved."

"Of course you couldn't," she replied. "But it's not you getting us involved. It's us getting us involved," she stated on a determined note. "You know that could be any of us. Just because it was Chrissy who died doesn't mean it couldn't be us next time."

"Are you thinking she really was poisoned?"

"The food here can be just awful sometimes," Nan replied. "I mean, there's that one cook here who we're pretty sure is not trained at all."

"That's not the same thing as killing a person," Doreen noted in exasperation. "Just because somebody's cooking might feel like it's killing you doesn't mean it is. That's like saying I could kill you with my cooking."

"You probably could," Nan replied.

Doreen gasped and Nan laughed. "You left yourself open for that one, dear."

"Nan, that's a terrible thing to say, even as a joke."

"Well, have you learned to cook better?"

"I'm working on it," she stated.

"Work harder and work faster. You know that the way to a man's heart is through his stomach."

"Well, that won't work then because Mack takes care of his stomach just fine."

"Oh, so you have accepted that you're working on getting closer to Mack? That's ... that's very good."

Doreen heard a bit of scratching going on. "Nan, you're not taking bets on my love life, right?"

"Of course not," she replied, as she continued to scratch away on paper.

"I don't believe you," Doreen stated bluntly.

There was a moment of silence on the other end. "I might not be taking bets, but I certainly don't want anybody else either."

"Meaning?"

"Well, people will talk, my dear. And, if I don't give them something to discuss, they'll make it up."

"Nan, I don't want anybody talking about my private

life."

"Of course not, of course not," she noted in that soothing tone that was immediately getting Doreen's back up.

"Oh, goodness, Nan," she stated. "You know how I feel about lack of privacy."

"Yeah. I wondered about that though," Nan replied. "Because really, you've been in the media an awful lot for somebody who doesn't want to be."

She snorted. "That's not fair. I didn't get there on my own."

"No, you sure didn't," she answered quietly. "You had lots of help. From Mack. And now we'll help you with this case too."

"Which case?" she asked.

"Chrissy, of course."

"But you can't go around accusing cooks of trying to kill you," she stated.

"Why not? That's what Chrissy did. And then look what happened to her."

Doreen cried out, "What do you mean, *what happened to her?*"

After a moment of silence, Nan asked, "Are you feeling all right, dear?"

"Nan, you're making me crazy."

"Sweetheart, I don't think anybody needs to make you anything. You're getting there yourself," she replied. "We were just talking about the fact that Chrissy has been poisoned. And so, therefore, that's what happened to her."

Doreen groaned, reached up, and pinched the bridge of her nose. "I know that you think she was poisoned, but we don't have any proof of that."

"No, but we'll get it," she stated quietly. "She was a

friend of mine. I don't know why I didn't think of this earlier."

"Think of what?"

"Chrissy never got any justice. She could have gone on for another six months."

At that, Doreen's eyebrows rose. "Was she that close to death?"

"Well, I don't know, but, in a place like this, we certainly don't measure time in years anymore. You know that lots of people can come and go in a heartbeat, who you thought could have lived for much longer," she stated in a harder tone. "No, we are quite happy to just judge by months."

"*Great*." Doreen wondered at the strange turn of conversation. "You also don't have to, you know, judge at all."

"Of course not." She laughed. "Don't you worry about it. We'll help."

"*Great*," she muttered. "You won't get me into any trouble though, will you?"

"No, of course not," she replied. "I mean, it's not like we'll deputize ourselves or anything."

"You can't," she said in alarm. "Nan, you know that, right?"

"Sure I do." But then Nan laughed and laughed and laughed.

Doreen wasn't sure if she was being teased or not. She sighed. "I looked into Chrissy's family and her death," she noted to change the subject. "I can't say I've found a whole lot yet."

"No, there's probably more on our little newspaper here."

"What do you mean, *your little newspaper*?"

"The one we have for Rosemoor. One of the residents

always takes it on for a while and does up a few local interest stories," she explained. "I'll have to see if I can find the copies from back then. I'll get back to you as soon as I can— if I find anything." And, with that, she hung up.

Doreen stared down at the phone in her hand. "Local interest stories," she said out loud. "And how is it I'm just hearing about that now?" she snapped to nobody in particular.

She looked over at Mugs, who stared at her, his head tilted. Goliath just ignored her, and Thaddeus appeared to be sound asleep on her shoulder.

"All this time and Nan hasn't once mentioned that to us," she muttered. "Why is that?" She glared at the animals, but they all ignored her. "Yep, that's the story of my life right now." She sighed. "Everybody's got all this information, and nobody tells me, so I miss out on stuff," she muttered. "That's just not cool."

And, with that, she brought out her notepad, flipped to a new sheet, and wrote down the little bits and pieces she knew about Chrissy. The fact that it wasn't even necessarily a murder made this whole thing more futile than anything. What she really wanted was something that she could bite her teeth into, and that seemed more to be like the guy who worked at the grocery store who had been poisoned. And then, of course, the *Poison in the Pansies* case that was Mack's.

She wanted to return to the beach park, but she'd already checked, and the poison was long gone. Since it was a public beach, there could be all kinds of traffic. So there could be all kinds of reasons and explanations as to who might have picked up the rat poison. She grabbed her phone and quickly sent Mack a text. **Did the police pick up that**

poison?

He snapped back a response. **It was a request. I don't know if it was followed through or not, but I'm assuming so.**

She didn't say anything. Then she sent back a message. **It's gone. It would be nice to know that the cops picked it up and not some random stranger.** She got a thumbs-up after that, which didn't tell her anything.

She groaned, as she stared down at the message. "Okay, this isn't helpful."

She didn't want to ask him any more questions. That would just piss him off at the moment. She sighed and headed back to her laptop and the notes that she was taking.

When Mack contacted her a couple hours later, he asked, "When did you go look for the poison?"

"Early Monday morning," she told him. "I wanted to make sure it wasn't still there to hurt anybody."

He replied, "Well, the cops went there today to find it."

"Only today?" she asked.

"Yes," he replied quietly. "So it might be gone already, but the cops didn't take it."

Chapter 5

Tuesday Afternoon

THAT AFTERNOON, DOREEN sat outside with a cup of tea on her deck, trying to appreciate being out of doors, trying not to worry. But she had things going on that were worth worrying over.

Good intentions and all of that did not necessarily provide good information. To think that somebody else had cleaned up the box of poison at the park near the beach— and had even dug up maybe some of the loose sand containing the spilled powder in and around there—could have just meant anything from the city gardeners to a concerned citizen.

Doreen would have been much happier if she and Mack had taken care of it themselves that Sunday. But, as soon as they had found the poison, Mack had put in the call to have it removed by a forensics team. Thus he'd thought, for sure, it would have been taken care of immediately.

And it had been, just not by whom they had expected and just not near fast enough. She found that newest tidbit hard to forget about.

Equally troubling was the fact that Nan and Richie were

working on Chrissy's supposed murder by poisoning, which was a whole different ball game. Trying to keep those two in control was like having two bears or lions in your backyard and trying to keep them out of trouble. Doreen didn't foresee that going well.

She let out a heavy sigh. Switching gears, she tried to figure out what on earth she could do to move either poisoning case forward, Chrissy's or Alan's, but she had no way to know what poison was used in either death – if Chrissy was even poisoned. Plus she had no tie to the rat poison at the beach. Really nothing came to mind. But, unless an eyewitness came forward, stating they had actually seen somebody down there near the beach with the box, well, Doreen had nothing to go on yet.

As she sat here at her deck table, her pen flicking back and forth in her fingers, she wondered, considering it was summertime, just how many steady go-to-the-park-every-day people were around here. Would many have seen someone hiding the box to begin with? What about seeing someone take off with it? Surely it took a while to bury the box initially and more time to clean it up afterward. Would somebody have commented on it? She wondered.

She wrote up a small sign on a sheet of paper, with her phone number added, and then, calling the animals to her, she hopped into the car and headed down to Sarsons Beach. She quickly affixed the sign to the message board, asking if anybody had seen the white powder in the box in the garden to contact her.

As she stepped back, an older gentleman joined her, read her note, turned toward her, and asked, "Do I have to phone you?" She looked at him, her eyebrows up. He shrugged. "I come here for my walk almost every day. Then I go home and have tea and biscuits," he confided. "It's the only way my wife will let me have my biscuits."

Doreen wanted to laugh, but, at the same time, she didn't want to offend him. But he saw the humor in her face.

"But you can't tell her that I don't walk," he stated, with a word of warning. "I just sit here and enjoy the view. Honestly, I think she's doing me as much of a favor as anything," he admitted. "I get to sit outside and just have a few minutes to myself."

At that, she did laugh. "Retirement a bit too much?"

He shook his head. "Fifty years of marriage is a bit too much." And then he cackled. "And I wouldn't have it any other way."

"Of course you wouldn't," she agreed warmly. "Did you see this box of rat poison that was in the garden?"

He nodded. "It showed up there Sunday."

She frowned. "I was here Sunday afternoon, when we found it."

He nodded. "Yep. And I was here in the morning. It wasn't there, and, when I came back in the afternoon, it showed up." He shrugged. "I did contact the city about it, and I'm glad to see somebody came and cleaned it up."

"You know what? You're right." She nodded. "I'm happy too. I just wondered if you saw who had put the box there."

He shook his head. "I didn't. A couple people were around at the time, but nobody I would have looked at and said, *Hey, he's the guilty party.*" Then he frowned. "Not that you can tell who's guilty anymore. It used to be the shifty-eyed bad guys were easy to spot but not anymore."

She smiled at him. "No, you're quite right. They tend to look just like you and me."

He laughed. "And how do you know I didn't put it there?"

She looked at him, her eyebrows shooting up. "Did you?"

He shook his head. "No, I wouldn't do that," he noted. "Children come around here to enjoy the park and the beach. You never know what they would touch."

"That was my thoughts exactly," she shared. "But it still would be nice to know who would have had that poison and why they would have put it out here."

"To get rid of it," he replied. "Why else?"

She chuckled. "Well, that makes sense. And did he just throw it, and that's the casual pattern it made as it fell, or did he deliberately circle the pansies with it?"

He stared at the garden. "Is that what those things are?"

She nodded. "That's exactly what those things are."

"Well, he must have hated the pansies to do that," he suggested. "Maybe the flower bed was full of ants. That rat poison would probably kill them too. I don't know."

She couldn't stop smiling. With him at her side, she walked over to the garden bed. "Whoever removed it did a good job too," she noted. "The bed barely looks disturbed."

"Well, wouldn't have been hard," he explained. Then he stopped, looked at it closely. "But most of the flowers are gone."

"Well, they were dying anyway," she stated, noting, in fact, a big patch of soil had been removed. "And I don't know if ants would have been affected by the poison or not. However, if you think about it, anything that's strong enough poison to kill rats should be enough to kill small ants."

He laughed. "Well, I'm old-school. We sure as heck

didn't hire anybody to take care of rats in my day. You took care of them yourself. And something like this was fairly common back then too."

"In other words, what you're saying is that a lot of people would have easy access to rat poison."

"It's an easy-enough product to buy anywhere," he noted, with a shrug. "So I can't imagine anybody would have trouble getting rat poison, if they wanted it." He looked over at her. "So is this your new case?" he asked, a curious twinkle in his eye.

She realized that he'd recognized her. "So, I'm Doreen, as you already know. What's your name?"

"Milford."

"Nice to meet you, Milford. And I'm so glad you stopped to speak with me." She shrugged. "As to your question about this being a new case, let's just say it's an oddity that's caught my curiosity."

"It is, at that." He frowned, as he thought about it. "An old guy sits here quite a bit. You should talk to him."

"Yeah? What's his name? How old is he?"

"Don't know names out here, but he's older than me," he clarified, with a laugh. "And that's saying something. I'm eighty-two. And this guy? Well, I think he's like ninetysomething."

"Wow. And does he come every day?"

Milford nodded at that. "He does. I often stop and say hi to him. However, he doesn't talk a whole lot. I don't know whether it's because he doesn't have any teeth or what, but he's not the friendliest sort."

"Are you thinking he might have dropped the box here?"

"No, I sure am not. He's old-school like me. You don't throw poison away. It's not even so much about hurting other people, but you might need it one day."

She winced at that. "I've seen that sentiment a time or two. Some of the older folks, whose parents and grandparents went through the Great Depression, are reluctant to let go of anything. Some come very close to becoming a hoarder."

He snorted at that. "I don't get those people." He shook his head. "I mean, when you think about it, keeping stuff that you can use is one thing, but keeping stuff that's garbage? Well, that's a whole different thing."

"And I think that's where the problem is," she agreed, sliding him a sideways glance. "I think the perspective is all about who owns it and what they actually think could be of value. What you think of value and what somebody else will think of value …"

He nodded. "Yeah, that's like my wife and me," he stated, smirking. "She seems to think that everything I've kept all these years has no value. Always trying to throw away my stuff, before I can stop her. I have to check the garbage constantly to see what she has dumped lately."

"Well, there you go." Doreen laughed. "If you think about it, that's exactly how hoarders feel. What they find in the garbage is gold, which is what other people throw away because they think it's useless."

He glared at her.

She just grinned. "Not saying that you're a hoarder or that your things are useless. Just saying that theory applies."

He shrugged. "Don't matter none. Anyway, this old guy comes around on a regular basis. But, like I told you, he doesn't talk much."

"Well, maybe he would have some ideas to help me," she added.

"And besides, what difference does it make if he does know who put the box there? What difference does it make about whoever put the box there?" he asked. "It could have been anybody's box. He might have picked it up out of the nearest garbage can, wondering what to do with it, and then decided he didn't want it around and tossed it."

"All good points," she noted cheerfully. "Just one of those things that I can't really let go of in my head."

He stared at her for a moment. "And that means, there's something to it."

"Not necessarily," she cautioned. "I'm just looking at a few things."

"*Hmm*," he replied, followed with a heavy *harrumph*. "Sounds to me like an excuse. You just don't want me interfering in your case."

She smiled at him. "I technically don't even have a case."

"Well, that's because you keep getting into the police's way," he noted, laughing at her. "You know what? If you would learn to be subtle, you wouldn't be getting into trouble all the time."

"Yeah, *subtle* has never exactly been something I'm very good at," she admitted.

At that, he burst out laughing.

She could see that he was thoroughly enjoying the conversation. She flashed him a grin. "See? Now wouldn't life be boring if I did nothing all the time and if I kept my nose out of things?"

"I don't know," he replied, still with that big laugh of his reverberating around them. "When you think about it, I'm sure the police work would be a whole lot more smooth sailing though." She frowned at that. He nodded. "You and that big detective, whatever his name is, I've seen you two on the telly a couple times."

She nodded. "A couple times I've been on there," she admitted. "And not like anybody asked me though."

"Nobody asks nothing in this world," he spat, with a sage nod. "As soon as they got a story, they run with it."

"Well, I'm not all about stories," she added. "I'm trying to be about the truth."

"Well, that's the other side of the story, isn't it?" he noted. "Your truth versus somebody else's truth—they're very different things." And, with that, he looked around, checked his watch. "I think I've been gone long enough. I think I can go home and have a cup of tea and some biscuits."

At that, she smiled. "By the way, this old guy who comes all the time, any idea what time of day he comes?"

Milford looked down at his watch. "You know what? He'll probably be along pretty soon, if you just sit tight and wait for a few minutes. But remember, I get the credit, if I helped." And, with that, still laughing, he turned and walked away.

She wandered to the nearby picnic table and sat down on the top of it, with her feet on the bench. The animals busied themselves, while Doreen waited. Mugs rolled around in the sand beside her. Thaddeus walked back and forth on the picnic table, and Goliath sprawled out beside her atop the table.

"Mugs, you can go in the water, if you want to swim." She quickly unleashed him and then noted the posted warning sign, saying dogs must be on a leash only. But, by then, Mugs was already racing into the water. Doreen groaned, realizing that, hey, if somebody wanted to cause trouble for her, it would be right about now.

And, sure enough, somebody spoke up. "Hey, dogs have

to be on a leash."

She looked up to see an old guy yelling at her, and, yeah, as far as she was concerned, he was quite a bit older than Milford. She winced and nodded and tried calling Mugs back. He wasn't very impressed, but eventually he returned to her, shaking tons of lake water off his coat. But he looked very happy. She apologized to the older man, who still glared at her. "You're right," she agreed. "I unclipped him, and then I saw the sign."

"Well, at least he didn't bite anybody," he admitted grudgingly.

"Mugs would never bite anybody," she replied, and then she shut her mouth. Because that wasn't true. Mugs didn't bite anybody *who was nice*. But, if anybody attacked her, well, Mugs was all over them. And she sure couldn't count on the fact that he might not bite anybody under those circumstances.

The old guy looked at her with a knowing look and added, "All dogs bite."

"Again, you're right," she agreed. "All dogs bite, depending on the circumstances."

"Exactly, don't ever expect an animal to do what you want them to do when the chips are down."

An absentminded tone filled his voice.

"I don't see you around here," he noted abruptly.

He probably considered himself the Sarsons Beach Police. She smiled. "I'm from the Mission Creek side."

"A little way away from home, aren't you?" he asked suspiciously.

"No, not a whole lot," she stated quietly. "I was here on Sunday and saw a box of poison in the garden bed, so I was hoping it had been cleaned up already."

He frowned at her, turned to the exact same spot she spoke of, and nodded. "I cleaned it up. You could have done it when you were here," he accused.

"And, if I had come by vehicle, I would have," she explained. "I came on a paddleboard, and we left the same way, so it wasn't an easy thing to collect it and to put it safely somewhere."

"You could have put it in the garbage," he stated.

"Maybe. I was also with a cop, and he called for somebody to come clean it up, so I assumed that it was being done immediately."

At that, the old guy laughed. "The cops? Do something? Something like that? No way. They probably phoned the city to come do a clean-up. You know? Like in the grocery store. *Clean up on aisle one.*" And then he laughed at his own joke.

For somebody who supposedly didn't talk much, he didn't seem to want to shut up anytime soon. She asked him, "Where did you put it?"

"Me? I just threw it—" And then he stopped, frowned at her, and asked, "Why?"

"I just want to make sure it was safely disposed of, so we don't have to worry about kids in the park getting at it."

"Well, that's why I cleaned it up," he snapped, giving her that look that said she should have as well.

"And that's why we called the authorities," she repeated quietly. "I just want to make sure that nobody else will get poisoned." And, of course, he pounced on that.

"*Else?* Did somebody get poisoned?"

The question was a little convoluted. She shook her head. "I don't think so, but I know a guy who died recently of poison. So, when I heard that, I was thinking of this stash of poison, and I didn't want anybody to get hurt from it," she explained, wondering why it was getting harder to talk to this guy.

Again he nodded. "Well, I put it away."

"You put it away?" she asked. "What does that mean?" He just glared at her. She held up a hand. "Sorry. I'm not trying to get too personal. I just want to make sure that it's disposed of properly."

"Well, I wonder if your *properly* done disposal is the same as mine," he snapped. "In my day, we never would have left that out in the open for somebody to grab. We would have put it away on the top shelf in the back corner of a garage." He just glared at her.

She nodded. "Well, hopefully nobody will have access to it there."

"Of course not," he retorted. "Pretty sure it was mine anyway."

At that, she stiffened. "Did you have a break-in recently?"

He shrugged. "In my day, we didn't lock up, like we have to now. Today it seems like just having a door means an *open* door. It used to be, if there was a door, locked or not, people respected it and didn't walk in."

"And so you didn't keep it locked, and somebody walked in and helped themselves, is that it?"

He didn't say anything, just continued to glare at her.

Doreen nodded. "Well, I'm sure the cops wouldn't hold anything against you, if that were the case."

"Cops? What cops?" he asked, frowning at her. "I don't talk to no cops."

"Right," she replied, wondering at the added crankiness. "I just meant that, if anybody had been hurt by it, nobody would blame you if somebody had come in and broken into your place to steal your rat poison."

"No, of course they wouldn't." He stared at her. "Why would you even think that? Rat poison can be purchased anywhere. Besides mine is old and at this point a mix of rat poisons."

"I don't know," she murmured. "It was just a thought that crossed my mind." She shook her head in confusion. "Why a mix?"

"Because I got some of a different brand from my brother way back when and forgot I had the box and bought a newer one a some point, but there was no point in keeping two so I dumped them altogether, not that it's any of your business," he snapped, then walked away, muttering something about "Stupid people. Interfering nosy-bodies …"

She watched him leave, and then, with the animals at her side, she hopped up to see just how far away he lived. She could hardly tell Mack that the poison had been picked up and was suspiciously taken from this old guy's house if she didn't at least have a name, and she highly doubted that the cranky old man would give her one—certainly not now. The only way she could get any evidence for Mack to pursue would be if she found out where he lived.

So, proceeding cautiously, knowing that this guy could cause her quite a lot of grief if he thought she was up to something, she watched as he disappeared into an cheap house that needed a lot of work at the end of the block. Well, not so much a cheap home but one which hadn't been properly kept and maintained, like the other ones on this street. After all, this was prime real estate, close to the park, close to the beach.

She casually walked past the house he had entered, jotted

down the number, without trying to make it look like she was, and then headed around the block, so that he wouldn't think that she'd come deliberately after him. As soon as she was clear, she and her animals hopped back into her vehicle and drove home.

At least the whole time that she'd been with the old guy, Mugs hadn't caused any disruption. Matter of fact, he just laid at her feet, ignoring the world going on around her. And that was a bit weird in itself too, but he seemed to be comfortable with the old man, so why wasn't she?

Chapter 6

BACK HOME AGAIN, Doreen sat down, added to her notes. She still didn't have anything concrete but was a little bit closer to something, even if she didn't know what that something was. She made herself a pot of coffee and waited in anticipation for it to be done.

When Nan phoned, just as she poured a fresh cup of coffee, she stared down at the Caller ID number and wondered if she should answer. If Nan invited her for a visit, Doreen would feel like she'd have to go—but she had just made coffee. ... A limited supply in her world.

Nan continued to let the call ring on Doreen's phone.

Doreen quickly answered it, before it went to her voice mail. "Hey, Nan."

"What were you doing? Sitting there with coffee?"

Doreen laughed because it was so close to the truth. "I just made a fresh pot of coffee," she admitted, "and I was afraid to answer the phone, in case you would want me to come down for a visit, and I would lose out on the fresh-brewed hot coffee." She had explained in such a woebegone voice that her grandmother laughed.

"I would have at least waited until you'd had your coffee," she noted, still chuckling. "Besides, you do need to come down. We have some information." And, with that, she hung up.

Doreen stared down at the phone with a gasp. "You did not just do that."

What was with everybody hanging up on her? And, of course, she wouldn't discuss the fact that she hung up on Mack all the time. That was Mack; he deserved it. But for Nan to hang up on her own granddaughter? Surely Doreen didn't deserve her grandmother hanging up on her all the time. Mystified at what they could possibly have found, and yet, at the same time, worried and wondering what Doreen should be doing about it now, she sipped her coffee, considering her options. When her coffee was cool enough to drink, Doreen almost chugged it.

She groaned. "And that's why I didn't want to answer Nan's phone call," she muttered to herself. She looked down at the animals, staring up at her hungrily. "And we didn't even eat," she muttered. She fed them a little bit of dry food and quickly made herself a sandwich. When everybody was done eating, and the prep mess was cleaned up, Doreen sent her grandmother a text. **On my way.** She didn't get an acknowledgment, but, hey, she was pretty sure that her grandmother had gotten the message and would wait for her.

At least this way Nan could put on the tea. She had the uncanny ability to figure out exactly when Doreen was coming or how long it would take her to get to Rosemoor because, every time she and her animals appeared for a visit with Nan, the tea was already steeping. By the time the group of them walked down to the center today, Nan was sitting outside, waiting for them.

Doreen smiled. "How do you always know when I'm

coming?"

"Well, you did text me," Nan replied, her eyes wide, as she stared at her granddaughter.

"I did," she agreed. "I just figured, when I didn't hear from you, I didn't know if you saw it."

"Of course I saw it," she stated, with a wave of her hand. "No point in responding since you were on your way."

"True." She sat down, as Nan gushed over Mugs and Goliath. Thaddeus, not to be outdone, walked down Doreen's arm onto the table and pecked a musical rhythm against the hot teapot. Nan just laughed at him.

"You are such a joy to have around." And, sure enough, he walked up her arm and sat on her shoulder and just cuddled in.

"I don't think he'll ever forget you," Doreen noted. "You two have quite a bond."

"So do you two." Nan chuckled. "And that's the way it should be."

Doreen wasn't sure what that meant but was happy to just wait and to let her grandmother talk when she was ready. By the time ten minutes had gone by though, Doreen was getting impatient. "So what information do you have?" she asked.

Nan looked at her. "I'm not sure I'm ready to share it yet."

Doreen stared at her, nonplussed. "I thought that's why you wanted me to come down."

"I always want you to come down and visit," she stated. "That's not the point."

"No, of course not," she agreed, and then she sighed. "So this is just a visit? You don't have anything concrete?"

"Well, of course we have something concrete," she stated

in astonishment. "I wouldn't have told you that we had something if we didn't."

At that, Doreen groaned. "Nan, could you just tell me what you found out?"

"Oh, sure." Nan smiled. "As long as you realize that our investigation isn't complete."

"Of course not," she replied. "Investigations are always ongoing. We aren't looking for complete as much as we're looking for information to lead us into the right direction."

"Well, in that case," she added, "I definitely have something."

Doreen looked at her and waited.

"Let me get my notes." Nan got up and went into the other room, and, when she returned, she had a notepad. "Chrissy started talking—as far as anybody here knows—months before she died."

"Talking about what?" Doreen asked, all down to business.

"Talking about being poisoned."

"And did anybody tell her to go to the doctor and to get checked out?"

"Oh, yes, of course, dear," she stated. "Several of us told her to call the police. But she was starting to, you know, get a little bit ..." Nan looked up at Doreen, looping her finger in a circle around her ear. "You know? She was getting quite forgetful, and she was quite *fanciful*, I guess is a good word," she noted. "So, over time, we all just stopped listening to her."

"And when you say, *over time*, you mean in the months before her death?"

"Yes, of course. It couldn't have gone on any longer. She died, dear. Pay attention."

POISON IN THE PANSIES

At that, Doreen let out her breath slowly and then nodded. "You're right. Go ahead."

Satisfied, Nan looked down at her notes, reading something before speaking again. "And then, about a month before she died, she started saying that it would happen soon. *It would happen soon.*"

"And do you know what *it* was?"

"She wouldn't clarify. She kept saying that she would be dead soon, and we all assumed that's what she meant. *It would happen soon,* as in, *she would die soon.* Which, of course, as you know, she was totally correct because she did."

"Right," she agreed carefully. "She did die soon, but it was still another month later, right?"

"Yes, exactly," Nan confirmed, "so it wasn't all that soon. Or it was, depends on your definition of *soon.*"

As Nan looked to be gearing up for another discussion on the perspective on *time* and *soon,* Doreen asked, "What other notes have you got written down there?"

Nan's focus returned to her notes. She mumbled through something, as she ticked off and crossed off a few things. "Her nephew inherited everything," she shared. "We thought that was suspicious."

"And why is that?"

"Because she has a daughter."

"Okay. Any idea why her daughter was excluded from the will?"

"No, that didn't make any sense to us," she replied. "Chrissy rarely talked about her daughter, but she was family, so we naturally assumed that her daughter would have been at least mentioned in Chrissy's will."

"Of course. And where does the daughter live?"

"I don't know." Nan looked up at her, with a frown.

"We haven't been able to figure that out."

"And what about her name?"

"Her name is Cassandra," she replied, as she pulled her glasses down her nose and peered over the top of them. "I think that's what I have written down somewhere here. I do seem to recall that name, *Cassandra*, but I don't know her last name."

At that, Doreen nodded. "Okay, so the nephew inherited everything from Chrissy's will. Do we know what his name is?"

Nan nodded. "Peter."

"Okay, that's an easy name to remember," Doreen noted. "Now we have Peter and Cassandra. What about last names?"

Nan shrugged. "We don't really worry about last names here very much, dear. Everybody at Rosemoor has been married two and three times. So we really don't bother to learn more than first names here."

"Right." Doreen smiled. "It still does help to get some history, when doing investigations like this."

"Oh." She thought about it and nodded. "I guess you can't just type in Cassandra and expect to get the right one, huh?"

"No, sure can't," she replied. "Does anybody here likely know what the last names are?"

Nan thought about it for a bit before answering. "You know what? Let me just call Richie." And, with that, she took out her phone. When she explained to Richie what she was after, she put her phone on Speaker and stated, "Doreen's here visiting, but I don't know how to find Cassandra's or Peter's last names."

"Let me think about it." He pondered that for a moment. "I'll contact Laura. I'll be down in a minute." And, with that, he seemed to disappear off the phone. Yet it sounded like he was walking down the hallway with his phone still on.

Doreen frowned at that. "Has he still got his phone on?" she asked her grandmother quietly.

Nan nodded. "Which is why his battery is forever running out on him." She shook her head. "And the one time you actually want the man to be there and ready and available, his phone's dead, and he doesn't get any messages," she complained loudly.

"I heard that," Richie growled from a long way away. "Of course I've got my phone on still. Then I don't have to redial to get you guys when I get the information."

Nan sat up straight in her chair and gave Doreen a bright smile. "See? He's perfectly fine."

"I'm sure he is." Doreen picked up her cup of tea and took a big sip of it. It was lovely tea. She sat back, closed her eyes, and just let the steam from the top of the cup bathe her face.

"You look tired, dear."

Her gaze flew open, and she stared at Nan. "I'm doing quite well. I had a pretty relaxing weekend."

"And now you're bored."

"I am?"

"Oh, yes. If we're looking into Chrissy's murder, you've only got this poisoning case to work on. So you must be bored. I'm surprised you haven't delved into those other files at your house."

"Well, it's under consideration," she replied. "I just wasn't sure I was mentally ready to handle a really big case."

"Oh no, that Bob Small matter? Oh my, you need preparation for that," she stated wisely. "And, of course, we're helping right now, just so that you can get a break and can get the rest you deserve, before you get on to those bigger cases."

Nan had spoken this with such a knowing air that Doreen had to laugh. "I don't know how big they'll be. According to Mack, we don't have that many cold cases anymore."

"Yep, but now that you've brought in the Bob Small stuff," Nan noted, "that's a whole different story. Plus, you still have Solomon's research files. You won't run out of work anytime soon. But you might run out of *oomph*, which is what this is all about. As long as we can help take some of the pressure off you with this legwork and initial research, you should be right as rain for the next one."

"Thank you for that," she said humbly. "It's nice to know you care."

Nan reached across, patted her hand. "Dear, I would be lost without you. Anytime you need me to help out, you just let me know."

Doreen grinned at her grandmother. "Thank you."

Nan gave her a wicked grin. "And I know perfectly well that you don't really want our help," she admitted in a conspiratorial whisper. "But it's equally important that we have something to do to keep us sharp."

"Of course." Doreen laughed. "It would never do for you to become anything less than sharp. If you were any sharper, Nan, you'd be cutting my hand every time we talk."

At that, her grandmother went off in peals of laughter. "I've still got it," she replied, tapping her brain. "So good of you to notice."

Doreen smiled at her. "Nan, you've always been a little

bit different, a little bit off, a little bit weird and unique, but, whatever it is that you've got, believe me. You've still got it."

And, in sheer delight, her grandmother laughed and laughed.

It went on for so long that it was hard to hear anything else, until suddenly a voice snapped, "Would you stop that?"

It was Richie, speaking through his phone.

"Good Lord. Here I'm trying to have a conversation with you, and all you keep doing is caterwauling."

"I'm here. I'm here," Nan replied smartly. "What did you find out?" And she heard voices in the background on Richie's end of the call. "Laura says, it's Peter Riley. R-I-L-E-Y. And it was Cassandra ..." Nan looked back at Doreen expectantly. "Richie, are you there? I can't hear what Cassandra's last name was."

"That's because we're looking it up," he replied. "Just give us a minute."

"Okay." Nan looked over at Doreen and shrugged. "At least we're getting you some names."

"Absolutely," she replied. "I still need to figure out why anybody would murder Chrissy though."

"Well, that's obvious," Richie responded testily on the phone. "That nephew wanted to inherit everything."

"But what did he inherit?" Doreen asked him curiously. "Was Chrissy wealthy?"

"Oh dear no," Nan answered. "There were some months when we had to pitch in to help her pay for her Rosemoor bill. She would overspend her account and then couldn't pay it off."

Doreen stared at her grandmother. "But, if that's the case, why would somebody kill her because obviously there wouldn't have been very much for them to inherit."

At that, Nan looked at her, frowning. "Well, there is that, I suppose." She stopped and asked, "What do you think, Richie?"

"We know people who would have killed each other for a cup of coffee," he explained, "so her argument isn't persuading me one way or the other at the moment."

At that, Nan nodded. "We really do have to trust in what Chrissy said. I mean, if she felt people were trying to poison her, you know I'm inclined to believe her."

"I hear you," Doreen agreed, "and that is a valid point."

"Of course it is," she confirmed.

At that, Richie's voice came through the phone again. "Aha, Cassandra Mason," he said in a triumphant voice. "Now, now you go do your thing, Doreen." He added, "And track down that nasty little nephew who stole everything." And, with that, he hung up the phone.

Chapter 7

Wednesday Morning

DOREEN WOKE UP and rolled over and stared across the end of her bed out the window at the gray weather. "Kelowna never has gray weather," she muttered.

But obviously, nearing fall—if one could count August as fall, which of course it wasn't; it wasn't even close— definitely some weather changes were happening. And that was okay. Doreen was totally okay to not have the crazy-hot weather that they'd had for some days. A few cool days would be nice.

She got up, had a hot shower, headed downstairs, feeding all the animals, and then putting on her coffee. She wondered if she would get to drink the whole pot herself while it was still fresh or if something would disrupt it.

As she settled at the kitchen table with her first cup of joe, her gaze landed on the notepad from last night. She pulled it closer and studied the last couple notes she had written down. She'd done a search on the two people related to Chrissy, using the names she had been given: Cassandra Mason and Peter Riley. Not a whole lot had come up. Doreen wasn't exactly sure how to do much in terms of who had inherited from Chrissy's will. What she needed was somebody close to the family, who might have known something.

Doreen did get the idea that Cassandra and Peter were both still in town—or at least nearby. With that thought, she quickly checked to see if either of their names were mentioned in the phone book. Nope. A quick search of the internet gave Doreen a single hit. She got a mention of a Cassandra at the Rutland pub, but it didn't tell Doreen much. She wandered outside onto her deck, with her cup of coffee and her animals, and then down to the bench by the river. Surely there would be a little bit more information available somewhere.

Hearing her weird neighbor's voice close by, she called out, "Richard."

She got a *harrumph* for an answer.

"Do you happen to know anything about Chrissy from the Rosemoor home? She passed away a few months back, said she was being poisoned."

Doreen heard a *bang*, as something was put against the fence that separated their properties, and then Richard's head popped up over the top.

"I know Peter Riley," he replied, "if that's who you're asking about."

She stared at him. "Okay. I understand he inherited everything from his aunt."

At that, Richard nodded. "He's a good guy." Richard paused. "Whereas his cousin, that Cassandra woman," he added, "wow. She's one of *those* women."

Doreen stared at him. "What does *one of those women* mean?" she asked.

"You know? She works at that bar there in Rutland."

104

Still not understanding what he was saying, Doreen frowned. "Like you know, like a girly bar. A sports bar." Doreen shook her head. He added, "Where they let things hang out."

"A stripper bar?"

"Yeah, exactly that," he confirmed, with a headshake. "She was always a little bit on the loose side of life."

"Interesting," Doreen murmured. "She apparently didn't inherit any of Chrissy's estate."

"What estate?" he asked, raising both hands. "That woman was broke."

"So you did know her."

"We went to school together," he noted. "She was a few years older, but they were from, you know, the wrong side of the tracks, and they were always broke. She married a handyman, and they stayed broke. The only good one in that family is Peter."

"Well, lack of money doesn't make someone bad though," she noted in a dry tone.

"No, not at all, but Chrissy was always a little bit, you know, kind of off in her head. All her life she was always saying that people were doing things to her."

"Like what?"

He shrugged. "In school she used to say things, like her daddy was touching her all the time."

At that, Doreen's mouth opened.

"Yeah, exactly," he agreed. "And yet apparently, no abuse was to be found. She used to make up stories about Cassandra being a bad little girl too. We never quite understood, but it was *that* family you avoided."

"That's so sad," Doreen replied quietly. "Maybe Chrissy needed some mental health assistance."

"Oh, she needed that plus," he stated, with an eye roll.

"Just before she died, she was telling everybody that she was being poisoned."

"Exactly," Doreen cried out. "Do we have any idea if she was?"

He stared at her. "Did you hear what I just said? She made up stories all the time."

"So, in other words, she was the kind of person who cried wolf?"

"Right. And, even if she *was* being poisoned at that point," he added, "no way anybody would have listened to her."

"And that's sad too," she replied quietly.

He shrugged. "But why poison her? No real reason to. She didn't have any money. It was all she could do to pay her Rosemoor bill. From what I heard, her government assistance money and her husband's disability pension went to pay for everything. Or at least, that's what Peter had said. And he had to top it up quite a bit too. So, I mean, if anything were to come his way at the end of the day, well, he was due," Richard stated. And he waved at her and added, "Go find some other family to torment."

"Torment?" she asked.

He shot her a gimlet look. "Yeah, *torment*," he repeated, with an eye roll. "Haven't you bothered the rest of us enough?"

"No, I haven't done anything to you."

He just snorted and hopped down from whatever he was standing on.

She settled back with her cup of coffee and pondered such a small town where they all went to school together and knew each other and kept tabs on everybody's goings-on around them while they grew up and went their separate ways.

She called out over the fence. "I wonder what Chrissy would have said about you?" At that, Doreen heard a harsh *bang* against the fence, and she snickered. "I guess not something you want to necessarily have me hear about, *huh?*"

Soon the back door of his house slammed shut.

Her presence alone had chased him inside. Still, her heart went out to Chrissy, who obviously could have used some support, maybe some professional counseling over the years. It wasn't an easy thing to always be mocked or laughed at or belittled. And Doreen understood.

Chances were very good that maybe Chrissy had had much less than an ideal life, and, as a result, maybe she'd made up stories in order to get attention? But would she have continued to do that at the end of her life? And then Doreen thought about it and realized that the end of life was often very similar to the beginning of life. Sometimes you were surrounded by people who you loved, and sometimes you weren't. Sometimes you had the advantage of good people to look after you, and sometimes it was more of a caregiver situation, which is how Chrissy ended up later in her life. And maybe in all of it, she was once again starved for attention and was making up stories.

Doreen had to admit that she'd been a little worried about Nan and Richie jumping on this whole issue as it was. Just because they wanted there to be a case didn't mean there was a case. And none of that was helping her to solve the other case on Alan's death. She pondered that for a moment. And then she sent Mack a text. **I know who cleaned up the box of rat poison and where it came from.**

When she got no immediate response, she wondered if he was tied up in a meeting or with a case or where he was.

She frowned, as she sat here and waited. Finally, after a long enough wait with no response, she stated, "Fine, see if I care."

She got up and headed back inside for her second cup of coffee. As she entered her kitchen, Mack was stealing the last cup of coffee from the pot. She stared at him, shaking her head, Mugs sitting at Mack's feet, staring up at him with adoration. "He didn't even let me know you were here," she complained.

He shrugged. "You left the back door open. When he heard me, he just came running, not even barking."

"Of course not," she replied. "You've ruined my watch-dog."

Mack laughed. "Mugs was never a watchdog, but he's a great companion."

At that, Mugs woofed and looked over at her, as if to say, *See? He appreciates me.*

She sighed. "And why are you here now?" she asked.

"Well, I was heading over anyway. I wanted to pop in and to spend a moment or two, but then you sent me that text." He narrowed his gaze at her. "What are you up to?" She opened her eyes wide, a picture of innocence, and he shook his head. "Oh no, you don't," he snapped. "I'm wise to that expression."

"Sure you are," she said, with an airy hand. "Besides, you don't know anything."

"No, but I keep hoping you'll tell me," he replied. "And then I won't have to drag it outta you."

She asked, "Can you do that?"

Such curiosity was in her voice that he burst out laughing. He shrugged. "I probably could because you'd feel guilty if you were to keep anything from me too long." She chewed on her bottom lip, and he nodded. "See? You're still one of the good guys," he noted. "You might withhold information for a little bit, but you would feel bad about it, just in case it was something I needed."

She sighed. "It's not much fun being a Goody Two-Shoes, you know?"

His eyes twinkling, he nodded. "Nope, I wouldn't know."

Chapter 8

D OREEN ROLLED HER eyes at him and led the way back out to the deck. "I was down at the creek."

"If you want, we can go down there."

She nodded. "That would be nice. As long as the weather holds."

"It should be really nice again soon," he noted.

"It's pretty early for fall weather. It's just overcast and grayer than I was expecting today."

"And maybe that's your mood?" he asked, looking at her inquisitively.

She shrugged. "I guess it's possible. Yet I don't have any reason to be upset or depressed though."

He nodded and didn't say anything. When they got to the bench, he sat down beside her and sighed happily. "It's a beautiful spot to sit and enjoy."

"It is, indeed."

As they sat here quietly enjoying the area, he looked over at her and asked, "Now you want to explain what it is that you're up to?"

"How come I always have to explain?" she muttered.

His lips twitched. "Maybe 'cause you're the one who's

always up to something."

She glared at him. "You know you're up to just as much."

At that, he laughed out loud. "Maybe," he agreed, "but what I'm up to is something I'm allowed to be up to."

She shrugged. "I don't see why I can't go do things like you do."

"If you want to become a cop and go through all that training, you can," he stated easily.

She stopped and stared at him, as she pondered what that would look like in her life.

He waited, one eyebrow raised. "Would you really consider it?" he asked curiously.

"No, I don't think so." She paused, then frowned. "It's not that I'm too old." And she looked at him pointedly.

He shook his head. "It's not that you're too old, but you might find it a bit more rigorous than you were expecting."

"Maybe," she noted quietly. "It also won't necessarily be fun."

"No, probably not," he agreed. "However, if it's something that you want to do, then you should do it."

She looked at him and then smiled. "See? You're a pretty good cheerleader yourself."

He rolled his eyes at that. "Can't say I'm trying to be a cheerleader."

"Nope, but it comes by you naturally." And then she reached across, patted his knee, and added, "No, I'm not coming after your job."

At that, he burst out laughing. "That's good." He nodded, with a smile. "Not that I was terribly worried about you coming after it though."

"You should be," she stated. "I would be good at it."

"You would be," he confirmed, his voice turning serious. "And you should consider that, if it's something that you want to do. I don't know what the requirements are right now to get into law enforcement, but we all know that you're a natural for it."

Pleased, she looked at him in delight. "Seriously?"

"Of course. I'm not sure that that's what you want to do with your life though."

"No, it isn't," she replied. "I mean, maybe if I were twenty years younger."

He just rolled his eyes at that. "And here you just said it wasn't about age."

"I know. I mean, there's no age limit," she explained.

"Well, there probably is, isn't there?"

"It's more about a heavy physical element required."

At that, she shuddered. "I'm not so sure I could do that part."

He chuckled. "It is a requirement though. You have to be physically fit for this job."

"So no jokes about doughnuts and cops, *huh*?"

"We laugh about it, just as much as anyone. It's a bit of a no-brainer in the movies," he teased. "But, at the same time, you have to be there, ready and physically fit to do the job."

She sighed, thought about it, and shook her head. "I wasn't really thinking about becoming a cop. That's not really where my heart lies." She shrugged. "Solving crimes, yes, but, unless I could go into the cold cases section, I don't know that much else would appeal."

"Most divisions have a Cold Case Department. But a lot of people really don't understand how that works."

"Even if I did understand that," she replied blithely, "I'd

just ignore it." He turned and fully faced her. She shrugged. "Sometimes you guys need things shaken up. So that you see how you used to do things isn't always the best way to continue doing things."

"Right," he teased, "so let's just completely ignore all the years of learning how to do something in favor of what?" he asked. "Just a slapdash attitude and go and do whatever you want?" She frowned at him. He just grinned back.

She sighed. "You're making fun of me again."

"What do you mean, *again?*" he protested. "Besides, sometimes you just leave yourself completely open for that stuff."

"Maybe," she admitted, "but I am good at rooting out information."

"That you are," he agreed. "You're also very good at getting people to talk to you, probably because you're not a cop," he noted, "so maybe just keep this as a hobby. And you'll do lots of good work that way."

"Do you think so?" she asked, noting with surprise the wistfulness in her own voice.

"Does it bother you to not have some job title or a label involved in this work that you do?"

"I don't know that it *bothers* me," she replied quietly. "For years I was just a *wife*." She punctuated the word with a wave of her hand. "And not even a wife who contributed anything."

"You mean, a trophy wife?"

She winced at that. "And yet, how can I get mad at you for saying what I'm sure everybody else said."

"Well, what they said before versus what they're saying now," he explained, "reveals you are a very different person today."

"I am. And I'm very happy to hear that. It's like I have to atone for all those wasted years," she shared quietly.

"Oh, I don't think so," he disagreed. "I don't even think that's a healthy way to look at it. You didn't do anything wrong."

"But I didn't do anything right either," she murmured, sending him a sideways look. She stretched her legs out, kicking up some sand in front of her. "It's almost as if there was *that* life and *this* life, and I'm still trying to figure out what this one's all about."

"You can, but there's no rush. Take your time, figure it out, do what you want to do. Enjoy life for a change," he added. "You'll never convince me that you enjoyed your life before, not with that jerk around." He finished with an eye roll.

She grinned at him. "You're still upset that I was even married to him."

He stopped, looked at her, and asked, "You figured that out, *huh?*"

"Every once in a while, it sounds like you're jealous."

"Yeah, every once in a while, I probably am jealous," he admitted quietly. "That guy had a lot of prime years with you," he noted. "And I don't think he appreciated any of them."

She smiled. "I think that's one of the nicest things anybody's ever said to me."

"Well, that husband of yours kept you as a pet. A trophy wife, sure, but definitely you didn't have any freedom to be who you wanted to be. So right now is all about what's good for you." He continued. "And it's a gift. You have the gift of time. Sure, I get it. You're broke for the moment, but you are getting through. You've got money coming in on the horizon from multiple sources. Not very many people can say that. Plus, you have done pretty well for somebody who didn't have anything to begin with."

"Yeah, well, without Nan, I don't know that I would have done all that well. Mugs and I would be homeless." She shuddered at the thought. "And that's without me counting the number of times you fed me."

He grinned. "And then there's the number of times that you've helped me out on cases or brought cases to our attention and closed them that I really haven't wanted to bring up too often," he acknowledged. "So why don't we just call it even."

"Is that instead of saying *thank you*?" He just eye-rolled her at that statement. She burst out laughing. "I admit, now that I've been here in Kelowna for several months, I am still not all that sure that I belong here, that I'm accepted here, and certainly having the ex show up hasn't been terribly comforting either. But I'm getting there." She looked up at Mack. "On all fronts."

"Good." He settled into the bench. "And now how about we go back to all that information that you seem to have dredged up that you haven't told me about."

She sighed, but then she explained about Milford, who led her to the older guy she also met at the beach.

"So you think he had the poison stolen from his garage and then what? Somebody threw it away at the beach?"

Doreen shrugged.

"It's possible, and, of course, an old guy like that? They often don't like calling the cops, and he probably would not want somebody to question his memory or to even accuse him of not handling the rat poison in a safe manner, possibly charging him for having left the poison lying around like that. We see it time and time again. Some of these oldsters, old-timers, they're fairly protective about their way of doing things versus us young whippersnappers," he teased in a mocking voice.

She laughed. "Yeah, that would be him too. And I did follow him home," she murmured, with a sideways look at Mack's face, seeing it darken. She refocused her gaze to stare forward. "Anyway," she added, "it's nothing solid to go on. Yet that rat poison, isn't exactly something I'm terribly happy to know was out in a public park."

"And yet, if anybody was up to something more than a prank," he replied, "I highly doubt they would have just tossed the box."

"Maybe not. I don't know if you can track poison from box to box, like they do on the TV shows," she noted. "They seem to have this magical little set of tools that make everything work."

Mack laughed at that. "We should be so lucky," he replied bluntly, "but real life isn't like that."

"So there's no way to know if that box had anything to do with your guy who died in Rutland?"

He stopped, gave her a puzzled look, and asked, "How do you know he lived in Rutland?"

She gave him a wide-eyed innocent look that didn't fool him for an instant. She shrugged. "I got that far. I was just looking to see if it was related to the box of poison."

He frowned at her. She frowned right back. "What did you find out?"

She hesitated. However, realizing his frown meant a whole lot more than just curiosity, she took his question to be more of a direct order to fess up or else. She sighed. "I really don't like that look on your face."

"Why not?" he asked, his gaze narrowing.

"Because it makes me feel like I'm in trouble."

"And is that a good thing or a bad thing?" he asked, looking at her. This time there was more curiosity in his gaze.

"It's neither," she noted, "but I can't imagine anything like that's ever good."

"Doesn't have to be bad either."

She nodded, but she wrapped her arms around her chest, as if feeling a chill.

"Did he ever beat you?"

"We've been over this," she snapped bluntly. "And there's an awful lot of things that people can do to you that has nothing to do with feeling their hand against your face."

"Very true," he agreed, "but you also know that I would never hit you."

She nodded, smiled, relieved. "I do know that," she stated brightly.

"And you're still not getting out of telling me what happened."

She frowned. "If you're talking about Rutland, fine. I'm not talking about my husband."

"Good. I don't like that man anyway."

She laughed. "Fine. But, as far as what's going on right now, I met an old woman in Rutland, and we talked by the grocery store where this guy Alan worked. This guy was pretty well loved."

Mack nodded. "Everybody deserves to be loved."

"Isn't that the truth, and it's just sad that he was cut down way too early in life. But he's the one who made a report to the police, so surely you guys have figured it out."

"Not yet," he noted cautiously. "Obviously we're working on it."

She frowned at that. "Sometimes you guys work too slow," she announced. He just ignored her. "But I know that you're not doing nothing."

"Well, right now, I'm sitting here, having a cup of coffee with you," he explained, "because we all need to catch a break sometime. We also need people to share information."

She groaned. "Well, nobody had a whole lot to say about it. And that is a problem."

"Sure it is," he agreed. "Nice guy and yet he was poisoned to death. The next questions are, *Who, how, what, and why?*"

"And what did you find out?"

He shrugged. "Not a whole lot to find out. He was married but now divorced, although not the partying type. He had been to dinner at a friend's house the previous night, but that wasn't found to be the source of the poison."

"Well, there had to be a source somewhere," she noted in astonishment.

"Sure. There has to be. That doesn't mean that we're seeing *where* and *what* though."

"Maybe not," she agreed, frowning. "What was his relationship at work like?"

"Everybody apparently loved him," he replied quietly, "just like your witness said."

"And that always makes me suspicious again," she muttered. "Maybe you need to check out the coworkers a little closer."

"Why?"

"Opportunity," she noted, looking over at him. "If the only constant in his life was work, then who else would have had that opportunity to administer the poison? And is it something that was administered once, or is it something that he was exposed to over time?"

"I'm waiting on forensics to come back with that." Just then his phone buzzed. He pulled it out and rolled through something on his screen.

When a frown lit his face and darkened his features, she leaned in closer to him. "And?"

He shook his head. "No *and*s," he muttered, "but definitely something to think about."

"You need to tell me more."

He gave her one raised eyebrow. "No, I don't," he bit off. "It's the autopsy report."

"It was rat poison – likely warfarin, wasn't it?" she asked.

He stared at her. "How would you know?"

"I'm really struggling with the word *coincidence* these days," she explained. "And it seems to me that that's too much of a coincidence. We just saw a box of rat poison in a garden bed by the beach."

"A long way away from where this guy lived and worked. There is no coincidence."

"So tell me flat-out, looking me straight in the eye, that it wasn't that what killed him."

He lifted his head and firmly stated, "It wasn't warfarin." But his lips twitched and his eyes slid to the side.

"So it was rat poison," she confirmed, even if he was being cagey with her. "You may want to go get that box," she muttered. "Test it for fingerprints not to mention ingredients."

He crossed his arms over his chest and glared at her. She mimicked his position and glared right back. He groaned and stared up at the sky. "Fine. It was a mix of ingredients used in rat poisons, not warfarin as an isolated ingredient."

"Cyanide?"

He shook his head. "No I don't believe so. You need to tell me which house it was. And I'll go talk to him."

"Good idea." She described the house, not far from the beach, and the address for it.

"It doesn't mean anything though," he cautioned.

"Maybe not," she noted, "but I would really like to get into Alan's apartment."

He stared at her and shook his hand. "You know that's not happening."

"Well, if there's nothing in his place to find …"

"I didn't see anything suspicious, and I was there yesterday, and," he added, "we looked for any kind of poison."

"Exactly, opportunity and all that, but you need to find somebody who works at the store who lives down maybe in the Sarsons area."

"I think we can figure that out," he stated bluntly.

"I know. I'm just stating the obvious," she muttered. "Sometimes it's better to state the obvious than to get caught up and forget the simple things in life. Still, don't you think Alan's poisoning happening recently and Chrissy's from a few months earlier are suspicious?"

"Chrissy?"

"She lived at Rosemoor. Always complaining about people poisoning her."

"Right." Mack nodded. "Died of natural causes." He shook his head. "You focus on Chrissy."

"Yeah, I will," she confirmed. "Speaking of which, I have to go up to Rutland and find Cassandra."

"Who's she?"

"Chrissy's daughter," she replied succinctly. "The woman who was left out of her mother's will. She works in a strip bar, apparently."

"You know that we've seen things like that time and time again," he noted, looking at her quietly. "Sometimes the parents can't accept what the children do for a living."

"Well, apparently, this Cassandra Mason—and Peter Riley, the nephew, who got the contents of the will—was also topping up her Rosemoor residential expenses and apparently is a stand-up guy," she explained, with a shrug.

"So what? Hang on a minute. You're telling me no murder was here?" he asked, giving her a bright grin. "No cold case to dredge up?"

She glared at him. "I don't know if there is or not, but you know I have to deal with Nan and Richie."

"Richie is involved?" he asked, a tone of alarm entering his voice.

She gave him a fat smile. "Yes, so looks like Darren'll have his hands full too."

Mack shook his head at that. "I tell you what. Things are bad enough down there with those seniors acting badly, but when those two get together?" He shook his head. "Like dealing with undisciplined teenagers."

"And somebody named Laura is involved in their investigation too," Doreen added, "but I don't know to what extent."

"Laura Hillman," he replied. "Another—" And then he stopped and fell silent.

"Another what?" She glared at him. "Don't you dare say something that'll insult Nan."

"Another nosy body," he said succinctly.

She winced. "Well, some people might call Nan a nosy body," she agreed. "I don't know if that's true or not, but she's definitely a caring woman, and, right now, she's feeling

POISON IN THE PANSIES

very guilty because Chrissy died. And, even though she'd
been telling everybody for months that she'd been poisoned,
nobody looked into it. Nobody raised any caterwauling
about her death either."

He stared at her. "Seriously? Nobody even thought to let
the police know?"

"Nope, not at all." She shook her head. "And that is a
trigger for Nan."

"Of course it is," he agreed.

"'Course Nan also tells me that I should probably go
home and start working on the Bob Small cases. I just know
that that'll be a lot of work to get my brain wrapped around,
and right now it aches."

He stared at her, a worried expression on his face.

She shrugged. "Okay, so it's not really aching," she admitted, waving her hand. And just then Goliath jumped up
onto her lap, surprising her. She snagged the cat, gave him a
big hug, and added, "But you know what I mean. Like, the
Bob Small cases will be fairly intricate and involved."

"Anytime you get a suspected serial killer," he noted quietly, "those cases can be convoluted. But that doesn't mean
necessarily that you have to get involved in any of it."

"Maybe not," she stated, "but it feels like I would be just
lazy if I didn't solve it."

"You know what? Just because you solve a whole pile of
these doesn't mean that you must do that Bob Small one
too."

"Yes, I do," she replied candidly. "An awful lot about
that case doesn't make any sense yet. But I'll get there.
Maybe it's not even so much trying to get my head wrapped
around it as much as realizing that parts of it need to jell."

"I've done that a time or two," he agreed. "You get all

123

the information in your head, and you just let things sit for a while until it comes together."

She nodded. "That's what I was questioning. It's also hard to know at what point in time to go back to it."

"Not until you're ready," he noted. "You are tired."

"Am I? I don't know. We took the weekend off and had quite a nice break."

"It was nice," he agreed. "You want to do something this weekend?"

"Sure, but what?"

"I don't know. Why don't we leave it open? We could try paddleboarding again," he teased, wagging his eyebrows.

She snorted at that. "Why don't we just go to the beach for a picnic or go for a hike first and then to the beach for a picnic, and we can go for a swim too?"

"That too," he agreed, "but I really enjoy paddleboarding."

She nodded. "It was nice to *sit* on the paddleboard," she agreed. "I don't know about the actual trying to do something with it though. It was pretty hard to stand up and paddle easily."

"Maybe." His phone buzzed again. He looked down at his screen and sighed. "I've got to get to work." He hopped to his feet, handed her his empty coffee cup. "Thanks for the morning coffee. I'll call you about the weekend."

She nodded. At that, she got up and followed slowly behind him. When he got up to the kitchen, he asked, "How about dinner tomorrow night?"

"Tomorrow night?" she asked, her ears pricking up. "Why not tonight?"

"I'll probably be busy," he replied in a deliberately neutral tone of voice, "but we can do something tomorrow."

"Like what?"

"What do you have on hand?"

She laughed. "Not a whole lot of anything."

He frowned. "Fine. I'll think of something." He stopped, stared at her, and asked, "What will you do now?"

"I should stop at Wendy's and see when I'll get the next check," she noted. "Not wanting to hassle her, but I did find a couple scarves and a couple pieces of Nan's clothing that I won't keep. Maybe we could sell them."

"Good enough," he said, and, with that, he was gone.

But he was distracted, focused. As if he'd gotten a call about another case or something important on this case about Alan. And considering the autopsy report on Alan, it could be a police meeting. She fancied herself contemplating where and what was possible, and then decided that she really should head to the consignment store.

She looked at the animals and thought about taking just Mugs or all of them, then considered walking there, although it was a longer distance. However, the walk might do her some good, and she was just unfocused enough that maybe that's what she should do. So she gathered everybody and put the leashes on Mugs and Goliath, then put on her good pair of walking shoes, grabbed the bag designated for Wendy at her front door, and headed out.

As she got outside on the front lawn, she heard a gasp from beside her. She looked over to see Richard's front door slamming closed. She rolled her eyes at that. "Good morning, Richard. Have a good day." And she walked past his house with a hand wave. There was just something about that neighbor. In fact, something was strange about all her neighbors on the cul-de-sac. She had pretty well made herself persona non grata after the Japanese tour buses started coming here, just to point out Doreen's house. Nobody wanted the notoriety that came with the media attention. Of course Doreen didn't either, but, hey, what was she supposed to do?

She enjoyed the walk. It took about forty minutes to get there today, with her and her animals taking their time and dawdling. When she walked up to Wendy's shop, Doreen saw lots of people in the front of the store, so she wandered around to the back alley. As she headed toward the back door, two men took one look at her and hopped up into the front seat of a nearby van, and they took off.

She stopped, her jaw dropping. That was fast. Matter of fact, it was too fast, as in suspiciously fast. Reminded Doreen of how odd Wendy had acted the last time Doreen had been here.

Doreen crossed her arms, her fingers wrapped around her upper arms, as she thought about it more. She just barely remembered the first three letters of the license plate on that van. *J-E-P.* She pulled out her phone and made a note of it, but she couldn't describe the vehicle. It just looked like a big moving van with a door that opened from the top down. The vehicle was white, and she hadn't seen any logos on it.

She got up closer to the back door and on impulse knocked. When no answer came, Doreen knocked again, and, just as she was about to leave, Wendy poked her head out, fear on her face as she looked around. When she saw Doreen, relief washed over her features.

"Hey," Wendy greeted her. "Did you bring some stuff?" she asked, pointing to the bag Doreen carried.

"I did, but I also had the animals, so I couldn't come in the front door."

She nodded. "Give me a second. I've got one last customer. And then I'll come back out here."

Doreen stood here and waited, and, sure enough, Wendy came back a few minutes later. "I'll leave the back door open, and we can hear if the front door opens again with the bells on it." And, with that, she pulled out the few things that Doreen had brought, and Wendy nodded. "These will sell," she noted. "I was hoping you would have a lot more to sell."

"You know what? I probably do," she confessed. "I just haven't gotten around to figuring out what else I want to get rid of," she admitted.

"Hey, I understand," Wendy noted, "but I'll definitely take these."

As she went to go back inside, Doreen stated, "I'm not exactly sure when the next check's coming."

"I'll do it at the end of the month, so it should be on a regular rotation now. That means, I'll do them up in about two to three weeks. And normally I'd pop them in the mail and send emails confirming that, or I will have them ready for everybody the last week of the month if people want to pick them up instead. However, if you need it earlier, I can do yours first."

Doreen's face lit up. "If you wouldn't mind, that would be awesome. I could use it."

Wendy nodded. But as she went to step back inside, her gaze slowly looked around again.

"They're gone," Doreen noted helpfully.

Wendy's gazed zipped back toward her. "Who?"

"The two guys in the big van." She hesitated and then offered, "Wendy, if you're in trouble, I could probably help you."

Wendy looked at her, shook her head. "No, I'm fine."

But she sounded anything but fine. And with another glance at the back alley, Wendy suggested, "It's probably better if you come to the front door next time." And, with that, she closed the door.

As Doreen stood here, she heard a discernible *click* on the back door as it was locked. She wasn't sure what was going on with Wendy, but definitely something was.

Chapter 9

THE DAY HAD crested into being nice and warm. Doreen's dinner for that evening would be a surprise, as she sat here, looking at the bit of food that she'd pulled out of her fridge. On impulse she typed her ingredients into a Google search, wondering what recipes would come up. She had two carrots, a little bit of broccoli, some green lettuce, and a couple eggs. The one thing that did come up was a frittata, although she didn't have potatoes, or a salad. She looked at that and wondered. But a salad wasn't a bad idea.

If she hard-boiled the eggs, she could certainly chop that up and cut the carrot into julienne strips or almost shave them. And, by the time she followed through on the instructions, she was looking at a pretty fancy salad. She quickly took a picture of it and texted it to Mack and then sat down outside on her deck. Her four-footed animals lolled all around her feet, both of them tired from the walk. Thaddeus usually hopped a ride on her shoulder, so he conserved his strength that way, as he was now. However, the animals had fared well in terms of spending the day walking to Wendy's.

Doreen's mind needed more information on these two poison cases, and it was getting a little harder to come up with something.

As she sat here eating her salad, Richard poked his head over the side of the fence. "Hey," he greeted her in a low whisper.

She got up and walked closer. "Hey," she replied in a low voice. "What's up?"

"Just a couple things. Apparently Peter bought a brand-new truck last week," he noted.

She stared at him. "And is that unusual?"

"Yes," Richard stated. "It is. He works as a bookkeeper for a small company, and he doesn't make tons of money."

"So maybe it came from Chrissy's estate?"

"I don't know." Richard frowned. "I can't figure it out. It's a big Chevy diesel," he noted, with a headshake. "Like that thing's tons of money." And there was such a note of envy in his voice.

She nodded, considering this new piece of information. "Any chance that he needed it, like maybe for work or something?"

He laughed. "Not as a bookkeeper."

"Right." She nodded and thought about it some more. "So maybe there *was* some money to inherit?"

"Maybe. Well, you'd think there had to be some for her to stay at Rosemoor. Plus, he did look after her, so, if there was anything, it should have gone to Peter. Did you check on Cassandra?"

"I thought I would go up there in about an hour," she noted, looking down at her watch. "I figured she would probably be on soon."

He stared at her. "I don't know that she still works as a

dancer."

"No?"

"No. I think she's behind the bar now."

"Okay," she replied. "I can always run up later and see."

"Let me know what you find," Richard stated. "I thought about it afterward, and I feel like I didn't, ... like I maybe didn't do her a service."

"It's okay," she noted. "I understand."

He nodded and disappeared.

Doreen took the animals back inside, washed up her dishes, said goodbye to her pets, and hopped into the car, heading up to the bar where Cassandra worked. Doreen didn't know if she could get a coffee in a place like that, but it was still early enough in the evening that she hoped not too many of the night-time goers would be there yet. She parked outside, in front of what looked like an attempt to be a railing-type fence, maybe to give it a western look.

As she walked in the door, it took her a few minutes to adjust to the shadowy atmosphere and to the heavy smoke. She was thankful to see that the place wasn't busy. Not too many people were here. However, they all seemed to be smokers.

A woman behind the bar asked, "What can I get for you?"

"Information," she replied bluntly. "Are you Cassandra?"

The woman's eyebrows shot up, and she crossed her arms over her chest. "Who's asking?"

"My name is Doreen Montgomery," she replied.

At that, the woman's eyebrows, already painted halfway up her forehead, seemed to disappear into her hairline. "The one with all the animals?"

"Yes," she confirmed, with a laugh. "Apparently I'm getting some notoriety."

"Not that that's a good thing for you," she noted, with an eye roll.

"Well, … I've been asked to look into your mother's death."

At that, the woman lowered her arms, took a step forward. "What?" she asked, her voice harsh. "Are you saying something suspicious happened with her death?"

"No, I'm not," Doreen corrected. "Just that, now, since she's gone, people are wondering about how she had repeatedly told people in the couple months prior to her death that she was being poisoned."

At that, Cassandra just stared at Doreen and then laughed and laughed. "Oh, honey, go on home and don't bother wasting your time. My mother was forever telling us something about that. Either somebody was poisoning her or something else equally strange." She shook her head. "Good God, I mean, it just never ended."

"And *was* somebody poisoning her all this time?"

Cassandra stopped, sighed, and shook her head. "I don't think so. But supposedly somebody was stealing from her, and somebody was trying to get her drunk. I mean, there was just always something."

Doreen nodded. "Did your mom ever get any psychiatric help? Anything like that?"

"Yep, sure did. She went to see Dr. Weatherby," she stated. "You can probably talk to him, although I'm sure he'd tell you that he couldn't discuss anything with you."

"They have a habit of doing that," she agreed, with an eye roll.

"I'm sure they do." Cassandra nodded. "But I can tell you there was nothing untoward about my mother's death."

"Well, an autopsy was never done."

"Why? She was an old lady," she stated quietly. "She was in relatively good health for her age, but, at some point in time, the body just stops. The fact that she went during her sleep is a godsend. I don't think she would particularly like having her body chopped up at this stage."

"On the other hand, maybe she would," Doreen suggested in a droll tone, "because generally, when people say all those things that you report that she said, they're looking for attention."

"She was always looking for attention." At that, Cassandra nodded.

"And what about Peter?" she asked.

Cassandra's face thinned down and turned mean. "What about that little thief?" she asked. "If somebody poisoned her, it would be him."

"Oh, so now she was poisoned?" Doreen asked.

"I don't know if she was or not, but, if she had been, it would have been that worthless nephew of hers," she spat. "He got all her money."

"What money though? From my understanding she couldn't make her bills on a month-to-month basis."

"And I think that was just her way, always buying stuff for other people," she noted quietly. "She certainly didn't give me two cents in my world, hated the fact that I worked in a bar. And I've been here for so long," she shared, "that I almost own the place outright. I don't need my mother's money. And she might have looked down on me for an awful lot of my life," she added, "but, in the end, I still did okay."

"I'm glad to hear that," Doreen stated. "It would be sad to think that she ended up going to her grave, ashamed and hating you."

"I don't know if she ever got over the fact that I was a stripper for a while," she admitted. "And she certainly didn't like any of the three husbands I had, … but, then again, if I'd been smart, I should have listened to her at least on that point. I'm not married to any of them anymore." She rolled her eyes. "Talk about losers. But, hey, I picked them up in bars. So what do I expect?"

Cassandra looked around the bar and shrugged. "I own this, along with my partner now," she stated, "and we're doing just fine. But it would really piss me off to think that somebody murdered her." She thrummed her fingers on the bar and studied Doreen for a long moment. "Do you really think there's anything to it?"

"I don't know," Doreen admitted. "My grandmother is in the same retirement home, and I know that she feels terribly guilty after Chrissy's death because she didn't get anybody to look into it," she explained. "So I promised her that I would."

At that, the woman nodded slowly and stared off at some distant point behind Doreen's head. "Well, if you do find something," she stated, "I would really like to know. I did brush off my mother all those years, mostly because she was always making up stories."

"And people tell tall tales because they're looking for attention."

"And that would have been her," she agreed. "I was an only child. And I couldn't give her what she wanted—that traditional happy well-adjusted daughter who goes university, graduates, gets a well-accepted job, gets married, has three kids and the white picket fence with a grandmother attached," she explained. "So she and I could never really connect in any way."

"I'm sorry," Doreen offered. "That would have been tough on you."

At that, Cassandra laughed. "It was really tough on me," she stated, "and I did eventually find a way out of that morass and to becoming myself." She paused for a moment. "For a long time I felt guilty about my worldly choices." She shook her head. "But it suits me. And I'm happy," she noted, but a defiant note was in her tone. Then her shoulders sagged. "I am at least happy now," she clarified. "But my mother would not have been happy with my choices, even at the end of her life."

"And do you see any reason why Peter would have done something to her?"

"Because he could," she replied bluntly.

At that, Doreen stared at her. "You need to explain that comment."

"Peter was one of those guys who, if you wanted to go left, he went right. If you were designated as a bad seed, he would be the good seed. If you stole, he was the Goody Two-Shoes. But if you wanted to be the good girl, he would steal and make it look like you'd done it."

Just something in the back of Cassandra's voice had Doreen probing a little further. "Are you saying that, somewhere in your past, he did something wrong, and you got blamed for it?"

"Many times in the past," she stated, with a headshake. "Peter comes from my uncle's family. His parents were killed in a car accident a long time ago. Peter moved in with Mum and me, so he's almost like a brother. And, in a way, I think Mum looked at him as her son. And, of course, since I was a complete write-off, he was a good thing."

"Right," Doreen stated. "And that's very important to know, especially later when we look at the will."

"Of course it is," she agreed, with a slight hand wave, as if none of it mattered. "But I was the only one who was her blood, her direct line. Of course Peter was her nephew, so, in many ways, that counted too. Plus, her brother was the apple of her eye."

"What about your father?"

"He took off years and years and years ago," she shared. "Our family of three was pretty happy when I was younger, yet I don't remember too much about those earlier years. Dad didn't take off until I was about sixteen—about the time Peter came to live with us, I guess. *Huh*, never made that connection until just now. Anyway, I did talk to Dad about it at the time, and he told me how he couldn't stand it anymore. He felt like he was choking. At the time I felt like I was choking too, so I understood. And I knew he wouldn't like my life choices either, so, when he took off, I basically did the same thing." She added, "I took off into my own world, and it was pretty tough on all of us."

"I know," she agreed.

"How would you know?" Cassandra snapped, looking Doreen up and down.

Doreen swallowed, raised her head, and faced Cassandra. "My husband of fourteen years had an affair and kicked me out and, after a couple months of lunch money handouts, cut me off completely. If not for my grandmother, I would be homeless." Doreen ducked her head for a moment. "So, yes, I do understand. And I'm sorry you had to go through that. How did Peter react when your father left?"

"I think he immediately stepped up and tried to be the father in the family. That didn't go over well with me, but I know Mum loved it because she didn't have to figure things out, since Peter was there to do it for her," she stated bluntly. "In fact, my mum was never somebody who paid the bills or looked after getting that electrician in or anything like that." Cassandra frowned, as if back in her childhood memories. "She'd vacuum and clean and cook, and that was about it. Honestly, I don't know what she did, even at the end of her life." She shook her head. "I never went to Rosemoor to visit with her. I know Peter always did, but, then, you know, Peter was in that Goody Two-Shoes mode."

"Would your mother have had any money to pass on?"

"I don't know. I wouldn't have thought so, but I guess the house may have fetched something, so that would have gone to Peter."

"Exactly," Doreen noted. "I heard from some people that there wasn't anything to pass on and that Peter had helped her out quite a few years paying some of the bills."

"I don't know about that. Peter came to me a couple times, saying that she needed money. And I didn't believe him. I did go to Rosemoor, and management told me that all her bills were paid and that there wasn't a problem. So then I didn't trust Peter anymore—not that I trusted him to begin with." She shrugged. "Sometimes you just can't trust anybody."

At that, the front door opened, and several customers came in and sidled up to the bar.

Cassandra looked over at Doreen. "Honey, you need to leave. This isn't your kind of a place. But, if you want to come back for a visit, come back in the daytime, and bring those animals of yours." She smiled and pulled out a card from underneath the bar. "That's my cell number. You can always give me a shout. I really would like to know if you find out anything. As you know, Mum and I didn't always have an easy relationship, and I know that I certainly never had her approval," she muttered. "At the same time though, I would not want to find out that something had happened to her at the end of the road."

"Good enough," Doreen noted.

She hopped off the barstool and walked out the door, and a couple whistles came from behind her. She just completely ignored them as she headed to her car. It was just that kind of a place. Outside, she took several deep breaths, trying to empty the second-hand smoke from her lungs and to clear her head a bit. What she really needed to do was talk to Peter and get some idea who and what he was like, as a person.

And, with that thought, she texted Nan. **Need a location for Peter. I just finished talking to Cassandra.** Her grandmother phoned as soon as Doreen got into the car.

"He lives down on Lambert Street," she said.

"Okay. And where's that?"

"Getting an idea. Out in Glenmore."

"What about a Dr. Weatherby? Do you know him? He was Chrissy's doctor."

"Oh my. Yes, we were just talking about him."

"Who was just talking about him?"

"Why you and me, dear."

Doreen shook her head. "When was this?"

"Earlier. When I told you about the skinny-dipping at Sarsons?"

"Oh my God, Nan. You went skinny-dipping with Dr. Weatherby?"

"I just told you that, dear." Nan laughed. "You should mention that when you call him later."

Doreen groaned. "I will do nothing of the sort."

Nan laughed heartily before hanging up.

Doreen almost lost her focus, as she headed straight to Peter's house. Doreen would call the doctor later. As she parked in front of the address, a single man, somewhat around her age, mowed the lawn. She hopped out, wishing she had the animals with her. She walked up the front sidewalk and waited until he saw her.

He shut off the lawn mower and walked over. "Hey, what can I do for you?"

She introduced herself and related how some of the residents at Rosemoor were upset about his aunt's death and how they'd asked her to look into it.

He asked, "Are you like a private detective or something?"

She burst out laughing, liking the easy personality and the smile on his face. "Or something," she agreed. "I just play around with it a little bit. But my grandmother and some of her friends are quite worried."

He nodded. "And that has to do with her constantly telling everybody she was poisoned, I suppose."

"Yes, exactly," she agreed.

"And, therefore, I must be the number one suspect," he stated, with a headshake. "And of course I'm the one who everybody looks to."

"Maybe," she noted, "since you did inherit."

"Right. I inherited what?" he asked, with an eye roll. "Sure there was some money, and it did help, but I've been saving forever, ever since I was this poor kid. When you save and finally manage to buy yourself something that you've wanted for a long time, it's a great feeling. Although it makes others jealous and small-minded."

She looked over at the big gleaming truck in the driveway. "That's one big shiny truck."

"Yep, just bought it." He grinned, rubbing his hands together in glee. "It's a beauty, isn't it?"

"It sure is," she agreed. "I've never seen so many big trucks like there are in this town."

He looked at her and shrugged. "Every boy likes his toys."

"Apparently." She nodded. "So can you tell me just what you inherited, and why you inherited and not Cassandra?"

"Well, if you ever saw Cassandra," he explained, "you'd know why. She and her mother didn't get along, whereas I was there for her, for Chrissy, the last couple decades." He shook his head. "It made sense to me that I inherited. But you know how the gossip nags will let their tongues wag."

"Maybe," she replied. "But no autopsy was done on Chrissy either, was there?"

"Why would there be?" he asked in astonishment. "She died in her sleep one night. And no matter what Chrissy said, no way anybody would have administered any poison to her."

"And why is that?"

"Because why would they?" he asked. "I already knew I would get everything. She wouldn't live too much longer as it was, so no need for me to kill her. I had no reason to kill her."

"Maybe not," she murmured, stumped. "Do you know anybody who hated her, anybody who didn't get along with her?"

"For that, you need to look at the residents in Rosemoor," he stated. "If ever a Peyton Place existed, that's it. I wouldn't be surprised if half a dozen of those people didn't plot her death."

"I thought she was harmless?"

"Oh, she was. And, as long as she was only telling stories about herself, it was great, but, when she started telling stories about everybody else, it wasn't so great."

"Did she tell stories like that about other people?"

"I don't know what stories she might have spread at Rosemoor, but I know that she used to tell me a lot of gossip. Stuff like, you know, some woman at that place gambles all the time, sets up all these betting pools." He shook his head. "Like how is that legal?"

Doreen's lips pinched, as she realized who he was talking about. She nodded. "I did hear that they were trying to get that stopped."

He laughed. "How do you stop something like that?" he asked. "Those old people can be a menace." He looked at his lawn mower, back at her, and said, "I don't know what else I can help you with. There wasn't anybody in particular in her world. Nobody could have passed her that poison on a regular basis." He paused. "I didn't see her all the time. I saw her maybe once a month, but that was it. I should have gone more often."

"No, understood," she stated. And slowly, feeling depressed, she lifted a hand and said, "Thanks for the talk." She gave him a weak smile, as she prepared to leave.

He nodded. "Anytime you want to talk about something other than my aunt," he offered, "just give me a call." He flashed that boyish grin again. "Always happy to go out with a beautiful woman."

Startled, she looked up at him again, but he had already turned on the lawn mower and was back to mowing the lawn. She got into her car and slowly drove home. When she walked inside again, all the animals were barking, meowing, and caterwauling like something crazy had happened.

She stared at them and asked, "What's going on? What's going on?"

They all raced to the back door of the kitchen. Even Thaddeus was already there.

So she opened the back door and let them out, and they all ran to the river, even Goliath. She was right behind them and then stopped and stared, as they all halted right at her property line and looked down the pathway toward Nan's place. They may have stilled in this spot, but they were still trying to tell Doreen something.

Loudly.

She frowned and looked at them, not sure what was going on here. "Okay, let's go."

And together, they fast-walked down the pathway toward Rosemoor; only they picked up speed the farther and farther away from her house they got, and thus they got closer and closer to Nan's. By the time they turned the corner, Mugs flat-out ran to Nan's patio. So did Goliath. That was a first.

Thaddeus was perched on her shoulder, looking at her, crying out, "Come on, come on, come on."

Doreen shook her head and picked up her pace. She didn't know what exactly was going on, but something was. And she dashed to a stop at the lawn outside Nan's patio. She found Nan sitting there, her eyes closed.

She walked nearer cautiously and asked, "Nan, are you asleep?"

When Nan didn't answer, Doreen stepped onto the small patio and reached out a hand to check Nan's pulse, while noting her breathing. Thankfully she had a good solid pulse, but she didn't appear to even be here. Doreen reached out a hand to gently stroke her hair, trying not to disturb her too much, in case she was in a deep sleep. When she withdrew her hand, it came away sticky and wet.

Doreen stared in shock at the blood. She stepped around her grandmother and took a look at her surroundings. On the ground behind her, on the patio, was a shattered vase.

Somebody had attacked her grandmother.

Now she had to, one, get help; two, call Mack; and three, find out who had a reason for hurting the most important person in Doreen's life.

Chapter 10

AS SOON AS Mack heard of Nan's attack, he turned on the flashing lights on his vehicle and exceeded the speed limit getting to Rosemoor, getting there seconds before the ambulance did. Mack hugged Doreen as the two of them oversaw the EMTs working on Nan. She had been unconscious when Doreen had arrived, but Nan was now alert and arguing with the medical staff. She very loudly proclaimed that she wasn't going to any hospital, that Rosemoor had nurses on staff here. There was no talking her out of that.

"She's raising her voice, so she must be feeling all right now," Mack teased, giving Doreen a squeeze.

Doreen looked up at Mack, still crying softly. "Or she's all bluster." She shook her head. "You know how she is. She doesn't complain about her own health. She's too boisterous about the wrong things."

Mack nodded, keeping a tight hold on Doreen. Once the EMTs declared Nan out of the woods, Mack and Darren seated Nan and Doreen inside Nan's little living room, with several Rosemoor residents gathered around. Mack and Darren represented the local authorities. Mack had been assigned as the lead investigator on this violent attack of

Nan. In general, Mack served as Doreen's "handler," when it came to cold cases. However, this was an active case and an important one to all concerned.

Darren had been assigned to assist Mack with this case involving Nan probably because, as Richie's nephew, Darren could hopefully handle Richie, who had a close relationship with Nan and could be his own handful as well. Both officials were talking to various residents of Rosemoor to see if they'd heard anything, since Nan's attacker had broken a vase over Nan's head. Somebody had to have heard something. Except Rosemoor was a senior living center. Unfortunately that could mean a lot of the residents were hard of hearing.

Mack shook his head, took a sly glance at Nan and Doreen, to see how they were holding up.

Richie sat quietly beside Nan, and Doreen held her grandmother's hand gently in hers.

"I'm fine, you know," Nan stated robustly.

Doreen wasn't so sure about that. She certainly hadn't been fine when Doreen had first found Nan.

At that look on her face though, Nan leaned over, patted her granddaughter's hand. "I know you'll worry anyway, no matter what I say." She sighed. "But it'll be all right."

"I'm not so sure it is all right," Doreen murmured. "You say that, but there's no doubt that somebody came up behind you and hit you."

"I was considering that too," Nan noted in a quiet tone. She looked over at Richie and asked, "Do you think it's because of our inquiries?"

At that, Doreen winced. "You know what? It quite possibly is." At that, both Nan and Richie brightened. She stared at them in astonishment. "That should make you more worried, not pleased."

"Nonsense," Nan argued, with a wave of her hand. "It means somebody is getting nervous."

Doreen stared at the two of them, as they shared a conspiratorial look, with almost glee on their faces. "If that's the case," Doreen stated sternly, "you need to back off immediately. Both of you." She glared at Nan and Richie.

They turned astonished gazes toward her, glaring right back.

Doreen raised both her hands in frustration. "I can't have either of you getting hurt."

"Why not?" Nan asked, narrowing her gaze at a granddaughter. "You get hurt all the time."

She stared, nonplussed. What could she say to that?

"And you know how Mack feels about that too," Nan added in a gruff voice.

Without Doreen realizing it, Mack had come up behind her, and he added, "Yes, you know exactly how I feel about that, don't you?" he asked Doreen, his voice hard. "And you ignore me too."

She turned toward him and glared. "Surely you're not condoning that these two should continue their investigation?"

He stared at her, frowning, and looked from one Rosemoor resident to the other. "Just what investigation are you talking about?"

Nan looked over at Doreen. "I really don't think you should have mentioned it, dear. Mack's not the kind to handle this well."

Mack pinched the bridge of his nose, even as Doreen's lips twitched. He glared at her. "Don't you start," he snapped at Doreen. "Keeping a rein on these two"—he pointed from Nan to Richie and back to Nan again—"in this place is hard enough, without you adding to it, Doreen."

She gave him an outraged look. "I'm not adding to anything. I've been trying to be the voice of reason."

He stared at her. "Seriously, you?"

She glared at him, before turning her back on him.

Richie gave a half-hearted chuckle. "She's right. Doreen has been trying to tell us to be a little bit more circumspect about our inquiries." He shrugged. "And, honest to goodness, we didn't think we would really do anything to seriously generate much interest about it. I mean, Chrissy has been dead for more than a few months already."

Mack looked at him and looked over at Doreen.

"Chrissy is the woman who told everybody she was being poisoned."

He nodded. "And I did look into that, and we don't have an official report of any complaint by her."

"No, of course not," Richie snorted. "Nobody ever listened to her. The trouble is, maybe somebody should have because she is dead."

"And yet, in this place," Mack explained cautiously, "dead is kind of ..." He hesitated, looked back over at Nan, and added, "I don't mean this in a vulgar way, but it's a common by-product."

She stared at him and then cracked a big smile. "You're right. It absolutely is common. But it's not that common after somebody has reported that she's being poisoned. I do blame myself."

"Why?" Mack asked in a reasonable tone. "Did you poison her?"

She stared at him and then slowly shook her head. "I hope, young man, you meant that as a joke," she snapped.

"Because there's really nothing funny about finding out that a friend of yours has been poisoned and that you ignored all the signs."

"What signs did you ignore?" he asked gently. "Because, from what I'm hearing, nobody believed her, then she died. And the coroner ruled it as a death of natural causes, and, for all you know, she wasn't poisoned at all."

"But what if she was?" Richie asked. "What if she was?"

Mack stared down at him, not sure how to answer.

"And that's where I keep coming to every time," Doreen replied quietly. "What if she was poisoned? And we get your point. Maybe she wasn't, but we always come back to the question, *But what if she was?*" She looked up at Mack. "An autopsy would settle this question right away."

"If she was being poisoned, then it would have been nice to have known ahead of time, in an attempt to prevent a death," he noted calmly. "Because, at this point in time, getting the forensic information will be non-existent. There's no way that any local poison that somebody here would have sussed out would have … would still be in the body."

Then he frowned and added, "I doubt it. Although, various toxins could be found in the hair even years later, I understand. I'll have to check with the coroner."

"Definitely won't be found now," Nan retorted, "because she was cremated." Mack turned and looked at her. She nodded. "And that was her nephew's doing."

"The nephew who just bought a very expensive brand-new truck," Richie shared, giving Mack a gimlet eye. "Maybe somebody should look into that."

"And I did talk to him about that truck," Doreen noted gently. "Just today, in fact."

At that, both Nan and Richie turned to look at her, their

eyebrows shooting up.

"And," Mack asked sternly, "did he tell you where he got it?"

"No, he didn't tell me where he got it, but that he had been saving for years and years, and he did get some money from Chrissy's estate. And just that he'd been so excited because he'd finally got what he'd always wanted."

"Well, of course." Nan sniffed. "I mean, inheritances are free money after all."

Doreen winced at that because she was in line to inherit whatever her grandmother had squirreled away and whatever Nan had not already spent on Doreen already. And she sure didn't want anybody else thinking that she would have had something to do with her grandmother's death in order to speed up any inheritance. At that thought, it's almost as if Nan had read Doreen's mind.

Nan leaned over, patted her arm gently, and said, "I know that wouldn't be you. Besides, we're having too much fun together for you to want to knock me off."

"Even if we weren't," she replied, "I would never want to knock you off."

Nan beamed. "That's because you're a sweetheart." She frowned. "However, it's not the same for everybody."

"Maybe not," Mack agreed, trying to corral the conversation, "but that doesn't mean that every person who's in line to inherit will turn around and try to knock you off."

"Maybe not." Nan turned and looked over at Richie. "Richie, what about your family?"

He shrugged. "I don't think so. But you know what? Every once in a while, Darren does say something about if I'm not, … if I don't smarten up and stop getting him into trouble at work …"

Nan frowned. "Maybe we should investigate *him* then," she stated in a loud voice, glaring at Darren.

Richie shook his head at her. "I think that would just get him into more trouble."

Nan thought about it and slowly nodded. "But, if you die," she promised, pointing a finger at him, "you can bet I'll raise Cain and have Darren looked at."

Mack sighed. "Darren's here to make things easier on his grandpa," he explained. "So I hardly think he's in any way a suspect, should Richie here decide that it's time to meet his maker. Besides, like we just said, a lot of deaths happen at this place."

"Sure, but Chrissy was relatively healthy," Nan stated in that know-it-all tone of voice. She wasn't prepared to listen to any arguments to the contrary. "So natural causes of deaths are understandable here. But *murder* never is." Nan was now laser-focused on Mack and Darren.

Mack turned, tilted his head, raised his palms, looking at Doreen.

She just shrugged. "I tried to explain."

"I don't think you did a very good job," he responded in an ominous tone.

She nodded. "I probably didn't," she agreed, "but you're not doing any better of a job at it either."

He groaned. "No, you're right there," he admitted. "Darren and I'll go talk to a few more residents. Then I'll meet up with Darren, and we'll see what we come up with."

"Good enough," Nan replied. "And then you come back and report to us."

Mack stopped at the doorway, looked at her, considering what he would say in response.

Doreen looked over at him, placed a finger against her

lips, and spoke up before he could. "Honestly, it's probably better to just walk away now."

He glared at Doreen. "We're the police. We don't report to any civilians." And, with that final parting shot, he turned and walked out.

Nan looked at her, looked at Richie, and announced, "Now we need to have a meeting."

"Sure," Richie agreed. "But I shouldn't say anything. I don't want you getting hit again."

"Nope, I don't either," Nan agreed, her fingers rattling away on the top of the nearby sofa side table. "How will we find out who did it though?"

"Well, it would have been nice if there were security cameras to access," Doreen noted quietly. "But apparently you don't have cameras in the hallways."

"Nope," she confirmed, "and I don't have any cameras in my suite." Then she batted her eyes at Richie and added, "Neither does Richie."

He had the grace to flush ever-so-slightly, and Doreen wondered just how close their relationship was at this point but then realized she really didn't want to know. "So that leaves us without any way to know who was in the hallway at the time, unless somebody saw something," she added quickly. "We need to find an eyewitness. And in order to find one, we need to locate somebody who may have seen something, so we have to talk to everybody. Even if it seemed not out of the ordinary, we need to know who was near Nan's apartment recently. After all, it could have been somebody who lives here in Rosemoor."

"Oh, good Lord," Richie groaned. "I'm tired already. And I'm not talking to that Magnus guy."

Doreen turned and looked at him and asked, "Who?"

POISON IN THE PANSIES

And Nan spoke up and replied, "I'm not talking to Maude either. Some of these people here are really crazy," she noted. "They'll invent information, if it makes them feel important, if it gets the spotlight on them, however briefly. Just ask the staff. They know."

Doreen wasn't sure what to say to that, so wisely kept her own counsel. But to think that anybody would have something to say to her about this, and that they wouldn't want to talk to her because they didn't happen to like the person in question who was viciously attacked, well, that would just make the case even that much more complicated.

"Maybe I should be asking," Doreen offered gently. "Who here would want to, you know ..." And then she stopped because she was going to say, *kill Nan*. That wasn't exactly something Doreen wanted to bring up.

"Hurt me?" Nan asked quietly.

"Yes."

"Nobody," she responded. "I get along here with every-body."

At that, Doreen frowned and added, "Except for this Maude and a Magnus."

"She's just a know-it-all," Nan retorted, with a wave of her hand. "He's just... weird. Can't stand those people."

Doreen stared at her grandmother, fascinated, because Doreen was pretty sure that a lot of people would say that her grandmother was a nosy body, a know-it-all, a gossip. She ran those bets about all manner of personal matters—who was dating whom, who was breaking up first, who was having a baby out of wedlock, how soon Doreen solved a cold case, how soon Doreen and Mack started dating, now how soon before Doreen and Mack were engaged. But obviously truth was in the eye of the beholder, and, in this case, it was all about Nan's version.

"And what about you?" Doreen asked, looking at Richie. "Do you have any idea who doesn't like Nan?"

He looked incredibly uncomfortable.

Doreen nodded. "Maybe you'd like to have this conversation in private?"

Nan, suddenly realizing that Richie might have some information, stepped up and demanded, "What are you talking about?"

He looked over at her and softly replied, "You have a tendency to make some people irate."

She stared at him, then shrugged. "So, what of it?" she asked. "Not everybody likes my flamboyant style, my popularity. And not everybody likes the fact that my granddaughter is here to see me all the time," she noted in a quiet tone. And she looked over at Doreen and added, "You have no idea how much that irks some people here, who never get to see their grandchildren, or in a lot of cases their own children. They are so jealous that they can't be happy that I have family who wants to come see me, who wants to spend time with me, who won't just forget about me in here. Maybe if they were more thankful that you came to see me, then maybe their own family would wise up." Nan gave an emphatic snort at the end of her diatribe.

Doreen stared at her. "But would they be angry enough to hurt you?"

Richie and Nan both turned and faced Doreen. Richie shrugged. "You know what? It's pretty hard to know what people will do at any given time," he hedged. "Definitely some crazies are out there."

Doreen frowned and shook her head. "But those crazies are not just *out there*. Those crazies could be right here, in

Rosemoor, living with you. Living where you sleep and where you eat and where you share tea and have dances." Doreen shared a frightened look with her grandmother. "Maybe, Nan, you should stay with me"—she held up her hand as soon as Nan opened her mouth—"at least until Mack finds out who did this and has them in jail."

"Oh, I won't argue with the crazy part," she replied. "And I appreciate the offer to stay with you, but I will be safe here with Richie, right, dear?" She smiled sweetly and patted Richie's hand, who just nodded. Then her personality changed, like she had two of them at the ready. "Who else doesn't like me? And give me some names." Nan glared at Richie now.

He avoided eye contact with Nan and instead looked at Doreen. "I can give you a few names, but these are people she particularly doesn't like."

Doreen nodded, as she looked over at her grandmother, and in a stern voice stated, "But *she* won't interfere because this is the next stage of the investigation, and we need to make sure it happens properly." When her grandmother maintained that stern look, Doreen added, "And we don't want you conked on the head again."

Her grandmother stared at her for a bit longer and then slowly nodded. "Fine," she snapped. "But, if any of those people say anything bad about me, I want to know."

"Why?" Doreen asked, a wry look on her face. "So you can stop them from partaking in your next betting pool?"

At that, Richie laughed. "Honestly, she's done that a couple times too."

"But then," Doreen added, "Nan wasn't provoking the anger. She was reacting to it. So that needs to be taken into account when I interview these people."

Richie nodded. "Most of the time these people think that Nan's cheating, not that Nan's retaliating for them cheating. They are projecting."

At that tidbit, Doreen stared at Richie and then back at Nan. "You know something? That's not good if people think you're cheating," she noted in alarm.

He shrugged. "Anybody who loses tends to look to see why they're losing. But they're the ones who are giving her their best guesses. It's not like Nan's writing it down wrong."

"Even though some people have mentioned that," Nan interjected. "And I would never do that."

"No, of course not," Doreen acknowledged, believing her grandmother on that level implicitly. "It's too important to you to mess up."

She looked at her and then nodded. "See?" She pointed to Richie. "My granddaughter understands."

He nodded. "But not everybody does," he noted cautiously. "And, of course, if you bring it up too much, a lot of people will get upset and quite possibly get Nan into trouble."

"Right, because you've been in trouble in this instance before." Doreen frowned. "Would they kick you out of Rosemoor?"

Nan shook her head and shrugged. "They're just old sticks-in-the-mud." She primped her hair with her hand. "I mean, honestly, why would anybody get upset over losing a few pennies?"

"It depends whether it's pennies or if it's big money," Doreen replied cautiously. "And, as I well know, your version of pennies versus my version of what are pennies are very different things."

At that, Nan's attention was completely diverted. "Are you broke again?"

Doreen winced. "Nan, that's really not something I want to discuss right now, and it's never been a case of *again*," she responded. "I still haven't gotten paid for a lot of things, so I'm still broke. It's not *again*. And, no, I don't need or want any more money from you."

But Nan didn't look at all convinced.

Doreen sighed and showed her palms. "When the antiques come in," she explained, "I'll be doing just fine." Doreen paused. "Heck," she muttered. "If any of that stuff finally comes in, it should be good, even Wendy's money." That thought reminded her entirely about the weird scenario at Wendy's. She sighed.

"Yeah, you're right there," Nan agreed.

Doreen looked down at her notepad and the very lack of information she had available. "Can we stop getting sidetracked and get back to the names of the people I need to talk to, please?"

Richie supplied four more names, as well as Maude, each one making Nan gasp or turn pale—or, in one case, pinch her lips.

"So these are all people you've had some problems with here, Nan?" Doreen asked, looking up from the list as she read through it.

Nan slowly nodded. "I guess you could say that."

"I'm not trying to hurt you or to upset you," she stated gently, "but I do want to know that whoever might have hurt you will pay for what they did."

Her grandmother gave her the tenderest of smiles. "You are a sweetheart," she replied gently, "but I'm as tough as nails."

"Maybe," Richie agreed, "but your head isn't."

And, at that, Nan went off in gales of laughter, as if it were the best joke ever.

Chapter 11

Thursday Morning

DOREEN HADN'T FORGOTTEN about Dr. Weatherby, Chrissy's doctor. She called him, trying to not get images of skinny-dipping in her mind as she did so. Regardless, when the doc answered, Doreen explained she was Willa Anne Montgomery's granddaughter.

He had coughed to collect himself, then asked what he could help her with.

"I know you can't talk about your patients, even dead ones," she began.

"*Yeeees*," he replied.

"I'm calling about Chrissy Smith. I understand that she died a few months ago and that her body was cremated without an autopsy, deemed a natural death, I believe. But can you tell me if she was depressed? If you were worried about her emotionally? I just need to get a feel whether an autopsy should be done on her remains, if that is even possible."

"*Hmm.* Well, you are bringing up many issues here. Some I have not enough knowledge of to give you an answer. And the others? I do believe they fall under doctor-patient privilege. Of course, if you wanted to file a lawsuit against me, the court would decide the matter."

Doreen sighed. "I was afraid of that. But thank you for speaking with me. My nan speaks ... well of you."

Again the doc cleared his throat. And hung up on her.

"I guess I deserved that," she muttered.

It was later Thursday morning before Doreen managed to get permission from not only the powers-that-be at Rosemoor to go talk to all the residents, looking for any eyewitnesses who didn't realize they had seen Nan's attacker right before it happened—but especially also the five people who seemed to dislike Nan the most, or at least the most publicly.

Her grandmother had been checked on several times throughout the night by the resident nursing staff, and, as Doreen talked to her grandmother this morning, Doreen was greatly relieved to confirm that everything was okay with Nan. That she had no problems through the night.

Nan offered, "Come down for breakfast. And we can set up a strategy for your interviews. I can give you targeted questions to ask those five haters."

Doreen had to smile at her grandmother's intensity. There was no keeping Nan down, at least not for long periods of time, thankfully. "Oh, I'll come down to see you anyway," she replied, with a giggle. "I wanted to check up on you, to see you with my own eyes."

"I'm fine," Nan replied, with an airy voice.

"Says you," she muttered. "You nearly gave me a heart attack."

Nan went off in gales of laughter.

That was a good sign that Nan had no headache or any pain when laughing. *Very* good sign. Doreen exhaled a long grateful breath.

"You and Richie." Nan snorted. "I don't know who he thinks would be his cohort in crime if I were to kick the bucket."

Doreen rolled her eyes at that. "Well, you know, you could consider the fact that maybe neither of you should be cohorts in crime. Anyway, Nan," she jumped in to say, "I'm packing up the animals, and we'll be down in a few minutes."

And, with that, she walked out in the backyard, stopped, noted a couple beautiful hydrangeas, returned inside to grab her garden shears and some twine, snipped those three big blooms—one white, one strawberry pink, and another one with a greenish tinge to it. Then she plucked two leaves, those long skinny ones from the daylilies, wrapped them around the blooms, and tied the bundle tight with the twine in a knot. And then she carried them down to her grandmother.

With the animals happily racing at her side, she walked toward Rosemoor, grateful that the animals had calmed down to the point today that they had been okay to just walk. She'd also forgotten to mention to Mack what they had done for antics to send her racing down to Nan's at top speed. But obviously they'd known something was up. As she wondered at the mentality and the intelligence of the animals, she noted that, chances were, they were much more intelligent than even she had suspected, given their ability to suss out that Nan was in trouble.

Nan was excited to see the flowers. "Oh my, you do have a wonderful green thumb, dear. Thanks for sharing these with me." She patted the animals as she spoke, not wanting to ignore them. "Let me put these in a vase." She returned shortly, placing the vase of beautiful flowers on the tiny patio table, then greeted the animals all over again and finally settled in her patio chair.

"I forgot to mention," Doreen said, joining Nan at the patio table, "but the animals knew you were in trouble yesterday, like they had this sixth sense of something being wrong with you. And, sure enough, we raced over here to find you unconscious and bloody." She quickly gave her more details about what had happened with the animals.

Nan stared at the animals with pleasure. "In that case, they obviously all need treats." And she quickly got up and raced back inside.

From the speed of her movements, it was obvious she wasn't suffering too badly. But still, it made Doreen a little uncomfortable to realize that her grandmother was walking and running like she was. Surely she should be moving at a more sedate pace. When she mentioned it to her, Nan just looked at her and waved her hand, as if to push away all Doreen's worries.

"That's just silly," she argued. "That would mean not being me."

"And of course that would never do, would it?" Doreen asked, with a smile.

"Absolutely not," she agreed, with a chuckle. "I still have to be me, even if it's uncomfortable for other people."

"Now that's true," Doreen acknowledged quietly.

Nan nodded. "Something for you to remember too. After your horrid husband abused you verbally for so many years, you need to watch out for that. Don't let others stop you from being you. You are just perfect as you are."

"Not that I don't need to keep improving where I can ..." Doreen added.

"Of course. Self-reflection is good. And more people should indulge in that painful exercise," Nan said, with a snippy tone, obviously mad at the five people who disliked her.

Doreen sighed. "It would be nice if your *uncomfortable other people* didn't push them to want to hurt you though."

Nan placed a pastry in front of Doreen and poured tea for two.

"What is this?" Doreen asked with interest.

"I had Richie get a selection of breakfasts from the Rosemoor cafeteria," she explained. "He's much better at pilfering food for you."

At that statement, Doreen's hand, hovering atop the two pastries, immediately pulled back.

Nan chuckled. "Honestly, I just had him tell them exactly who it was for. And they're totally okay with you having a treat," she noted. "Besides, it's my breakfast too, and I told him to go get some more because I'm really hungry today."

"You just sent Richie for more breakfast?" Doreen asked incredulously. "The way you're bouncing around here, why didn't you go get breakfast yourself?"

"Because *we* have a meeting," Nan stated, with that self-important air. "And that's obviously way more important than me making my way down there for breakfast and trying to make my way back again without everybody wanting to stop and gab about my attack."

"Oh." Doreen stared at her grandmother. "And is Richie joining us?"

"Of course, of course. I told you. I was just sending him down to get breakfast."

"You just sent him down to get you some breakfast. That doesn't mean that he's joining us for the meeting."

"Well, of course he is, dear," she replied. "That wouldn't make any sense to have a meeting without him, would it now?"

Considering they'd had lots of meetings without Richie—but maybe not in regard to this one particular scenario where Nan got conked on the head with a vase—so Doreen figured it was just easier to stay quiet. And, sure enough, a few minutes later, Richie walked in, and he had a basketful of stuff.

He looked over, saw Doreen, and a big smile beamed across his face. "There you are," he greeted her in a hearty voice. "Nan was afraid you would starve."

Doreen shot a glance over at Nan, caught her with a guilty look, right before she managed to wipe it off her face. She sent a disparaging frown at Richie. But Nan didn't say anything, which also added much validity to her guilty state.

Richie put down the basket and stated, "And look what I've got for you. I snagged them from Peggy, who works in the kitchen." He had a big grin on his face, obviously having had tons of fun getting this stash. "I hope you share."

Doreen watched as he peeled back the napkin on the top to what looked like a half-dozen croissants, cheese croissants, and maybe even ham and cheese croissants.

Doreen smiled. "Absolutely I share," she confirmed, looking over at him. "Do you get enough to eat here?"

He patted his tummy. "Well, the doctors say I do. But I wouldn't be averse to having more," he noted. "I do like my groceries."

And, with aplomb, he reached into the basket and pulled out the biggest and fattest of the croissants. Doreen managed to withhold her grin, but Nan wasn't having anything to do with it, and she smacked his hand and told him off.

Doreen burst out laughing. "Wow, you too are just having so much fun," she noted, chuckling.

"Of course," Nan stated. "We have to. At our age, that
fun can come to an end really fast."

That sober reminder of Nan's accident yesterday immediately had Doreen looking over at her grandmother and
saying, "Are you sure you're feeling better?"

"Of course I'm feeling better," she replied. "Don't I look
better?"

"You look marvelous," she agreed gently, "but then you
always do."

Her grandmother beamed. "Thank you, child," she
heartily responded. "I'm so happy to have you around."

Richie just muttered around the croissant that he had
stuffed in his mouth. "That's because she keeps giving you
compliments."

Nan gave him a frown and argued, "Well, it's much nicer to get honey from people than it is to get lemons."

Not sure exactly where that conversation was going, but
Doreen wanted to stay out of it as much as she could. "I
came, hoping to talk to some of the residents."

"And you probably can," she agreed, "but you probably
want to do it on the sly."

Doreen looked over at her. "Why is that?"

"Because I think Mack told them that they didn't have
to talk to anybody else."

"Oh, *great*," Doreen moaned, followed by a sigh. "Mack
again."

"Well, he was here to do his own investigation," Richie
confirmed. "I don't think he wants you interfering."

"*Me* interfering?" she asked, looking at him. "What
about you guys?"

"He didn't mention us specifically," Richie noted, with a shrug of a shoulder. "So I don't think it applies to us."

"Oh, I see." Doreen stared at the two of them in fascination, as they completely ignored the fact that they weren't supposed to be doing *any* investigating. Shaking her head, she asked Nan, "How many of them will listen to Mack?"

"Not many," Nan answered in a cheerful voice. "Besides, you're the one with all the notoriety. So they figure, if anybody'll solve this, it'll be you."

"Well, that's nice to know," she replied and then sighed. "No pressure though, *huh*."

"None at all." Nan chuckled. "Just all of it."

As it was, the three of them finished off the breakfast goodies, Doreen keeping Nan and Richie from sparring too much, and asked her to keep the animals at her little suite while Doreen talked to the residents. And then, with her list of names, Richie led Doreen to the common room and pointed out three of the people he'd mentioned. And Doreen headed to the first one, sat down beside Maude, and introduced herself.

The woman looked at her in delight. "Oh, I was so hoping you'd come," she stated.

"And why is that?" Doreen asked cautiously, not sure, as these would all be questions about the rift between Maude and her grandmother.

"Because I don't think you understand just how bad your grandmother is," she snapped in a severe tone. "I really do think you need to smarten up to her ways."

"Ah," Doreen replied, as she massaged her temples, realizing just what her day would be like. "And I suppose you have some concrete evidence of some problems?"

"Oh, absolutely." And then Maude went on a lengthy

166

discourse of all the things that she had deemed to be wrong with Doreen's grandmother. Not that there wasn't something about her grandmother that rubbed others the wrong way because, of course, Doreen could see how her grandmother had probably irritated an awful lot of people. But it would be nice if somebody had more than just ill will involved.

By the time Doreen got through that diatribe with that Maude woman—and then the other two in that same common room—it was obvious that Nan was not well loved by any of them and that these three women were all best friends. When Doreen asked specifically about anybody hurting Nan and if they had seen anything, almost verbatim, the three of them basically said the same thing: that they hadn't seen anything, but they did certainly understand the sentiment.

Her grandmother could be very irritating, and it was all they could do to stand to be in the same room with her. So, if somebody had hurt her grandmother, well, this trio certainly understood that. But, no, they hadn't seen any likely suspects and hadn't done it themselves.

As Doreen studied the three ladies, with their pencil-stick-thin arms and the frail looks to them overall, Doreen realized that, with her grandmother, if she had been sitting there quietly or even snoozing, could they have knocked out Nan? Granted, it's not as if much strength was required, especially when the prey was just completely unaware. Plus, the EMTs and Mack had both confirmed that Nan had no defensive wounds.

Yet the thought of any of these three women doing something like that to Nan didn't fit. And maybe it's because they were so skinny and scrawny that it looked like they couldn't lift even a poker to smack Nan over the head with or at least to hit her hard enough to render her unconscious.

Heads were still notoriously hard, even if they were on older people. By the time Doreen had finished talking to those three, she asked one of the ladies if she knew where to find Patsy Simmonds.

"Oh, Patsy." She shuddered. "You should find her in the billiards room. As if there weren't enough people here at Rosemoor who have problems, but we've got Patsy too."

"And what's the problem with Patsy?" Doreen asked.

"Everybody knows what girls like that are like," she snapped, with an ugly sniff.

Doreen was fascinated at this insight into the small community where her grandmother lived because, of course, it was just a sample of what the real community, or rather the larger community, around Kelowna was like too. But it was a part of the community that Doreen rarely dealt with on this level.

As she wandered toward the pool table area, it took a bit to find it. But finally, after asking somebody else for assistance, she did. And there was, true enough, one little lady with—and then Doreen stopped, studied her, realized that she was lean and short, but the hat? The hat got to Doreen. It was like what she'd imagined a bookie hat would be, from the movies.

The woman looked up at Doreen, and Patsy's gaze narrowed, as if seeing her as a mark, and she motioned Doreen into the room. "It's all right, sweetheart," she said, "I'll be gentle."

At that, Doreen had to laugh. "Well, I won't be playing with you," she noted, "because I wouldn't know one end of a stick to another."

At that, the other woman rolled her eyes. "Wow. How is it nobody has anything to do with the best sport in the world?"

"It's not anything I was ever exposed to growing up," she replied honestly. "And, by the same token, some things are just, you know, easier for others than what we would expect."

The woman looked startled and then shrugged. "Life's what you make it, but you're probably too young to understand that."

She winced. "Maybe. But believe me, I'm getting older by the day."

And, for some reason, that struck the other woman as absolutely hilarious. And she went off in peals of laughter. "Oh my, you're a pistol, aren't you?"

Another phrase Doreen had never really understood. "I'm Nan's granddaughter."

At that, the other woman nodded. "Of course you are. I heard you were out wandering around, talking to people."

"Somebody did attack her," she noted gently. "So obviously I want to find out who did."

"And what will you do then?" she asked, eyeing her carefully. "Because, you know, this place is full of misfits."

"Until yesterday, I hadn't realized just how much that was true," she admitted. "I would like to think that my grandmother is safe here."

"Ah." Patsy nodded. "Well, I hadn't considered that, but she's as safe as the rest of us."

"And what does that mean?"

"Well, if somebody was trying to hurt her, they could have done it in many ways. So you have to look at the why of the timing and the why of the location."

"Well, the location's because it was private, and nobody would see the attack. But anybody could have seen her attacker coming and going."

"Not really," Patsy replied, "because the other thing about Nan's place is, she has a ground-level patio, and they could have just stepped onto the patio, hit her, and left."

At that, Doreen looked at her in astonishment, and then a knowing gaze came into her eyes. "You know something? Now that makes more sense. I couldn't quite figure out how anybody or why anybody would bother doing that because surely, with everybody wandering up and down the hallways at all hours of the night and day, surely the person would have been seen. But what you're saying is that an outsider had a great getaway."

"So, in that case, I revise my opinion. You're not as dumb as you look." And having delivered that coup, she returned to her pool stick and the balls on the table.

"So does that mean you have any idea who might have done it?"

"Nope, sure don't," she said cheerfully. "If you're looking to see if I did, I don't have any reason to."

"I heard that you and my grandmother don't always get along," she noted cautiously.

"In a place like this, nobody *always* gets along." She gave a shrug of her shoulder. "Cramped surroundings, not enough air for a lot of us to breathe all the time," she explained. "Lots of personalities coming and going—some of them, ones who you wish would go—but it's always the good ones who seem to go early," she muttered. "And that's just too bad. But, for the rest of us, we're here for the duration. This is a one-way portal here." She put down her stick and stared at Doreen. "And you have to remember. All of us know that.

We don't get out of here. This is a life sentence."

"Oh, wow," Doreen replied. "I hadn't considered it that way."

"Of course not. That's because you're young. You don't have to stay here. This isn't a life sentence for you, but, for the rest of us, it's a one-way street. We're here, and we're only going to leave in an ambulance or in a plastic bag," she noted succinctly. "And that makes our life, our living, our day-to-day activities here, very different from what yours is. You go home, think that you're fine and dandy. You still got another fifty, sixty, seventy years ahead of you, until a bus comes down your side yard and just slams into you and takes you right now."

Patsy sighed. "Other than that, you're not bothered. You think that you'll live forever just because you're young and stupid," she said, without appearing to mean any insult.

Kind of like Patsy was on autopilot, and this was her daily spiel.

Patsy continued. "Those of us in here, we already know that we've lived longer than we should, and a lot of times people here don't care about the consequences of what they do or say because they know that there's really nothing anybody can do about it that'll make a difference. So what? They'll take away our perks here?" She shrugged. "Big deal. So I can't play pool for a day or two? I've got a mini one in my room anyway," she stated. "They can't touch that. They'll make me not eat breakfast? Well, that's not allowed. That's against the law, so obviously they can't do that." She shrugged. "They'll put me in jail? Maybe, but I highly doubt a judge will do that either. Anybody here in this place has exactly the same knowledge that I do. So they can pretty well get away with murder."

At that, Doreen sucked in her breath. "And that's one of the reasons that I'm going around and talking to people," she stated carefully. "Did you know Chrissy?"

"Of course I knew Chrissy. Everybody knew Chrissy, mad as a hatter." And she picked up her cue stick again and whacked it into her other hand. "And, if you think she was anything but that, you're wrong."

"Okay," she noted. "Why would you say that she's mad as a hatter?"

"Because she was," she stated, waving the stick and then turning to point it at Doreen. "You have to be here to understand, but very quickly you recognize who's got it all up here." Patsy tapped her temple. "And who doesn't. Your Nan? She's got it up here." Patsy pointed again. "That's why the two of us sometimes don't get along because I do too. We're both sharp as a whistle. But I respect Nan. Your grandmother's good people, just not always good people for me. And that is probably something you can't quite understand yet either. Maybe in another thirty, forty years, you will." Patsy laughed.

"I think I understand just fine." Doreen liked and appreciated the woman's forthright honesty and humor. "It still doesn't change the fact that somebody attacked Nan, and potentially somebody killed Chrissy."

At that, the woman looked at her in astonishment. "Good Lord, who would want to hurt Chrissy? She was harmless."

"Sure she was harmless," Doreen agreed.

"Besides, even if somebody did murder Chrissy, I don't think anybody cares."

At that, Doreen raised an eyebrow. "Well, I care. Nan cares."

"Why does Nan care?" she asked curiously. "I mean, like I said, Chrissy was off her rocker."

"Because Nan feels guilty," Doreen noted quietly.

"Ah. So she was ignored, with all that talk about somebody poisoning her, *huh*?"

"So you heard that too, did you?"

"Sure did." Patsy nodded. "I considered it for a brief moment and then let it go because, even if somebody was trying to murder her, there's not really any way to prove it. Chrissy's been talking like that for a long time. Sometimes it was for attention, and sometimes it makes you wonder."

"Makes you wonder what?"

"Whether it's true or not. At one point in time, you just give up because you can't tell fact from fiction. Chrissy lived in her own head a lot of the time."

"Did she ever say anything else to you?"

"Yep, she did. She said it was justice."

At that, Doreen's antenna twitched. "Justice?"

"Yep, justice for something she'd done. Somebody was poisoning her to get back at her for something she'd done."

"Interesting."

"That's what I thought. I did try to talk to her about it little bit more, but I never got any further. You had to pick your moments with her, and then she would go down the rabbit hole very, very quickly, and it could be days before she came back out. Part of that was the medication they kept her on. I did question her medication a couple times and talked to the nurses a couple times, and they just said that she was losing her grasp on reality, and that's a real big *duh* moment for all of us because of course she was. Was it a good thing? No, of course not. Was it a sad thing? Yeah, sure was. But it was also the facts of life here. We have a lot of people who lose their grasp on reality." She yawned. "So boring. So predictable. I hope whenever I die, it's definitely not in the same vein."

"You don't want your death to be predictable?" Doreen asked, then she smiled.

"Or boring," she added. "Like your Nan, I'd rather hit the home plate, skidding in at the last moment, with a glass of scotch in my hand and holding a winning poker hand in the other, only in my case, make it be a pool cue." She chuckled. "And there's enough shenanigans going on this place to keep even the two of us going."

"Shenanigans?" Doren asked quietly.

At that, Patsy rolled her eyes. "Sex." She shook her head. "Everybody's bed-hopping with everybody. It's as if we all hit our second childhood, with absolutely no rules or regulations." As she looked at Doreen, Patsy chuckled. "And look at that? You're blushing. Nobody your age ever wants to think about anybody our age having sex," she noted, "but it's rampant in these homes." And she went off in peals of laughter again.

"Well, that's a good question though," Doreen noted. "Was Chrissy seeing anybody?"

At that, Patsy's laughter stopped; she looked at Doreen. "You know something? That's a really good question." She thought about it and frowned. "I think there was somebody, and he was quite a bit younger than her. It did cause some consternation among the residents though."

"Why is that?"

"Well, we don't really worry about age gaps, when we're here," she noted. "I mean, why bother? We'll die anyway, so who cares? And, if we can get it on with somebody that much younger, all the more power to them. And, for the old guys, they don't really care what age you are anyway. As long as you're still breathing, they're good to go."

"Seriously?" Doreen asked. "So they don't change much in old age, right?" Patsy guffawed so loudly and long. Doreen found herself grinning like a fool. Something was really likable about this woman. And, yes, Patsy reminded Doreen of her own Nan.

And when she finally calmed down, Patsy was still laughing, but added, "No, they're exactly the same here too. They're just trying to wear us women down a whole lot faster because, you know, hey, there's no more time for them, so they have to work a little bit harder. But most of the women here don't have to be convinced too much," she noted. And then she looked over at Doreen. "But I won't bore you with the details, or you'll turn fifty shades of pink as it is."

Her reference to the fifty shades part had to be deliberate, and, sure enough, Doreen felt her own ears turning pink at the comment. "Do you remember who it might have been?"

"Well, obviously I haven't forgotten," she replied. "I just told you that he was younger."

"And is he a resident or staff?"

"Quick comment," she said approvingly. "You're sharp. I like that. He used to be staff. And now he's a resident. Or was? So, in your case, both of those apply."

"Name?" Doreen asked, knowing this Patsy woman knew exactly who she was talking about and was just trying to decide whether she should help Doreen or not.

"What's in it for me?" Patsy asked.

"And what is it you want?" Doreen asked. "Considering that you're at this stage of life and pretty well don't care what you have or don't have," she said equally bluntly.

At that, Patsy smiled. "Your grandmother took me off the betting charts. I was really miffed at that."

"What did you do to deserve it?" she asked.

Patsy looked at her with a crafty glance. "I might have cheated."

"Then I'm not surprised she took you off. I'll mention it to her, but, if you'll cheat, I don't think she wants you in her orbit."

Patsy nodded. "It was foolish. And I didn't do it to win money I wasn't due. I just wanted to test her."

"And now?"

"Yeah, now I know who she is and what she's like." Patsy sighed. "But I didn't think getting back in her good graces would be this hard."

"Well, I'll talk to her, but no guarantees. And of course you have to give me something seriously good in order to warrant that." She wondered at why she had to negotiate the truth out of somebody like Patsy, but Doreen somehow understood that that implicitly was part of this game.

"His name is Xavier, Xavier Zelnick."

"Interesting, and why do you think he could possibly be a suspect?"

"I have no idea," she replied, looking over at her. "You didn't ask me for any suspects. You just asked what the name of her boyfriend was."

"Fine. Do you have any idea of anybody who would be a suspect?"

"No, sure don't." Patsy gave Doreen a fat grin. "But you're still going to talk to your grandmother, aren't you?"

"I will. A deal's a deal." And, with that, Doreen turned and walked out, leaving Patsy cackling behind her.

More than tired and fed-up, Doreen headed back to her

grandmother's place to see her sitting on the couch, resting gently and alone. Her eyes were closed, as Doreen came around to look at Nan but hesitated.

"I'm fine," Nan said, without opening her eyes. "Stop fussing."

"That'll be the day." Doreen sat down beside her grandmother on the couch.

"How did you make out with everybody?" Nan asked, looking over at Doreen curiously.

"Well, I had some interesting talks with some very interesting people."

"Place is full of them," she replied. "Just when you think you got them all figured out, somebody comes along and changes the dynamic, and people do things that you just didn't think were even possible." Nan shrugged. "I can't tell you how many times I thought I knew somebody, until they did something so wildly out of character."

"You mean, like Patsy?"

She snorted at that. "Did you talk to her?"

"I did."

"And what'd she say?"

"That she would give me the name of Chrissy's boyfriend, who I wanted to talk to, if I told you, … if I asked you to reconsider letting her in on your betting again. She knows she cheated, but it was more a test to see how you'd handle it."

At that, Nan looked at Doreen, a twinkle in her eye. "Of course it was a test, but I was hoping for more out of her than that."

Doreen sighed. "You guys are playing lots of games here."

"Sure, nothing else for us to do, well, except for *that*,"

she noted, with an eye roll.

"Well, Patsy was pretty clear about *that* being a pretty prevalent activity here too." She studied her grandmother closely.

But Nan just gave her one of those beaming smiles. "Sure, people are bored. What can you expect them to do? No people here to moan and groan and to tell them how to behave themselves. They get to finally have a chance to kick up their heels and to do what they always wanted with whomever they wanted." Nan shrugged. "You can't blame them for that."

"No, I wasn't planning on blaming them for anything." Doreen smiled. "Now what do you know about this Xavier guy?"

"Ah, Xavier," Nan replied. "He's a heartthrob. And once he and Chrissy broke up, I have to tell you that more than a few ladies, with happy sighs and hopeful looks, were heading in his direction."

"Okay. When did they break up?"

"Pretty quickly before Chrissy died, now that I think about it." She frowned.

"Oh?"

Nan nodded slowly. "She was pretty upset. She said he broke her heart."

"Do you know why he broke up with her?"

"Somebody said something. … In this place it's hard to know what anybody said."

"But what did Chrissy say they said?" Even that was getting Doreen confused.

"She thought somebody had told Xavier that Chrissy was cheating on him. So she wasn't being faithful." Nan paused, then added, "He got pretty upset and broke up with her."

"So he didn't trust her?"

"I guess that would be the main thrust of it, yes, but the bottom line is, he broke up with her, and that devastated Chrissy."

"So I got a question for you," she stated. "What was Chrissy's mental state in the days leading up to her death?" She wondered if anybody had even asked that question yet.

At that, her grandmother stared at her. "Oh." And then she added, "*Ooh.* I didn't think of that."

"No, and maybe it's something we do need to think about," Doreen replied quietly.

At that, Nan sat back on her couch and went really quiet, as if going through what Chrissy's last few days were like. "I ..." And then she stopped. "You know? I just don't know." Then she shook her head and looked over at Doreen, and, for the first time, Doreen saw tears in Nan's eyes. "I guess it's possible that she was very depressed."

"I'm not saying that it happened," Doreen murmured. "I'm just wondering if her mental state was such that maybe she did something to herself. Would she have taken her life over this breakup with Xavier?"

"She was really upset," Nan whispered, wiping the tears away from her face.

Doreen got up, walked over to the kitchen counter, grabbed the box of tissues, and brought it over for her.

Nan dabbed at her eyes and whispered, "That would be absolutely terrible, if that's what happened."

"But we also have to understand that sometimes, at the end, what we think we're looking for is not the end that we find," she murmured.

Nan shuffled so that she was closer to Doreen, and

reached over and picked up her hand. "If I'd even thought that we would go down this pathway," she said, "I wouldn't have gone here."

"Maybe not," Doreen agreed gently. "And I can understand being terribly upset to think that your friend might have done something like this willfully, but it is something we have to consider."

Nan sniffled again and then took another Kleenex and blew her nose. "Maybe," she muttered. "But I won't believe it," she stated defiantly.

"And why is that?"

Her grandmother stopped, looked at her. "Because she was very much in love with him. I think she fully expected to explain it away and that he would forgive her."

"And what if she had that talk with him and what if he didn't believe her?" she asked quietly.

At that, Nan shook her head. "I don't know," she replied. "I can tell you that she would have been very, very upset."

"Exactly," Doreen agreed quietly with her grandmother. "And that is then something that we do have to consider."

"I don't want to consider it," she snapped.

She reached over and gripped her grandmother's hand. "Remember. We're doing this for Chrissy's sake, not for our sake. We're trying to get at the truth, not just create something that fits the truth you want it to be."

At that, Nan's gaze widened. "Oh dear, is that what I'm doing?"

"You're looking for something to … something to justify the guilt, to ease the guilt that you're holding in your heart," she explained quietly. "And we can't always do that. Maybe your friend did need a friend to listen to her at the time.

Maybe she needed more from somebody. Still, that doesn't mean she needed it from you. But it may feel like that, especially if this is what ended up happening, but we don't know for sure."

"No, of course not." Then she wrapped her arms around her chest, as if she were cold.

Doreen got up and grabbed the crocheted afghan from behind the big recliner and wrapped it around her grandmother's shoulders. "And I'm sorry this is so upsetting for you."

"Well, of course it's upsetting," she noted. "Last thing I want to think about is a friend of mine having been so upset that death was an easier answer than facing tomorrow."

"And yet," she reminded her, "for many people, the tomorrow here isn't necessarily all that happy."

"Maybe not," she agreed, "but Chrissy wasn't like that. You know how she really lived in her own world."

"And maybe that inner world of Chrissy's suddenly turned sour on her," Doreen suggested, "and it was hard for her to come to terms with the reality that she had to get to tomorrow."

"Meaning, Xavier?"

"Yes, I mean Xavier." There wasn't a whole lot of point in staying any longer, but she asked, "Do you know if this Xavier guy is still here?"

She shook her head. "After Chrissy's death, he moved."

"Oh, interesting. Do you know where?"

She nodded. "He went down to something called Riverview Manor. "I don't ... I don't even remember if that's the name of it, but it was something like that."

Doreen nodded. "Maybe I'll ask Richie."

At that, Nan snorted. "Yeah, you go ahead and ask

Richie about that one. He wouldn't have given Xavier two times a day."

"Sorry?" Doreen asked in confusion.

"Well, if someone wouldn't give Xavier the time of day, then Richie hated him so much that he wouldn't have given him two times a day."

Still confused, Doreen nodded, as if she understood. "Do you mind if I leave the animals here, while I go talk to Richie?"

"Of course not. They are welcome here anytime. And especially when I need more hugs."

After a teary hug with her grandmother, Doreen quickly stepped out of Nan's place and walked down the hallway to Richie's room. At the knock on the door, he called out to come in. She poked her head around. "Hey, Richie."

He motioned at her to come in. "Come on in. Come on in. Have you got any news?"

"Just a couple questions at the moment." She asked, "Do you know a Xavier Zelnick?"

He nodded. "Wish I didn't though. Talk about a ladies' man."

At that, she stifled a smile. "In what way?" she asked. "Apparently he was Chrissy's most recent boyfriend."

"Yep, and they were an item for quite a while, but he broke it off when one of the witches in this place started up a rumor about her having an affair behind his back."

"And was it a rumor?"

"Absolutely. Chrissy was just head over heels in love with him. And I don't even know why," he said, with a sniff. "I mean, obviously he wasn't worth it, and she was some-body special."

"And did you have any hope of a relationship with her?"

she asked curiously. He looked at her, and she almost thought she saw a blush forming.

"Of course not. I was too old for her anyway."

"I see," she murmured. "So, after that, do you know what happened?"

He looked at her. "What do you mean? What happened?"

"Well, they broke it off. So did he have another girlfriend after that?"

He thought about it and added, "Well, Chrissy died really fast after that." He frowned. "So I'm not sure if that was exactly ... if that's exactly when he left or not but he, ... he moved out pretty fast. I don't think he even gave much notice here."

"*Hmm.*"

He frowned, then shrugged. "Maybe he did it, and that's why he ran."

"Maybe," she noted on a cautionary tone, "but we can't jump to that conclusion." Yet it was obvious that Richie was quite excited about his conclusion. "Remember, Richie," she explained. "We need facts not just fiction."

His face fell. "Well, good luck getting facts. He's not here anymore."

"Do you have any idea where he is now?"

"Yeah, Riverview," he said, with a wave of his hand. "No idea what it's like trying to talk to anybody there."

She winced at that. "No, that's a good point. I get a lot of leeway here because everybody knows me."

"Exactly," he agreed, "but down there, you'll be persona non grata." And then he chuckled. "I always wanted to use that phrase."

She smiled. "Well, now you did, and it's up to me to

figure out how to talk to him."

"You'll let us know, won't you?"

And such anxiousness was in his tone that she nodded. "I'll let you know what I find out, if I can," she stated, adding a cautious note at the end.

"Of course, of course." He gave her a sage look. "Once you talk to the police, that is."

"*If* I need to talk to the police," she reminded him. "We don't know who's behind this, if anybody's behind this." And then she stood up, walked back to the door. "Now you have a good afternoon, okay?"

With that, she returned to Nan's to get her animals, before they all headed out toward the river. Doreen just wanted something completely different for a change from all those gossipy tales going on at the seniors' home. It was not exactly an easy place to ask questions, and yet they all had so much information. However, most of the time, they really didn't have a clue what to do with the information.

As Doreen slowly wandered down the river, she picked up a few rocks and tossed them in. With Goliath racing to catch the rocks on the path and Mugs racing to catch the rocks in the water, she ended up with two very wet animals—Goliath very unhappy as he stalked ahead of her. Thaddeus had apparently not had a chance to sleep at all at Nan's and was curled up against her neck.

She reached up, stroked his beautiful feathers and whispered, "We'll be home soon."

"Home," he murmured. "Home."

She smiled, tilted her head so that she could cuddle him a little closer, as she walked them home. Pretty quickly she saw the bench at her place, and, calling the animals to her, they headed up her garden pathway to the kitchen. When she reached for the kitchen door, she heard the front door slam closed. It took her a second to realize just what she heard, and then she raced out to the front door in time to see a small dark car tearing out of the cul-de-sac. That's all she saw. But it was obvious that somebody had been in her house. As she turned around, she studied the chairs that were upturned and the few items on the shelves tossed.

"Good God," she told Mugs, who was sniffing around the floor and at all the items on the floor. "I think we just had a break-in."

Chapter 12

MACK STARED AT Doreen in shock. "You left the house, and you didn't set the alarm?"

Since this was the third time he had questioned her on that, she glared at him. "I already apologized," she snapped, her hands on her hips, as she stared at him. "You can't make me feel any worse than I already do."

He shook his head, snagged her in his arms, and pulled her in for a hug.

"You should have done that in the first place," she muttered against his chest.

He chuckled. "You're right. I should have. I'm sorry."

She sniffed but let herself sink into his embrace.

"And did you see anybody?"

"No, as I came in the kitchen," she stated patiently, knowing he would ask her over and over again, "all I saw was, … all I *heard* was the sound of the front door banging shut. When we raced out to the front yard to see, a little black car was taking off."

"And did you see two people in the car?"

She frowned. "I'm not sure. What difference does it make?"

"Well, somebody got into the vehicle, and to turn it on first would take a little bit longer. Whereas, if they had somebody already in the getaway car, and this guy just had to get in the passenger side, and the engine was already on, then they could have gotten away that much faster."

"Oh." She felt foolish for not having considered that. "I guess it's possible. I don't know."

Mack nodded. "Maybe your neighbor saw something."

She sniffed at that. "I doubt Richard saw anything. Even when I went out the front door yesterday morning," she noted, "he raced back inside, as if afraid I would see him."

"You do have a strange relationship with that person," he muttered, turning to look in the direction of Richard's house.

"That's not the word for it," she argued. "And more or less it works because we don't get in each other space."

His lips twitched at that.

"Okay, fine," she quickly amended. "I try not to irritate him too much. And in return he's had a helpful tidbit or two."

He nodded. "You are you, and, once again, I don't want you to change."

She smiled at that. "Every once in a while, you do say nice things." She gave him a gentle pat on his back, and then she stepped away. "But I really don't know what I'm supposed to do now."

"What brought all this on?"

"You mean, besides the fact that I've been down talking to everybody at Rosemoor, right?"

He winced. "Of course you have." He sighed. "And did you come up with anything?"

"Chrissy's old boyfriend may or may not have had something to do with her death. Nobody knows anything about who attacked Nan with a vase. She's got several enemies at the senior's home," she noted. "As much as I hate to admit it, not everybody adores my grandmother like I do."

He gave her a commiserating smile. "I don't imagine everybody would like her style, but she comes from the heart."

"She does, indeed." Doreen smiled. "And surely that's worth something."

"It is to a lot of people and isn't to a lot of others." Mack shrugged. "So anything concrete?"

"Nope, absolutely nothing."

And he had to laugh at the wealth of disgust in her voice. "That's the fun of investigating."

"Nope, not really," she disagreed. "You know that somebody knows something."

"But do they?" he asked. "I'm sure you've already considered who was attacked and where."

"Absolutely," she stated. "Nan has one of the few ground floor corner apartments, and, therefore, it has an easy access and an easy exit for anybody wanting to do something—whether from inside or outside."

"Exactly."

"And whether it was triggered by her investigation into Chrissy's death, that really doesn't have much bearing on it."

"And why is that?" he asked, looking at her curiously.

"Because apparently she has enough people down there at Rosemoor who don't particularly like her anyway," she replied. "And that just confuses the issue. I had to make a couple deals with people to even get them to talk to me." She shook her head. "That Patsy is something else."

He grinned at her. "I even know that one. Patsy's very

much like your grandmother."

"Yeah, I recognize that." Doreen nodded. "Both of them always trying to work the angles." He just looked over at her. She added, "Fine, fine. I probably come by it honestly myself," she admitted, with a sigh.

"You do, indeed." Mack laughed. "But not to be outdone, Patsy is generally a good-hearted person."

"I won't argue with you there," she admitted. "It did appear that she wanted to get back into my grandmother's good graces. Whether that'll work or not, I don't know."

"And what did she do to get out of it?"

"She cheated," she replied succinctly.

At that, even Mack winced. "Not sure that'll work with your grandmother. She doesn't tolerate that very much."

"Nope, she sure doesn't." Doreen laughed. "And I can't say I really blame her."

"No, maybe not," he agreed, "but, if we don't have anything to go on with Nan's attack and if we don't have anything to go on here with your break-in"—he paused—"it does make me wonder if any of these are connected."

"And why would they be connected?" she asked.

"Because you're pushing the boundaries again."

"Actually," she clarified, "more than the boundaries there at Rosemoor. Don't forget I've been asking a lot of questions about the poisonings."

At that, he turned and stared at her. She shrugged. "Didn't want you to lose sight of that fact."

"Great, thanks for that," he said. "So, just like your Nan, you have an awful lot of people who might want you to butt out of their business."

At that, she glared at him. "I'm not a terrible person," she muttered.

"Not at all," he replied. "Yet not everybody'll have the same viewpoint."

And of course he was right there. Whether she wanted to admit it or not, a lot of people didn't like her methodology—her meddling. "So what's the answer?" As he went to open his mouth, she said, "And, no, I'm not staying home and staying out of trouble."

His mouth clicked shut, with more force than necessary, and he glared at her.

She shrugged. "You know perfectly well that's not something I can do."

"You could try," he suggested. "You don't always have to be the one in the middle of the danger."

"No, I don't," she agreed. "However, something here is definitely off."

"I won't argue with you there," he noted, "because I agree. Something is off. I'm just not sure what's off about any of it. And whether any of it's connected."

"Well, in my world, it seems that they're always connected. I just don't know if that recent poisoning of Alan and Chrissy's earlier poisoning, *supposed* poisoning"—she corrected at a look from him—"but a few months earlier and now possibly Nan's recent attack could all be related. That seems a little bit far-fetched."

He nodded. "And I can't blame you for getting involved in the poisoning cases because we were together at the beach when we saw the box of rat poison."

"Exactly," she said in delight. "So really you can't blame me for this one."

"No, I would like to though."

It took her moment to understand, and then she gasped in shock. "You don't get to just blame me," she stated.

"No, it doesn't work that way," he muttered. "But I will have to talk to my captain about this."

"*Great.* We already know how he feels about me being involved."

"He's been very tolerant with you so far." Mack gave her a hard look. "Let's not push it."

"That's what I meant about how he feels about me being involved. I mean, *let's not push it* isn't the same thing as being lenient."

"No, of course not," he replied quietly. "So what we do is, we have to ensure that we get to the bottom of this and fast."

"Any leads on the poisoning of Alan, the poor man who died?"

"Nope. Nothing concrete. Wouldn't it have been nice if he'd left us a roadmap to say, *Hey, this guy did it.*"

"Right?" she agreed. "And it seemed like everybody loved him."

"Exactly. But death sometimes smooths over people's rough edges." At Doreen's frown, he explained further. "Some people overlook another's shortcomings, once they're dead. Like you do, with your former divorce attorney, Robin."

Doreen shrugged, but she understood what he was trying to say.

"Still," Mack added, "that doesn't mean that everybody really loved him. It only takes one person to make something like this into a very ugly scenario."

"Agreed," she noted quietly. "And it sure seems like we have more ugliness than is fair." He looked at her. She shrugged. "I don't know. It just always seems like there's so much ugly around."

"Getting a little bit depressed about humanity?" he asked quietly.

"Sometimes, yeah." She stopped, thought about it. "Wonder if there's any connection among the people? Maybe you should do that," she said thoughtfully. "Check out associations between the three different scenarios—Alan, Chrissy, Nan."

He looked at her, then shrugged. "I can do something along that line," he agreed, "but it still doesn't mean that we'll get a list of known associates, much less anyone in common with all three victims."

"What about … did Alan leave a will?"

"I spoke to the lawyer this morning," he relayed. "He's not being terribly cooperative."

"Yeah, well, maybe the lawyer did it too then," she noted in exasperation. "I don't get it. Why are these guys causing us so much trouble?"

"*Us?*" he asked, with a raised eyebrow.

She glared at him. "You know what I mean."

"I do, indeed. But they're trying to cover their own selves and make sure that they're staying within the confines of the law."

"So maybe they should have done that in time to keep their clients alive," she stated.

"In this case, he's checking into his own legalities. And then he'll talk to us."

"Sure he will. What, as long as you sign some sort of disclosure agreement?"

He chuckled. "No, I have a meeting with him tomorrow, and that'll only happen as long as he cooperates."

"Fine." She sighed. "But keep these names in mind, just in case somebody pops in that will."

"And the will's already been read, I believe," he noted.

"In that case the lawyer should be perfectly capable of handing off any information about it, shouldn't he?"

"Maybe," Mack said cheerfully. "Not your problem."

She glared at him again. He shrugged. "It's not."

"Fine," she muttered. "I really don't like it when you get official and kick me out of it."

At that, he smiled. "I wouldn't have to, if you would stay out of it voluntarily."

She waved her hand. "That's just details."

He burst out laughing. "So you had breakfast, but did you eat anything else?"

"Nope, not yet. Oh—" And then she stopped, looked at him. "I have another problem."

"*Great.*" He walked to the fridge, opened it, and took a look. "It's not dinnertime, is it?"

She checked her watch and gasped. "Oh my God, I missed lunch."

He looked over at her, grinned. "Yeah? Why do you think I'm looking in your fridge?"

"And you were supposed to cook today."

"I was," he said, with a nod. "Remember that part about checking your fridge?"

"Yeah, remember that part about there is never any food?"

But he kept rummaging through the fridge, the freezer, and the cupboards, gathering stuff.

When he came back with two chicken breasts from the freezer, mushrooms from the fridge, and pasta from the pantry, she nodded. "Well, anything with pasta is always good." But she looked at his selection and asked, "Can you really make something out of that?"

"Absolutely." Then he stopped and said, "Nope. You'll make something out of this."

"Oh, and here I thought you wanted to eat tonight," she grumbled.

He burst out laughing. "We will be eating tonight, and it's not hard."

"Yeah, *right*. I'm pretty sure I've heard that before."

He smiled and waved her over. "Come on over here. Let's get to prepping. And, while we're cooking, you can tell me what you found out about whatever this other problem is."

"Oh." She stopped and looked at him. "It's Wendy."

"What about Wendy?" he asked, as he sliced up the chicken. And then he stopped. "Oh no, you don't. You'll do this." He changed places with her, handed her the knife, and said, "Slice it like I did."

So moving carefully and much slower than him, she slowly sliced up the couple chicken breasts until they were thin. He nodded. "Now get your fry pan, toss in some butter, add some minced garlic, maybe a chopped onion." He watched as she heated the pan and the butter. And then he nodded, got an onion out of the pantry, and—before she had a chance—he had it diced and threw it into the pan already. Then he quickly mashed a couple cloves of garlic.

She said, "I thought I was making it."

He winced. "Sorry. Yes, now stir that."

And they went back to her following his instructions. But it was pretty hard on him to take a back seat and to watch her do this for the first time, when he could have finished it in no time. Still, she needed to know that she could do this—even if he weren't here standing over her. So he'd handled his lack of patience and his growing hunger pretty well. By the time she had the onions simmered and the chicken mostly cooked, she already had the pasta pot on and smiled. "Hey, cooking this meal, so far, isn't too bad."

"The rest of it isn't bad either," he noted.

And, before she knew it, she was seriously busy making a sauce.

"And you still haven't told me about Wendy."

"Oh, yes." And she quickly told him about what she'd seen in the alleyway behind Wendy's store.

He stopped, turned toward her, and asked, "Seriously?"

She nodded. "A couple days ago when I was down there"—and then she winced—"okay, so I was there recently, but I was there a couple weeks ago maybe. It seemed like something weird was going on that time too." She shrugged. "I should have told you straightaway, but I didn't really have any theory, didn't really understand it," she noted. "And I know how you hate it when I jump to conclusions and operate on a hunch with no evidence. So I didn't mention it the first time it happened. Yet I kept thinking it over in my mind, but I had no answers. Still, it kept nagging at me. But obviously there was some problem again more recently. I should have mentioned it to you then."

"Not a whole lot I can do if there's a personal problem, not a legal problem," he noted. "Remember. These people have a right to their own life too."

"Maybe," she noted, with a sniff, "but this was definitely odd."

"*Odd* happens a lot, as you should already know," he teased. "So what is it that you think was odd?"

"Well, last time she just looked like she was … *nervous*. She kept watching over her shoulders, as if something was seriously wrong. And when I told her that she could always, you know, tell me whatever was wrong and how I might help, she did tell me that there was nothing I could do." And then she stopped. "How is it people always say that?"

He smiled. "Because they don't want, for one, to get people in trouble with them, and, for two, they don't know how to explain the trouble they got themselves into, revealing their vulnerable moments," he noted quietly. "A lot of the time they're just ashamed of it, or they think there's no way to get out of it, regardless of who helps."

"Maybe," she noted. "But I would have thought that maybe she would let me help a little bit."

"Why, because of your reputation?" he asked, with a raised brow. She glared at him. He smiled. "Get back there, stirring your pan."

She stepped to the pot with the sauce and stirred it vigorously.

He reached out a hand on her shoulder and added, "Gently."

She sighed, slowed down her movements, and noted, "There's really an art to this."

"No, it's not so much an art, more science. It's a matter of relaxing and letting the pan do its thing and the heat do its thing," he explained quietly. "And going with the flow instead of trying to force it."

She nodded but wasn't sure that he knew exactly what he was talking about.

And obviously he could guess at her thoughts from the look on her face because he laughed. "I'm not lying, honest." He smiled.

"Are you sure?" she asked. "Because it sure seems like everything here could be going a lot faster."

"You can turn up the heat," he suggested, "and then the rest of it will cook faster, but you're pretty well done. However, if you don't stir it every once in a while, things will stick."

"Right, and then we get those horrible pans to clean."

He snorted. "Exactly why I told you to stir."

"Okay, got it," she replied. "I am getting there, you know?"

"You're doing quite well," he told her. "And considering where you were when we started," he suggested, "you're doing very well."

She smiled up at him. "That's a lovely lie, thank you." He burst out laughing. She grinned and added, "I am worried about Wendy though."

"Maybe the next time you're at her shop, see what she's like, how she's acting, and you could offer your assistance again," he suggested. "But, if people don't want help and if they don't want to confide in you, then there isn't a whole lot you can do about it."

She nodded, but she didn't like anything about that. "I hear you. I just don't think it's fair."

"Why? Because you don't get all the answers that you want from people?" His voice cracked with suspicious laughter.

She shrugged. "I get it. You think it's funny, but there's an awful lot going on right now."

"There is, indeed," he agreed. "So let's focus on all that and not so much on everything else."

"Wouldn't that be nice?" She sighed. "I really don't know what's happening at Rosemoor though."

"And what do you think *is* happening?"

"Well, people hate Nan. She was conked on the head

POISON IN THE PANSIES

with a vase. She's not safe there. I offered for her to stay here
for a few days, but she'd rather be with Richie. She'd rather
be there in the middle of Rosemoor and all its secrets. I don't
know." She raised both hands in frustration. She looked
down at her animals and added, "The other thing is, Mugs
didn't bark or didn't even seem upset when he came into the
house today, right after the intruder left. I thought that was
odd."

He looked at her, stared at Mugs, and asked, "And how
much of it is because he might have known this person?"

She frowned. "I don't know. I just don't know. I didn't
recognize the car," she admitted honestly. "So ..." She shook
her head. "It's just very strange. It's not like there's anything
to steal here."

"Maybe they thought that some of the antiques would
be back."

"Why?" she asked. "I'm still waiting to get that stupid
catalog, showing me all of Nan's items."

"Good," he nodded. "And, assuming you trust these
people, it should be all coming together soon."

"*Assuming I trust these people?*" she repeated ever-so-
slowly. "Are you saying there's a chance that they're not
trustworthy?"

He winced. "No, that's not what I'm saying. All I'm trying to do is keep in mind that an awful lot is going on in
your world right now, and, if you focus on the good, the rest
should fall into place."

She frowned suspiciously at him. "You sound an awful
lot like Nan, when she's trying to calm me down."

"Gee, is it working?"

"No," she replied, "but I do want to know more about
the guy who recently died, Alan."

"Why is that?"

"Because I still think his death is connected to the poison that we found down at the park."

"I did talk to the old guy you found at the park, but I found him at his home. As you can imagine, he wasn't happy to see me and wasn't all that cooperative. However, he finally showed me where the rat poison was," he explained, "*but* the box is missing."

She stared at him in shock. "So, even after he put it away, somebody came back and took it again?"

He nodded. "That appears to be the case, if we can believe him."

She frowned at him. "Right. And, of course, if he had anything to do with the poisonings or if he's trying to protect somebody, he would have lied about even having the poison."

Mack looked at her, grinned. "You sure you don't want to go into law enforcement?"

She thought about it and replied, "A part of me would love to go into law enforcement, but I think all those rules would really hamper my style."

Chapter 13

Friday Morning

THE NEXT MORNING, Doreen thought about the conversation with Mack from the previous night. They'd hashed up a lot of different ideas, but they hadn't exactly solved anything. And that was the part that would drive her nuts. She wanted to know more about this young man who had been poisoned, but she also wanted to know more about the box of poison that had gone missing from the old guy's garage yet again.

On that note, she looked down at the animals, with a determined nod. "Let's go back to Sarsons Beach, guys. Then we'll hit Nan's and see how she's doing." But she wanted to get to the beach early enough to see if this old guy was there. And, sure enough, when she got there, he toddled toward the beach.

She parked, got out, with her animals racing at her side, as she walked up to him. "Hey."

He looked at her and frowned. "I don't want to talk to you."

"Maybe you don't want to talk to me, but apparently it's possible the poison used to kill a man did come from your place."

"So what? It's gone anyway."

"And I wondered who you might be protecting when you say that."

He stopped, stared at her, and then got really angry.

She winced at how absolutely crass and awkward her accusation had come out. "And you're right," she replied. "None of my business and how dare I accuse you of something like that."

And it's like she took the words right out of his mouth. He stared at her before speaking. "Are you always like this?"

"Yeah, kind of," she muttered apologetically. "I do sometimes say things without really thinking about it."

He nodded. "That is quite a failing."

She smiled at him. "You could be right, but, at the same time, people are dying."

"One person's dead," he corrected, "and I didn't have anything to do with it."

"Maybe not," she agreed, "but I suspect you know more than you're telling."

He just stared at her. "And why is that?" he asked. "Because the poison *might* have came from my place?" He shrugged. "You know how many times people steal from my garage? I don't even lock anything anymore because it's easier than having to replace windows and locks. I just don't keep anything in there."

"Right," she noted, thinking about that. "I had a break-in at my place just yesterday."

He looked at her in astonishment. "Well, you probably do piss off a lot of people."

It was her turn to glare at him. "Well, they didn't take anything, since I interrupted them," she stated. "I just have no idea why they were there."

"I guess it depends on how much you piss them off too," he quipped, with a fat grin.

She sniffed. "And somebody attacked my poor grandmother in the old folks' home."

"What?" he asked. "Good Lord, what's going on?"

"I'm not sure," she replied quietly. "But if they thought attacking my grandmother would get me off the case, they're wrong."

He nodded. "Absolutely, we have to look after our own."

"And now you know why I'm here again," she stated. "She was at Rosemoor, just sitting, resting on her patio, and somebody came up and clunked her over the head with a vase."

He looked at her. "Is your grandmother Willa Anne Montgomery?"

She looked at him in astonishment. "Do you know my nan?"

"Well, maybe," he replied, "at least if that's who we're talking about."

She nodded. "That's who we're talking about, and, yes, she was hit over the head two days ago."

He shook his head at that. "She's a lovely lady." And then he looked at Doreen suspiciously. "And, if somebody hit her over the head, I would have gone looking for her next to kin."

"That would be me," she declared, glaring at him. "And I wouldn't hurt her."

"Maybe not," he admitted grudgingly. "I did hear something about you being an interesting character."

"If you mean because of my animals"—she pointed to them, even now staring up at him—"I'm getting a lot of criticism over that."

"I didn't say *criticism*," he argued. "Could be all kinds of reasons why people look at you as different."

"Sure," she noted. "And criticism is usually the first."

He looked at her and nodded. "That could be." He hesitated. "Are you the one who does all that detective work?"

"Yep, that's me," she said. "And that's another reason I'm back. I don't know if this is connected to my grandmother's attack or to something else."

He frowned. "It shouldn't be, but I don't know anymore." He fretted for a moment and then added, "I didn't tell that big detective anything."

"Well, this is your chance to tell him, without actually telling him," she offered. He looked at her. She shrugged. "I work with him all the time."

And then he chuckled. "I wonder if he would agree with that."

"No, he sure wouldn't." She laughed, giving him full points for having sorted that one out. "But it doesn't change the fact that I do often work with him, and I often get told off by him."

He nodded. "Yeah, I think you'd be quite irritating."

"*Thanks.*"

He shrugged. "What do you expect? People like you, who get in our faces? Like, who wants that?"

"Maybe I see your point," she murmured, "but, at the same time, I am trying to solve several cases."

He thought about it for a long moment. "I don't know who it was for sure, but I thought I saw one of my neighbors' kids in my garage."

She looked at him, a whisper of instinct prodding her. "And you know which one?"

"Well, that's the thing," he explained. "I couldn't testify to it, so that would be out."

"No, I understand that. Yet I wonder why he would have been in your garage."

"I figured he was after something quick and easy to sell."

"But you've said that you don't keep anything in there."

"No, I sure don't," he confirmed, "but I'm not sure he knew that."

She thought about it. "And do you know what his name is?"

"Why?" he asked. "So you'll go talk to him?"

"Maybe. Do you know anything about him?"

He shrugged. "I know he works in Rutland."

She stared at him. "And how do you know that?"

He looked at her before deciding to share more. "Because, at one point in time, I heard his mom yelling at him to bring groceries home, and he said that he worked at the store, but he didn't own it. So, if she wanted groceries, she needed to give him some money for it. Besides, the gas to Rutland was killing him."

"*Aah*," she replied, with such a wealth of understanding that he looked at her.

"Why?"

"Because the guy who was poisoned," she said, "worked at a grocery store in Rutland." And watched as all the color fled from the old man's face.

He hid his face from her, bending to visit with Mugs for a minute.

Her phone was in her car. She needed to call Mack and turned to head that way, although Mugs wasn't too thrilled about the idea right now.

When the old man finally straightened up, she still saw

the fear in his expression.

She shook her head at him. "Let me talk to Mack first. And we'll see where we go from here."

He looked like he wanted to say something, but then he pinched his lips together and just nodded.

She smiled gently. "I don't think you'd be in any trouble."

He looked at her hopefully.

"Again, let me talk to Mack." And, with that, she raced back to the car with her animals, and, once inside, she phoned Mack.

"What's the matter?" he asked.

He thought it was yet another emergency. She sighed. "You probably won't like this," she began, and then she told him what the old guy had figured out.

Mack swore on the phone. "Good God. I can't leave you alone for five minutes without you getting in trouble."

She stared down at her phone. "It's been longer than five minutes," she snapped. "And you're welcome." With that, she hung up.

When the phone rang a few minutes later, she ignored it. She was already heading to a whole new location. She was looking for Riverview Manor. And the man who had somehow convinced Chrissy to fall in love with him. As she reached the address, it looked like just another retirement home, although not quite as nice as the Rosemoor seniors' center, yet quite respectable. She got out, walked up to the front reception desk, and asked to see this Xavier person.

The woman looked at her. "He doesn't get visitors," she noted. "Not sure there's been any since he moved here."

"Maybe I'll be his first," she noted.

"And who you are?"

"I'm a friend," she replied.

The woman looked doubtful but shrugged and made a phone call, while just out of her hearing. A few minutes later she sat back down at her desk again. "He'll meet you outside in the back garden," she said, with a bright smile.

"Oh, good." Doreen turned back to the woman and asked, "Am I allowed to take the animals?"

"Because you'll be in the garden, yes," she explained, "but please don't go through the building with them."

"No, of course not." Following the woman's instructions, Doreen headed outside to meet up with Xavier. As she reached the gardens, she didn't see anybody, so she stopped and looked around. She wasn't even sure what this guy looked like. Seeing somebody approach who looked like they worked here, she asked, "Can you tell me where Xavier is?"

The orderly pointed to a resident, sitting off at a small table. "That's Xavier."

"Oh, thank you," Doreen replied. "I'm supposed to meet him out here for a visit."

The woman looked at her and then shrugged. "Whatever, he's harmless enough."

Doreen frowned. Maybe things here were a little bit different than at Rosemoor. "So are the members, the patients, the residents here," she asked, quickly cycling through the terms to find one that was less offensive than the other, "are they harmless?"

"Oh, yes." The orderly chuckled. "But you know, like every group of people, each one has their own little idiosyncrasies."

"Right." Doreen looked over to where Xavier waited. "Hopefully he's friendly."

"He's friendly all right." The woman laughed. "Probably

too friendly."

And, with that, the orderly took off, leaving Doreen to approach the man, sitting all alone on the far side. When she got closer, he looked up at her and stared. She asked, "Are you Xavier?"

He nodded slowly. "And who are you?" He frowned, not recognizing her, but then he stared at the dog, the cat, and the bird with her.

"I'm Doreen," she stated. "Nan from Rosemoor is my grandmother."

His astonishment went to acknowledgment and then immediately to suspicion. "What are you doing here?"

"I wanted to ask you a few questions about Chrissy."

His face fell. "Chrissy's dead. And there's nothing to ask questions about."

"Well, you're not dead," she noted, as she waited for an invitation to join him. Without one, she sat in the nearby chair, her animals right beside her. "And, if you know anything about what happened to her, I would very much like to know."

He stared at her. "Surely you won't go on about her being poisoned to death."

"I have no idea what I'll go on about," she replied carefully, "because I'm still not too sure I've gotten to the bottom of all this."

He frowned. "Well, if you talked to anybody at Rosemoor, I'm sure you got a snootful of information, most of it wrong."

"Maybe," she agreed. "I heard that the two of you were an item."

He nodded. "Until she stepped out on me."

He used a phrase that, in any other circumstances,

would have made Doreen smile.

"I never expected it of her. Broke my heart."

"And are you sure that that's what happened?"

"She didn't deny it," he replied. And then he stopped and frowned. "Well, she did deny it but not convincingly."

"And maybe she didn't think that was an issue and that you should have just believed her," she suggested.

"Maybe. But—" Then he stopped again. "I'm sure you really don't care," he muttered, "but she was very special. And it hurt me that she would do something like that."

"Well, the rumors that I have heard about it," she added, "are that she didn't step out on you and that it was just gossipmongering from some very jealous women."

He stared at her for a moment. "I had heard that at the time too, ... but I didn't believe it."

She nodded slowly. "You didn't at the time, but how about now?"

He winced. "It did occur to me afterward, after she was ... that maybe she hadn't really done what I thought she'd done. The trouble was, at that point in time, it was already way too late to change my mind or to ask forgiveness or to turn back the clock. She was already gone."

"Right. And do you think she died of natural causes?"

He stared at her, swallowed carefully, but leaned forward, then slowly shook his head. "No," he said quietly, "I don't."

Chapter 14

D OREEN LEANED BACK in her seat and stared at Xavier. "If you don't think she died of natural causes, what exactly do you think happened?"

"I have no idea."

But she was having none of that. "No, I don't believe you. You must believe something."

He shrugged, stared off in the distance, and then glanced around to make sure nobody was close.

"I know she was always telling anybody who would listen that somebody was poisoning her, but I didn't believe that. I didn't think of it, anything of it, until the day before she died."

"But did you see her then?"

He shook his head. "I didn't see her, but I did talk to her on the phone. And she was feeling pretty rough. But she wouldn't give specifics. She was already on a mix of medications and the doctors had been changing doses trying to get a better handle on her nosebleeds, headaches, even indigestion."

Doreen stared at him. "Nobody has mentioned anything about that yet."

"She was in her room, alone, and she hadn't gone down for dinner because she wasn't feeling well."

"And how is it that you two were talking?"

He winced. "I wanted to see how she was doing. I just had a bad feeling."

"And was she surprised to hear from you?"

"She was surprised. She was happy. I hate to say it, but she was almost grateful. And that just makes me feel like an even bigger loser. Normally I wouldn't have even called her, but there was just *something*, you know? Like, when you get that feeling, where you need to do something? So I followed through on that nudge, and I talked to her, and it was an okay conversation, I guess. I felt fine about it, and then, the following morning, I found out she was dead."

"And how did you find out?"

"I tried to call her again and got no answer. I tried for several hours that morning and still no answer. Finally I phoned the front desk of the home, and they told me that she'd passed away the previous night."

"And did you say anything then about her symptoms?"

"No, of course not," he stated. "I wasn't even thinking straight at that time. I was too shocked. I mean, I'd actually been thinking that maybe we could try again. I hadn't said so to her, but it occurred to me that maybe I'd been too rash— maybe I'd been too harsh. It's just one of those regrets that I'll have to live with now." He glanced around, leaned forward again, and whispered, "Do you think she was murdered?"

"I don't know," Doreen admitted. "The other option is a little less pleasant too."

He stared at her. "I don't think she committed suicide," he argued in a more robust tone.

"And why not?"

"Well, when I was talking to her, and she told me about being sick to her stomach, I think she would have confessed to me then, so she could get help or something."

"I guess it depends on whether she thought that you were literally being nice to her and maybe there was hope for you two again."

"I don't know. I didn't say anything outright like that, but, I mean, we were talking and happy and laughing," he replied. "She didn't sound in any way depressed or suicidal," he stated in shock.

"Maybe after the phone call," she suggested, eyeing him carefully, "maybe she realized what she'd lost and couldn't live with it."

He stared at her, and she watched the sickly gray color slide over his face.

"I'm not trying to upset you." Mugs stepped up to Xavier, rubbing along his leg. When Xavier went to pet Mugs, Doreen wasn't sure Xavier was even aware of the interaction. Mugs just didn't want Xavier to be upset.

"Good thing," he murmured. "I can't imagine if you were."

She sighed, wondering how anybody could gently talk to people regarding something so emotional, especially what could obviously end up being a very guilt-ridden issue. Thaddeus rubbed his head along Doreen's cheek, probably picking up on her stress too. "I just wonder what she would have been like mentally and whether that would have had something to do with it."

He wrapped his arms around his chest, a motion she hadn't seen very many men do. But his hands were shaking now, as if he had really settled into the idea that maybe he'd had done something to cause her to do this. "She kept saying that her stomach was hurting and that she'd been on the toilet a lot."

"And did she tell you that she thought she'd been poisoned then?"

"Not then." He frowned, looking at Doreen. "I didn't even think to mention it either."

"Did you suggest that she go get help?"

"I did," he replied, happy that he'd thought of that. "And she said that it should be fine, that she just needed a good night's sleep."

"I think we all have said something like that to somebody to push off their concerns at the time," she noted. "And you know what? In some cases that is exactly what is needed."

"Exactly," he agreed. "So I didn't really think anything more of it."

"No, of course not." She pondered what he'd shared. "And she didn't say anything about vomiting? She didn't say anything about a smell or her senses being off or anything like that?"

He shook his head. And then he stopped. "There was one thing she said that made me wonder at the time because it was such a funny thing, but it wasn't then in our last phone conversation. It was a couple months earlier."

"What was that?" Doreen asked.

"She said that she used to love almonds and that now she hated them. Even the smell of them."

"Did she say why?"

"She said something about how she kept smelling almonds all the time, and it, ... it had turned her off. Although she did admit that she watched too much tv and it likely was nothing."

"So do you think she would have eaten anything that smelled of almonds?"

"I don't know. They were a favorite of hers," he stated. "I used to get her almond cookies, and, even though they had a lot of fake almond flavorings in them, she said it didn't matter. She loved it all but once she started telling everyone that she was being poisoned she stopped eating anything almond."

"Right," Doreen noted quietly. "Of course, it could be a case of allergies that build up in time. Or just her sense of smell not working as well. However"—Doreen paused—"it does go along with the idea that maybe she was poisoned."

"And how do you figure that?" he asked in astonishment.

She gave him a wry smile. "Because some poisons can smell like bitter almonds. Cyanide for one."

He sank back with a look of horror on his face. "I don't want to hear that. I really don't want to hear that."

"Good. I agree." She stood, handed him a note with her phone number on it, and added, "If you think of anything else—no matter how slightly connected—let me know, will you?"

"Only if you do the same for me," he stated, taking the note with shaking hands. "She didn't deserve that."

"We don't know for sure that that's what happened," she clarified, "but, no, if that *is* what happened, she definitely didn't deserve to have her life cut short. She was just a lonely older woman, looking to find somebody as a companion."

He nodded. "And I'm just a lonely old man who's a fool," he snapped bitterly. "I should have given her a chance to explain."

"And why didn't you?" she asked curiously. It always amazed her just how much human nature kicked in and how hard it was for people to find the Reverse gear.

"I felt humiliated," he explained quietly. "Everybody had always talked about me having this way with women all my life." He shrugged. "I never really saw it the way other people did. I was just the guy who had lots of women friends around, but they weren't the one woman I wanted, and that became a bit of a problem, even at Rosemoor."

"In what way?"

"Well, because I really cared about Chrissy, and some of the other women weren't terribly nice about it. They were really nice at the beginning, and then, you know, it's almost like, over time, they showed their true colors, as jealousy set in."

She pulled out her notepad and asked, "Do you remember anybody who was particularly difficult about it?"

He stared. "They wouldn't have hurt her."

"Why not?" she asked. "You think just because they're in an old folks' home that they don't think about murder? Do you have any idea how many murderous people are in retirement homes?"

He swallowed hard, shook his head. "No, I really don't want to know either."

She gave him a knowing smile. "In that case, I'll save you the statistics. But the fact of the matter is, just because people are older doesn't mean that they don't have the same instincts that they may have had when they were younger. In a way they're even a little freer to do things—if they can physically do what they're considering—because they don't care about the consequences anymore. So who were all the women in your life that you ignored because you were with

Chrissy? And when Chrissy was gone, who was the first person to step up and say something to you?"

"That would be Laura," he replied instantly.

Her head came up, and she looked at him. "Laura Hillman?"

He nodded. "Yeah."

"And what did she say?"

"Just that she wasn't surprised."

"In what way? That Chrissy died?"

He nodded. "I didn't say anything about it. I was there that morning. I went immediately over to her place."

"And please tell me that you weren't trying to take anything away from her room or do anything like that."

He shook his head. "No, I wasn't." He sighed. "I just … it was such a shock that I wanted to be closer to her. I did see a bunch of people on that day, and I hadn't moved out of Rosemoor at the time but was in a hotel short term. So I certainly saw everybody, and their reactions were mixed. Some people, like your nan, were quite bereaved, and others were almost happy. I couldn't understand the happy part. Some of them were just smug, said it served her right, that she shouldn't have been carrying on as she was. I thought they meant carrying on with whatever male she'd chosen to replace me," he explained quietly, "but I never thought to ask."

"Any idea who it was who said that?"

He frowned, then shook his head. "At the moment, no, but it might come to me later."

Doreen nodded. "Anything that comes to your mind about that in particular would be good. And did anybody there hate Chrissy?"

"Several of the women did. You have to understand

Chrissy was one of those beautiful china dolls. And, even as she got older, she became more graceful, more fairy-like almost," he said, with a smile. "Whereas some of them got harder, uglier, *haggard*, for lack of a better word."

She just stared, contemplating that.

He shrugged. "You know how some women age beautifully and how some women don't? Chrissy aged beautifully," he noted quietly. "It was a joy to be around her. She got softer and more fun. Her laughter was very delicate." He gave a long sigh. "I really hope she wasn't murdered, and please, I really don't want it to be because of anything I did or didn't do."

"I hope not too," she replied, "but I'm still in the stages of sorting it out."

He got to his feet, and Mugs returned to sit by Doreen again. "I'll head back inside." Xavier looked over at her and added, "You know what? Maude said something too."

"Maude?"

He nodded. "Over at the home. She said something about it served her right."

And Doreen thought about that. "Yeah, Maude's had some interesting times in her world."

"She sure has, and she's not the nicest of people, so, in a way, I expected that." Then he stopped and added, "You know something else? One of the women I used to see before Chrissy"—he flushed slightly at that admission—"she worked in the kitchen."

At that, Doreen just stared.

"I've always liked women. Younger or older. It didn't matter to me."

"Sure," she noted quietly. "And, if that were the case, then maybe the younger ones didn't understand you choosing an older woman."

"Peggy is maybe sixty-five," he shared. "No, maybe sixty-eight. I know she was supposed to retire but couldn't live on the money that she had. Anyway, we had a lot of fun together, yet it wasn't a serious relationship," he noted. "Once I met Chrissy, honestly, it was all over for me."

Right," Doreen said. "And how did Peggy take it?"

"Terribly, but that was months earlier."

"*Right.*"

"Months and months earlier," he stated, with a wave of his hand. "No way it would have been her."

Doreen just stared at him for a long moment.

And he added, "At least I hope there's no way it would have been her."

"I'll probably find out soon enough," Doreen noted. With that, they made their way to the side door.

"I'll go lie down."

"Are you all right?" she asked. "You look a bit shaky."

He stared at her. "You do realize the conversation we've just had for the last hour, right? I have a right to be shaky." And, with that, he stepped smartly inside, leaving her outside with the animals.

She looked down at Mugs and said, "Guess what? We're heading back to Rosemoor."

And she and her pets returned to her vehicle.

Chapter 15

INSTEAD OF GOING to Rosemoor directly, Doreen headed home and had lunch and a chance to update her notes. As she sat here wondering about what to do next, yet knowing where she needed to go, Mack called.

"Hey," he said. "I got this really weird feeling about you."

"Oh yeah?" she asked brightly. "I hope it was a nice one."

"It was one that said you're in trouble," he noted in a dark voice.

"Oh, those." She frowned. "You should be used to them by now."

He snorted. "*Fun-nny.*"

She grinned. "I'm sitting at home. I just had a sandwich, and now I'm thinking about going to see Nan."

"So you haven't done anything wrong? You're not in any trouble? I won't get any phone calls saying that you're doing something illegal, right?"

"Not that I know of," she replied, with a bright smile. "Why?"

"Oh, just something I was thinking about."

"In what way?" she asked. "What could I possibly be getting into trouble over?"

"Depends which of these cases you think that you should be investigating," he replied.

"All of them," she stated. "Anything new on the young man who died?"

"No."

"What about the kid who worked at the grocery store with him and was the neighbor to the old man?"

"I talked to the kid today," Mack admitted. "He was working with the guy, Alan. The kid did know him, and they both worked at the same grocery store, which I find odd. The kid has been living at home with his mom and hasn't yet moved out, although his mother has told him to several times."

"Ah, and he hasn't moved out, why?"

"Because he doesn't have enough money to live on his own, apparently."

"Well, I understand that, but, if I can make it, he can make it. He at least has a job. And what was his relationship with this Alan guy like?"

"According to him, it was great. They were buddies."

"Interesting," she noted. "Did they hang out much?"

"Yeah, usually at the kid's place though."

"*Interesting.* Any particular vibes going off on this one?"

"Lots," Mack stated cheerfully, "but none that I want you interfering in."

She sighed. "That's fine. I'll stick to my case then."

At that, he got suspicious. "The only reason you'd do that is if you thought you had something."

"I have a couple lines to tug," she admitted. "But do I have something firm? Nope, no such luck."

"Are you sure?"

"Absolutely. And, by the way, if this guy was friends with Alan, any chance a girl came between them or something?"

"Not that I know of," he said, "but I can find out today."

"I suggest you do. Seems to be one of the biggest reasons for a fallout among friends."

"Yeah, love is one of the big reasons for murder too," he stated, "but for a young man like this kid, he must have one good reason to throw his life away."

"And maybe …" She stopped, thought about it a bit. "You know what? Could be something as easy as this Alan guy agreeing with the kid's mother that she should kick him out of the house. That would upset his lifestyle and the apple cart."

"Well, I think it would have been a lot more than that," Mack stated. "Remember. This Alan guy was being poisoned over time."

"Yeah, I find that interesting," she noted, "because it's like Chrissy too." She paused, then asked, "And how much poison's required to poison someone over time?"

"I guess it depends on the weight of the person and how soon someone wants to kill them, yet not be obvious that it was murder. Alan just thought he was being poisoned. He didn't say how long or by whom or in what way."

"Probably didn't know any details yet," Doreen suggested.

"Maybe not, at least not enough to share with anyone."

"So nothing on my intruder yet?" she asked.

"Not yet. Anyway," Mack added, "I have to go." And, with that, he hung up.

Doreen stared down at the phone, thought about it for a long moment, and then contacted Nan. Her grandmother answered in a bright, cheerful voice. "Good," Doreen said. "It sounds like you're feeling better."

"I've been playing bocce balls," she shared. "Outside of a bit of a headache from the sun, I'm doing fine."

Doreen frowned at that.

"Stop frowning," her grandmother ordered through the phone.

Doreen laughed. "How did you know I was frowning?"

"Because I mentioned a headache, and immediately you went quiet. I knew you would start to worry."

"I just want to make sure that you're doing okay after getting hit over the head," she stated. "You know it'll break my heart if anything happens to you."

"I do," she agreed, "and that, believe me, makes me feel tons better to know that you worry about me, but I'm okay. So nothing to be worried about here."

"Well, I'm glad to hear that," she replied. "Do you know Peggy?"

"Yes, she works in the kitchen. Why?"

"Oh, I was just wondering. I'm trying to figure out how to get a few moments to talk to her. Whether she's the friendly kind or maybe not so friendly."

"Peggy is pretty friendly. Honestly, she's often here in the common area, trying to get away from the kitchen for a few minutes. If you want, I can ask her to come down and to have a cup of tea, and you could casually pop on by."

She laughed. "Well, I was thinking about *casually popping on by* anyway, so that just might work." Their call ended, and she looked down at the animals. Goliath lay on the kitchen table beside her, disgruntled that her plate was empty. She hadn't even offered him a piece of cheese or anything. She reached over and stroked the beautiful golden fur. "Sorry, bud."

He just glared at her, hopped off the table, and sauntered into the living room, where he threw himself down in the hallway. She sighed, as Mugs stared up at her, his tail wagging like crazy, as if waiting for his treat. "Wow, I really just ate that and didn't even think about you guys, did I?"

She got up, walked over, sliced a piece of cheese, split it into thirds, and gave one to each of them. Thaddeus looked at it, his head cocking from side to side, and then picked it up with his beak and walked in front of Mugs, who followed him, trying to get it away from him. But Thaddeus wasn't having anything to do with that. He flew up to his roost in the living room, and both Goliath and Mugs sat on the floor, staring at the bird, while he crowed with this thing in his mouth, finally managing to eat it.

She distributed the rest of the cheese and watched all of them and their antics, while eating the cheese, then asked, "You want to go to Nan's?"

Mugs barked and did circles, chasing his tail. Goliath stood, just to throw himself on the ground again, this time with his tail twitching as he stared at her.

"Well, Goliath, you can stay here, if you want." Doreen walked over at Thaddeus to get his reply. "Thaddeus loves Nan," he cawed at Doreen and hopped onto her shoulder and rubbed against her cheek.

"Well," she added, "Doreen loves Thaddeus."

He cuddled up against her neck and whispered, "Thaddeus loves Doreen."

She smiled, grabbed the leashes, but Goliath was just looking at her like, *Don't bother.* She shrugged, hooked up

Mugs, opened the kitchen door, and stepped outside. Just at the last second before the door closed, Goliath raced through and out the door. She quickly set the alarms and shut the door, remembering Mack's warning about the intruder last time. The whole intruder thing just bothered her because there was absolutely no reason for anybody to come into her house to get something.

As she headed down to the river, she stopped to look at the water, finding a sense of peace that it always brought her. It was really shallow though, so theoretically, if she weren't on her way to see Nan, she could sit here and spend a few hours. She looked down at Mugs. "When we get back," she promised.

And, with that, she started in the direction of Nan's. The animals were well accustomed to this pathway. They'd probably dug in a lot of this groove just with their own footprints. As she walked, she looked at all the fences and the beautiful rocks and just admired the area itself; it was so pretty. She really loved it. If they put a proper pathway in here, it would ruin it for her. It would also make it a lot more accessible to other people.

A certain number of kids and strangers were always wandering through the area as it was, but to have it as a proper pathway for the public would be hard for Doreen. She wanted to see more of Mother Nature every day, not less. And she was doing pretty well with that, considering her walks with the animals and her gardening, whether her own or for others. *I need to check on Millicent's garden*, she reminded herself.

With that thought, she looked down at her phone, wondering if she should contact Nick, Mack's brother. She quickly sent him a text, asking how her divorce settlement papers were going. But instead of getting a text back, he phoned. She wondered as she answered, "Hey."

"I've been trying to get a hold of you," he stated. "I was really surprised when I got your text."

"Mack said something about that," she noted. "I haven't been avoiding you."

"No, because you've been leaving me all kinds of messages, so I gather we just haven't connected."

"I guess so," she agreed, "and, once I get on a case, you know I can get really focused."

"You mean, *obsessed*?"

She snorted. "Yeah, you're Mack's brother all right."

He chuckled. "I am, indeed. Now the question is, have you got a moment?"

"I'm on my way to Nan's," she said. "And we're meeting up with somebody else, so I have just the duration of this walk."

"Ah," he noted.

"Where are we at with the divorce?"

"Your husband's refusing to deal with the property division."

"Of course he is," she stated, with a sigh. "So where does that leave us?"

"We can have it presented to a judge and see what he says, and I think, if we get that far, your husband would cave in because, by law, you should get half of everything."

"Seriously?" she asked. "You know he'll never let that happen."

"Which is one of the reasons why I wanted to bring it up. Do you feel like you would be in danger if we did this?"

"Absolutely," she cried out. "You don't understand what he's like. I mean, as far as he's concerned, what's his is his, and I'm no longer his, but, boy, oh boy, he sure will control what I get."

"The thing is," Nick explained, "the way the divorce works in this province, you are entitled to half of everything."

"Even if I don't want it?"

"No, you may not want it in theory, but he's not giving you a very good option."

"And that's because he doesn't think we'll go through with it. That I'm just bluffing or don't know the law or whatever."

"Exactly," he stated in a cheerful voice. "So I suggest that he keeps on thinking that, and I will file to have this settled in court, and I know that you'll still get a fair shake before a judge, even if it's not quite half. And your husband will have to fight long and hard to not give you that much."

"Interesting," she murmured. "You know that I never wanted half, right?"

"I know that, but you must have something to live off of. And you did a lot to aid your husband's business during your marriage. Plus, you were married for a long time. You assisted him in his business dealings for fourteen years."

"Right," she said, with a sigh. "I mean, if he'd even offered me a decent amount when he first kicked me out, I would have been okay with that."

"The thing is, what you consider *a decent amount* and what I consider a decent amount and what I know you'll need for the rest of your life are all different. He is wealthy," Nick stated quietly. "As in mega-megawealthy. To give you enough to live on for the rest of your life, he wouldn't even note the lack of it. He would have absolutely no problem financially giving you several million dollars."

She froze in her tracks. "Seriously?"

"Absolutely. And that's the thing. The judge will see that as well, and he will make sure that you're well taken care of."

She gasped. "Oh my God, I think he'd try to kill me over that much for sure."

There was silence on the other end of the phone. "Now that wouldn't make anybody happy," Nick finally said. "But you do have direct access to Mack, and, if at any time you feel threatened or in danger, don't hesitate to speak to him." He paused. He didn't get any response from her. "Doreen? Promise me."

She knew she should do this. "I promise. I will contact Mack if I'm scared."

"Good," Nick said, blowing out a breath. "At the same time, I don't want you to buckle under his threats. He is a bully, as you well know."

"Has he threatened anybody yet?" she asked. "Like you?"

"You ask that like it's a guaranteed reaction."

"If you could lose millions of dollars, and you thought you already had the divorce matter sewn up ..." She stopped, not sure how to get Nick to understand.

"Well, that'll be another reason—two, three reasons— why the judge doesn't go easy on him," he added. "Besides his greed and failure to disburse marital assets, plus the improper lawyer conduct in reaching the original divorce settlement, which the judge will hear all about, there is also your husband's physical and verbal abuse of you during said marriage, his marital affair, even stalking you here."

"Oh my. Look. I don't, ... I don't even know what to say," she replied, as she started walking again.

"Well, just let me handle it, and we'll see if we can get your husband to bring in a decent offer. Because he will know, especially with his new lawyer's advice, what'll happen in the court, so I suspect he'll come up with a much healthier offer for you. I'll keep you apprised." And Nick hung up.

She slowly pocketed her phone. But it was a bit much to consider that a judge would let her have millions of dollars. She still thought of it as his money, mostly because he had always made it clear to her that it was his money. And yet, as Nick reminded her, they'd been married for fourteen years. She deserved something from that. Doreen shook her head. "I was an idiot and a fool," she said out loud, "but I don't want to be a fool anymore."

She also didn't want to take what wasn't hers rightfully, and, because of the way he had kept her so enmeshed, so controlled, so verbally belittled during their marriage, it was hard for her to see if any of it was hers or if she was entitled to any of it. But to consider that he can give away that kind of money and not have it hurt him in any way, shape, or form financially, well, that was a bit too greedy for her. The least he could do was share.

But this man didn't have a generous bone in his body. In his mind, it was his money, and she wasn't entitled to any of it.

She arrived at Nan's, still confused and off-center. As she stepped onto the small patio, she heard voices inside.

Chapter 16

DOREEN STEPPED INSIDE, calling out, "Hey, Nan."
Nan bounded to her feet from the couch. "There
you are," she said. "How nice to see you and the animals."

Doreen gave her grandmother a hug. Then Nan had to
pet all the animals. Doreen noted an older woman sitting on
a chair. She smiled at her. "Hi. I'm Doreen, Nan's granddaughter."

The woman looked at her and gave her a beaming smile.
"She talks so much about you," she said warmly. "I'm Peggy.
I work in the kitchen here. I'm just taking a few minutes to
get off my feet." She waved at her obviously swollen ankles.

Doreen took one look and winced. "Ouch, they look
very sore."

"They are," she confirmed. "My doctor wants me to get
a different job, and I just want to retire. But, hey, neither
one of us will get what we want. So there it is."

"I'm sorry." Doreen nodded. "I certainly know what it's
like to not have enough money."

At that, Peggy stared at her and asked, "But do you?"

The money conversation was guaranteed to upset people
either way, so Doreen backtracked. "Obviously each situa-

tion is different. I hope you come up with a solution soon."

"I thought I had a solution," she added, with a heavy sigh, "but it wasn't to be." Peggy looked over at Doreen. "Nan probably won't want to share," she teased, "but I did bring over some almond croissants."

And Doreen's nose twitched, as she could smell it. "Oh, wow. The food here's been absolutely marvelous. Anytime I've had a chance to try it, I love it." She winced, looking over at Nan, realizing that Doreen probably shouldn't say anything about all the food that she was getting here.

"Oh, that's nice of you to say," Peggy replied. "We do work hard in the kitchens. Sometimes the recipes work better than others, but most of the time we can hit everybody's favorite dishes without too much trouble." She chuckled. "I understand Nan gave you some assorted croissants the other day."

"Oh, yes, she did. I hope that doesn't get her into trouble."

"Oh no, not at all," Peggy said.

Nan got up and announced, "I'll go put on the teakettle. Peggy brought a few treats with her, so we'll sit outside and have them."

"That was very nice of you," Doreen told Peggy, as Nan disappeared. She looked over at the other woman. "I know my grandmother gets quite lonely here sometimes," she mentioned in a lowered voice. "So thank you for taking the time to visit."

Peggy nodded, a conspiratorial look on her face. "That's all right. We look after one another in this place," she said gently. "Your nan's a beautiful person."

"She really is," Doreen agreed. "She's got a heart of gold too."

And, with that, Nan popped back in again. "Let's sit out on the patio."

As they got up, Peggy looked at Nan and asked, "Where are the cookies I gave you?"

Nan flushed. "I ate them for breakfast," she admitted. She rubbed her hands together. "Chrissy gave me that wonderful little bowl," she said, "I put them in there. And then I scarfed them."

"What little bowl?" Doreen asked Nan.

She looked at her, walked over to the cupboard, pulled it out, and said, "This one. It's more of a large sugar bowl, but it's just perfect for a couple cookies too."

"I thought you gave that to your granddaughter already," Peggy said to Nan.

"Well, I am," she replied. "And I guess I forgot to. But you're right. I said I would." She handed it to Doreen. "Here. This is for you."

Doreen held up her hands. "No, no, no, no. I can't take that."

"Why not? It was Chrissy's sugar bowl," Nan stated. "I dumped out the sugar because I don't add sugar very often to my tea, but I so wanted to give it to you. Then after all this discussion about what happened to Chrissy, I just hung on to it."

"And so you should hang on to it," Doreen stated firmly. "It's much more important that you hang on to it for memories' sake."

At that, her grandmother just put it back in the cupboard. "I'll think about it." She gave an eye roll, as she looked over at Peggy. "I'm just a foolish old woman."

"You really liked Chrissy, didn't you?" Peggy asked.

At that, Nan nodded. "I did, indeed. She was always

really nice to me."

Peggy didn't say anything to that, and they made tea, sat down, and Doreen turned to Peggy and asked, "How long have you worked here?"

"About ten years," she said, with a smile. "Seems like a lifetime. I wanted to move in here, once I retired. But I don't think I'll have the money."

"Oh my." Doreen frowned. "Surely they could give you a break on the price, after you worked here all these years."

She looked at her. "You know what? I never even thought of that."

"I'd ask them," Doreen suggested. "I don't know what your situation is like, but, if you're close to retirement age or something along that line, you might talk to them about part-time work, in exchange for some of your care."

Peggy stared at Doreen. "I really hadn't considered any of that," she muttered. "Maybe I'll talk to them later," she stated, giving Doreen another odd look.

She shrugged. "I'm all about making things work."

"Glad to hear it, but you're right. I hadn't even thought of it."

At that, Nan jumped in. "My granddaughter, she's got quite a brain on her," she stated proudly.

"*Hah*," Doreen said. "Sometimes I think I'm out to lunch."

At that, Peggy laughed. "That's me all the time. You think you're okay, and then one day you just wake up and do something foolish, and you think, *What was that all about?*"

"Exactly." Doreen nodded.

They had a nice visit, and then Peggy stood. "I've got to run and to get back to work." She looked down at the empty plates. "I'll see if I can bring you a few more croissants later today," she said to Nan. "Doreen here's eaten them all."

At that, Doreen flushed. "I guess I was hungry." She winced. "I'm sorry. I had a sandwich at home, but the croissants are just always so good here."

"Absolutely they are." Peggy smiled, turned, and left.

At soon as she was gone, Nan leaned forward. "What do you think?"

"What do you mean, what do I think?" Doreen asked.

"Do you think Peggy killed Chrissy?"

Doreen stared at her grandmother, considering that question. "I'm not sure. She seems nice enough. And I did meet with Xavier this morning," she shared. "I really can't say that I see Xavier and Peggy as a couple."

At that, Nan nodded wisely. "None of us did. But Xavier confirmed they were dating?"

"He said that they were friendly, but, once he met Chrissy, it was all over for him."

"You know what? That's quite true. That's how I saw Xavier and Chrissy too. He very much fell in love, and, after that, I don't think it would have mattered who he had been seeing, if he actually was seeing Peggy in that way," Nan explained. "And I'm not saying there's anything wrong with Peggy, but you understand that Chrissy was quite beautiful, inside and out."

"I do understand that. Xavier thought she was gorgeous."

At that, Nan looked at her and nodded. "That's a very interesting comment, but you're right, isn't it? Beauty is in the eye of the beholder, and sometimes we look at couples and think, *What on earth is keeping those two together?*"

Doreen chuckled. "Yeah, like me and my ex."

At that, Nan winced. "I didn't mean that, dear."

"Maybe you didn't mean it," she stated, "but I'm not foolish enough to ignore the fact that, for a lot of people, it was probably part of what they were thinking."

"Well, it doesn't matter now," she stated loyally. "You're well away from him, and that's a good thing."

"It is, indeed. It's all right, Nan. You haven't insulted me."

"Oh, I'm glad to hear that," she replied, "but still, you should have left him a long time ago."

"*Thank you*, Nan," she quipped, with an eye roll.

Nan grinned at her impudently. "Anyway, if you can figure out what happened with Chrissy," Nan said, "let me know." And she hopped up, grabbed the sugar bowl again, and handed it over. "Here. Take this."

"No, I thought you would keep it."

"Oh no, I'd rather you had it," she stated. "I have my memories."

With that, Doreen accepted the sugar bowl, not sure what she should do with it.

Nan added, "I don't think it's gold, dear, but I think you could probably sell it."

At that, Doreen burst out laughing. "Nan, are you just taking things from your friends in order for me to make a few bucks?"

She nodded. "It is an antique. She bought it because I told her to, many years ago," she admitted. "So, by rights, I didn't have a problem accepting it back. Her nephew gave it to me to remember her by."

"Okay." And Doreen leaned over, gave her grandmother a kiss. "I'll see you tomorrow or the next day." And she called out to the animals, "Come on, guys. Let's go home."

And, with that, all of them got to their feet, looking a little more tired than normal.

She smiled down at them. "Okay, we'll go home, and we'll stay home this time."

At that, Mugs barked, and they headed across the lawn, calling goodbye to Nan.

Chapter 17

DOREEN POCKETED THE sugar bowl, and she and her animals headed back to her house. Doreen considered everything she'd learned so far. When she got to her property, she stopped for a few minutes here at the river with the animals and sat on the bench, looking for all the world like everything had calmed down and was much more peaceful now. And yet she knew that she probably did understand what had just happened, and *peaceful* was not exactly the answer she got. When her phone rang, she sighed and looked down to see it was Mack. "Hey."

"Are you okay?"

"I am," she murmured. "Are you coming by tonight?"

"I can if you want me to," he replied. "Why? What's up?"

She shook her head. "I don't know, just a weird feeling."

"I'm coming by then," he said instantly.

She chuckled. "Thank you."

"I'll be there in a little bit. Have you eaten?"

"I haven't eaten dinner," she noted, "but I did just have some croissants, almond croissants, down at Nan's place."

Mack whistled. "Wow. I think I'm jealous."

"You should be. They were delicious." She burst out laughing. "So I don't really need dinner."

"In that case, I'll bring pizza just for me."

"What?" she cried out. "You wouldn't do that."

"You just told me that you're full."

"No, I didn't say that," she argued. "I said I probably didn't need to eat, but, if you're bringing pizza …"

"*Hah*," he said. "I'll see." Somebody in the background called out for Mack. And, with that, he hung up.

With her animals in tow, she headed up to the house and put on coffee. He hadn't exactly given her a time frame, but she carefully pulled the sugar bowl from her pocket and sat it on the counter and phoned Xavier. It took a few minutes to get through to him, and then she had to explain who she was.

"Oh, right. Did you find out something already?"

"I just wanted to ask you a couple questions," she explained. "Did Chrissy have a sugar bowl she used all the time?"

"Oh my yes, it was an antique," he replied. "At least she thought it was. I wasn't so sure." He added, "A friend of hers recommended it as being a good investment, so she bought it. And she used it all the time."

"Interesting. But what did she use it for?"

"She was a tea drinker, and she added sugar to her tea constantly."

"Ah," she replied. "And what kind of tea?"

"One of those fruity blends," he noted. "I couldn't stand it myself."

"Any chance it had an almond flavor to it?"

He stopped and then said, "You know what? It did, kind of. Sometimes it was stronger than others, and I never really

POISON IN THE PANSIES

understood why, yet there was never really a strong flavor to it. I did have tea with her once, but it wasn't anything that I liked. However, she loved it."

"Right. And did somebody from the center get the tea for her?"

"Well, she had to order it through them. Everything was ordered through Rosemoor," he noted, "so I don't know if she got it specifically from one place or not."

"Right." Doreen looked at the sugar bowl distrustfully. "Thanks for that," she said, and she quickly hung up.

She heard a vehicle drive up, raced to the front door to see Mack carrying a pizza box.

"Did you already have that in hand when I talked to you?" she asked suspiciously.

He grinned at her. "Hey, be nice, and I will share."

"But you weren't going to, if I didn't ask you to come over, were you?"

"Technically you didn't ask me to come over, did you?" he asked cagily.

She rolled her eyes. "We're quite the pair."

He nodded and dropped the box on the table. "You sounded odd on the phone."

"Yeah, it's always hard to understand what motivates people," she murmured.

"Ah, yes," he agreed. "Sometimes we find out things that we wish we hadn't."

"You're not kidding," she muttered.

He looked over at the table where he had the box of pizza, walked to the counter, grabbed a couple plates, came back, served her a piece and then himself two pieces. He handed her the plate and said, "Here you go."

She picked up a piece and took a bite.

Mack asked, "So what's going on that has you all in a funk?" She pointed at the bowl on the table. He stared at it. "Godawful ugly."

She burst out laughing, feeling a sense of relief at that. "You know that's one of the reasons I really like you," she admitted. "You're always honest."

"Well, it is ugly. I mean, I don't know what it is, but why would you want it?"

"It was Chrissy's," she noted quietly. "And when she and Nan were out shopping at a garage sale one time, Nan encouraged Chrissy to buy this, since it was an antique and a good investment."

"I guess that makes sense, particularly if Chrissy liked things like that."

"And, in your sense," she added, "I was thinking the same thing. It's really ugly. Yet everybody was oohing and aahing about it."

"Even Nan?"

"Well, I don't know. We had a bit of an audience when we were there," she noted. "Peggy from the kitchen was there."

"Don't think I've met her," Mack noted.

"Well, you should," she said. "You really should." And she took a deep breath. "You should take that sugar bowl, and you should get it tested for rat poison."

He froze, his hand holding a slice of pizza in the air, and he slowly lowered it, looking at her first, then staring at the ugly sugar bowl. "What the ...?"

"Yeah, that's my reaction," she replied. "Lean over and smell it."

He leaned over and ever-so-gently sniffed it. And then he bolted upright and stared at her. "Smells almost like... a hint of garlic."

"Yeah," she agreed quietly. "Not sure what rat poison smells like, but I'm pretty sure somebody was putting the rat poison, into her sugar. Possibly a little bit at a time, over months. She was already on anticoagulants so that just exacerbated her problem possibly eventually killing her. Plus, and I don't know this as the box is missing, but strychnine was used a lot in rat poison and it's odorless and colorless and doesn't take much to kill. And this was a very old box of rat poison and who knows what levels of poisons were used. It was certainly before the days of dyes and other additives now used to make it taste terrible to stop people from unknowingly ingesting. The old guy also said that his particular box was a mix of several that he'd just dumped into one so that explains several things."

"Good God." Mack stared at her. "But who? Why?"

"I think it's Peggy, the woman who I saw today." And she quickly explained the story about Xavier and Chrissy.

He sat back, munching away on his pizza, his gaze going from her to the sugar bowl and back again. "Did you touch it?"

"I did," she admitted, "but I held it on the outside, and then I did wash my hands when I got home." She sighed loudly. "I don't know how long it would take to test it, and then, of course, you'd have to come up with a way to prove it. Because you know that a lot of people at Rosemoor had access."

He put down the crust from the slice of pizza he had just eaten to pinch the bridge of his nose. "Crap!"

"Yeah, that's how I felt," she agreed. "Two other women were miserable about Xavier's relationship with Chrissy too, but not everybody would have had access."

"Well, what difference does … How would Peggy have access?"

Doreen explained, "First, she works in the kitchen at Rosemoor, but here's the other thing. When I got home, I quickly looked up her name and address, where she lives." She brought it up on her nearby laptop, clicked on the satellite view, and then stated, "This is her house."

He leaned forward, stared at, and said, "Oh, no, no, no, no, no."

She looked back at him. "Oh, yes, yes, yes, yes."

"No."

"Yes."

"No."

"Yes. Then I wondered if Peggy had a son living with her. If so …"

Mack sat back, looked at her, opened the pizza box, picked up the biggest piece, and shoved a huge bite into his mouth, chomping furiously, as he stared at the satellite image of Sarsons Beach and the house right next door to the old man who'd had the old box of rat poison stolen from his garage.

Twice.

Chapter 18

LATER THAT EVENING, after Mack had gone, Doreen was wide awake in bed, thinking about everything and how sad it was if she were right. There wasn't any way to know for sure, but, in her gut, she knew it. She didn't quite know how it related to the young man, Alan, who'd been poisoned at the grocery store, but the fact that Alan had been to Peggy's house to visit with her son, Alan's coworker, was suspicious. As was the fact that Peggy's house was next to the old man's house. And Peggy's son could have been the one the old man saw getting into his garage.

Well, all that was just too coincidental, until they sorted out exactly what had gone on. But this was just way too much connection between Alan and Peggy and Chrissy. Even Mack had been quite perturbed by the whole thing. He kept swearing during dinner.

And finally he said, "You know that I was hoping to have an evening off."

"Yeah," she agreed. "I was too."

He nodded. "And, from that tone of voice, I can hear how sad you are."

"Chrissy didn't need to die. She could have had a nice

ending to her life, spending it with Xavier," she explained. "There was absolutely no need for somebody to do something like that to her." She looked over at him, as he got up.

"I have to leave," he stated quietly. "I'll check in with you, as soon as I run some of this down." He picked up the bagged sugar bowl.

Doreen nodded. "Yeah, you do that."

He stopped as he went to walk out the front door and then turned around, headed back, pulled her onto her feet, and wrapped her in a hug. "You have to consider these things, if you want to keep doing this," he noted. "For every time somebody commits murder, there's always a story. There's always a loss. There's always greed, envy, hate, or some other stupid excuse for taking a life. Always something shows up in these murders that will turn you inside out and upside down. It's the cost that you pay for looking into this stuff," he murmured.

His chin rested on top of her head, and she nodded slightly. "I know," she acknowledged, "but I still feel like I need to do it."

"I was afraid you would say that," he noted. "And I do understand. That's why I'm in law enforcement."

She tilted her head back, looked up at him, and said, "And you do such a fine job."

He rolled his eyes. "You make me feel like a fool constantly."

"No, not true," she argued, "but I have more time to do this, to focus wholly on one case at a time. I have some connections to do this, and I have some things that I can do to make your job easier."

"You think this makes my job easier?" he asked in astonishment.

"To help you make your job easier." She stepped back and added, "Go do what you have to do."

He looked at her and asked, "You'll be okay?"

"I am, until I'm not."

He winced at that. "I'll call you just before."

She nodded. "Before what? Before you leave?"

"Yes," he said. "I'll make sure you're all right."

"You probably should," she replied in an odd tone.

At that, he stopped and stared at her.

She shrugged and said, "Don't mind me."

"I do mind you," he stated, "and I want to keep you alive and safe and well."

"Good." She crossed her arms over her chest and waited till he left. And then she took a cup of herb tea and went down to the river's edge. She didn't want to talk to people, didn't want anything to do with anything, just to admire Mother Nature and share a little bit of peace and quiet. Mother Nature could be quite a capital B apparently, considering she put humans on this planet, and all they ended up doing was hurting each other. Or God maybe did that? She didn't have any proof either way, and so everything just seemed like conjecture at this point.

But, in her heart, she knew she was right about Peggy. Maybe that was just the voice of experience over the last few months of dealing with cold cases, as everything slowly pulled together in her world. And, at the same time, it had been, … it had been tough. She'd done a lot, maybe too much in some ways. By the time she wandered back to her house and went upstairs, had a hot shower, then curled up in bed, she still hadn't heard from Mack.

She wondered whether he was leaving yet or if he was still at work. She texted him, to see if he was still at work. He sent a curt **Yes** right back. She realized that he was still fussing with whatever it was he was fussing with. And that was a good thing.

She drifted off to sleep, her heart sad and feeling an overwhelming grief for Chrissy, an older woman who had just wanted to be loved at the end of her life. Something everybody wanted, no matter how old they were. Something everybody had a right to expect and to enjoy, particularly when they already had somebody special in their life. To think that whoever had transferred all that gossip to the person in Chrissy's life—Xavier, who was supposed to trust Chrissy unquestioningly—had been one thing, but to think that whoever, possibly even the same people, had worked to kill Chrissy, to make her pay for being the one chosen by Xavier, that was something else entirely. And it just made Doreen sad.

Finally, with a lot of effort, she fell asleep.

Chapter 19

DOREEN WOKE TO something wrong. Mugs growled right beside her, his head coming up off the blankets. Thaddeus slept soundly on the roost, and Goliath was stretched out, his face tucked into his paws. But Mugs? Mugs was not sleeping.

She raised her head from the pillow, looked at him bleary-eyed, and whispered, "What's the matter, buddy?"

He just growled again and then again, this time hopping off the bed and racing over to her bedroom doorway. He stopped at the closed door and looked at her, whining. She got up, grabbed her housecoat, and pulled it on her shoulders, noting it was only 11:00 p.m.

There was no sign of Mack yet, although she really didn't expect him to come over this late at night, not with him having such a long day at work. But she did expect a text. As she checked her phone, she found no further texts, and he hadn't tried to call either.

With Mugs in tow, she quietly opened her bedroom door, slipped down the stairs, and realized that Goliath had come with them. Thaddeus, well, he just stayed sound asleep. She wished she had because she knew she'd have quite the time getting back to sleep now at this time. But she wandered into the kitchen, and Mugs, not to be outdone, went to the back door. She opened it for him and let him out. Almost immediately he started barking like crazy. She stepped back as a man stepped inside, holding a gun.

She stared at him in shock. "I don't have anything to steal."

"I know, and how bad is that." He shook his head. "This place is frickin' empty. Like pathetically empty. You're worse off than I am."

She didn't know who he was, and she didn't recognize him at all. "I don't know who you are. Do you know who I am?" She wished she had some way to contact Mack.

"How could I not? I mean, the town's been agog about you, but you're not all that smart."

She winced, as she could hear the boasting about to come. "No, I'm not. I think I'm just lucky."

He nodded. "I'd agree with that."

"And I'm not sure what you're here for, but it's not here."

"Well, if you don't know what I'm here for, how can you tell?" he asked curiously.

"Because I have a good idea." He stared at her. She shrugged. "Your mother sent you to get a sugar bowl, didn't she?"

His jaw dropped. Literally. She'd never seen it happen in real life, but wow.

She sighed. "And you killed your coworker Alan. I don't even know why you would do something like that. I mean, what is it with this world?" she cried out. "You're supposed to be nice to people, and here all you, … you and your mom, all you're doing is murdering people. Taking out people who are in your way in life."

He stared at her, his head shaking. "Good God," he said. "What are you talking about?" But he'd already exposed his tell.

She nodded. "You know exactly what I'm talking about, and how sad is that? Did Alan really deserve to be killed? Did poor Chrissy? I mean, so what if your mother didn't get the relationship she wanted. I get it. That must have been heartbreaking. It always is when we lose somebody who we care for," she explained. "But to kill Chrissy?"

"Shut up," he snapped. "Don't you say nothing about my ma."

"Good Lord, your ma? I get it. You're just helping out Peggy, but did you have to go and take her methodology and use it yourself?"

"You don't know anything about it." He glared at her.

"I know that your mother told you to move out and that you don't want to."

"Of course I don't want to move out now. I can't afford to either. But that doesn't mean I'm not going to when I get back on my feet."

"Well, that's good to know," she noted. "You should live on your own. You know that, right? I mean, you're supposed to be independent."

"You don't know anything about me." He stared at her in disgust. "You just need to shut up."

"Well, I'm trying to figure out why you would do this for your mother."

"I didn't have a choice," he stated.

"Right. Because Peggy knows what you did to your friend Alan. But you also know what Peggy did to Chrissy. So what is this? Like a mutual admiration society?"

"No," he snapped. "Not at all. She was really angry when I found out what she'd done."

"And how did you find out?"

He shrugged. "I saw her taking a box of the rat poison into work and when I asked her about it, she said that somebody needed to learn a lesson. I had heard her complaining about Chrissy a lot already and then how she'd stolen Xavier from her. So then, when Chrissy died, I asked Ma point-blank about it. Actually I accused her of murder. And she had to admit that it was true."

"And yet you turned around and did the same thing to poor Alan."

"How do you know that?" he asked, staring at her in horror. "Nobody knows that."

"Not even your mother knows, does she?"

He shook his head. "No, I've been getting the rat poison box for her from the neighbor's. So one time I took a little container of it myself."

"Of course you did. And yet it was your friend, somebody who came over to your house all the time."

"Exactly. But he was getting sweet with my mother. And that was just disgusting."

"So you killed him because he was sweet on your mother? I thought he was a younger man."

"Maybe for my ma but not to me. Mid-forties."

"Maybe he wasn't sweet on her. Maybe he felt sorry for her."

He shook his head. "No, I asked him about it, and he said she's got a nice house, and she wasn't all that bad-looking. He might make a play for her himself."

"And you don't think he was joking?"

"I was sure he was joking," he replied. "At first. Yet I

could see him considering it, wondering if she'd go for it. And he started to flatter her a little bit, and she started responding. Like it was disgusting," he snapped, his face twisting. "She was obviously vulnerable and too dense to realize he was just playing and making a fool out of her. But what would happen if he succeeded?" he asked, staring at her. "I mean, no way I could let that happen. I mean, it was just gross. Not to mention he'd make sure I was kicked out and cut out of the will. He'd get the house and everything."

"So hang on a minute. You killed this supposed friend of yours so that he couldn't have a relationship with your mother?"

He nodded carefully. "Yes, that made the most sense. Besides, it was pretty easy to do. He always came over, and he ate with us some. Plus, we always had cans of pop in our house. And we mixed a lot with booze. I just dumped some into the can one day."

"Did you know he told the cops that he thought he'd been poisoned."

He stared at her. "He said that to the cops?"

"Yeah, he did," she replied quietly. "He knew. He may not have known it was you, but he knew somebody close to him was poisoning him. How long do you think it will take for the cops to find you?"

He just shook his head, wordless. His phone buzzed.

"That's your mom, asking if you got the sugar bowl."

He swallowed and stared down at the gun in his hand.

"Did you really think you could do the job with a gun? I mean, you've been killing by poison," she noted quietly. "That's something hands-off, not personal, not messy, and you don't have to see the results."

He shook his head. "That won't matter because Ma's

outside."

"Oh, *great*," she muttered, thinking about the large woman. "And now I suppose you expect me to do what?"

"Give me the sugar bowl," he stated, "and that'll keep her happy."

"I can't," she said quietly.

"Why not?" he cried out. He looked around, frantic. "I have to get it. That sugar bowl has to be here."

"She'll know which one because she mixed the rat poison in the sugar constantly." He nodded. "Did you ever think that she might do that to you too?"

He stared at her. "No way, I'm her son."

"Yeah, you are. If she ever got a life insurance policy on you," she noted, "I'd run."

"She just did," he admitted, staring at Doreen in shock.

She shrugged. "Your mom wants to move into Rosemoor and to retire, but she doesn't have the money. Although her house should be worth a fair bit."

"She'll never have the money for that place," he replied.

"It depends on how much the life insurance is."

He swallowed hard. And suddenly the kitchen door opened, and there was Peggy.

"What is going on here?" Peggy snapped.

Doreen smiled at her and nodded. "Oh, just Old Home Week," she noted quietly. "Just letting your son know what the odds are of him surviving this right now."

Watching Mugs sniffing around at the base of his legs, she asked, "And how is it Mugs knows you?"

He shrugged. "Sometimes when he's outside, this last week I've come in, and I've given him some treats. And some pats."

"I haven't even seen you."

"Besides, it's easy to keep some of your hair on my pant leg. A trick that my mom told me to use." He looked over at Doreen. "From your hairbrush. You almost caught me that time."

"Did you just tell her everything?" Peggy asked in shock.

"I didn't have to, Ma," he stated. "She already knew."

At that Peggy looked at her, stunned.

Doreen nodded. "Yeah, it was pretty easy to figure out. So you might want to consider what your choices of action are right now. Because the sugar bowl is not here. The cops have it."

She shook her head slowly, as if in denial. "No way," she declared. "No way a cop would even look at that sugar bowl." Peggy turned to argue with her son.

"Except for a cop who trusts me," she replied quietly. She looked down at her phone, noting Mack had been the last one called, and she quickly hit record then Redial and put the phone down on the table. The buzzer was off, but maybe, with any luck, Mack would realize that she needed him.

But Peggy was still berating her son. "What did you do?" she asked. "You realize you'll go to jail for life for this."

"You both will," Doreen cut in before her son could reply. "Although I understand that you think you're going to get away with this but you're not. I mean, you two each killed somebody. And the way it's going, like I said, I wouldn't be at all surprised if your mother here wasn't thinking about killing you next."

"He's nothing but a lazy layabout failure," his mom snapped, followed by a heavy snort. "The money he's cost me all these years, while he sat at home, doing nothing, didn't pay any rent." She glared at him. "I'd be in Rosemoor myself right now. Instead I'm still working, still trying to pay the bills. Once I sell that house, I'm out of there."

At that, her son looked at her. "You're not serious, are you?" he asked, his tone faint. "*Mooomm?*"

"Why not? It's not like you'll give me grandkids anyway. At least not while I'm still alive. You couldn't even dispose of that rat poison like I asked you to," she said in disgust.

"There are always rats at the lake and they come to our house too," he protested. "so I dumped it one of the garden beds figuring that would take out a lot of them. How was I to know old Gorman would find it and bring it back home again."

"How could he not. That crap is dangerous. You don't just leave it out where anyone can find it. What if a child found it?" She glared at him then twisted that glare in Doreen's direction. "And you. You're nothing but a pain in the butt. Do you really think I haven't heard all the stories about all the stunts you've pulled?"

"Yeah, there have been a few of them, I'm sure." Doreen grabbed her phone. Mack wasn't answering her call, so she quickly texted him—typing out **911**. She hit Send, right as Peggy grabbed the phone out of her hand.

"You just sent it," she snapped, glaring at Doreen's phone. Only to quickly add a second text message. **Just kidding**. She laughed. "Now he won't come."

"Yeah, he will," Doreen confirmed. "I mean, when there's a day that I kid, it won't be about something like that." She glanced at Mugs, who stared up at Peggy. Maybe Peggy's son had befriended Mugs with treats, but Mugs wasn't having anything to do with Peggy. He growled at her. Peggy looked down and kicked out at him. He just growled again, skittering away from her.

"Leave the dog alone," her son cried out. "He didn't do anything to you."

She stared at him in disbelief. "You need to shoot her. And we need to get out of here."

He glanced at the gun in his hand, looked over at his mother, and said, "Not me. I didn't do nothing."

"Except for killing your friend and stealing the old man's rat poison," Doreen noted.

He glared at her. "You need to shut your mouth about that."

Of course his mother had no idea about that. Something Doreen planned to fix. "Peggy, you didn't know that your son killed his friend *Alan*, because the guy was sweet on you, *huh?*"

She stared at her then spun to look at her son and roared, "You what?"

"Like mother, like son apparently," Doreen replied. "Or did you not realize that your son was using the same poison. And of course now we're all suspicious because there's been more than one death."

The color faded from Peggy's skin, and she turned and looked at her son. "Please tell me that you did not do that," she cried out.

"He was trying to get in your pants," he yelled. "It was disgusting. You were just simpering around him, like you were a sixteen-year-old."

She stared at him in shock, and then she smacked him hard on the side of the head. "Don't you ever talk to me like that again. He was just being nice."

"He was trying to see if he could move in and could take the house from you," he said, with a sneer. "But you were too hooked on him to even understand. And he was too hooked on the idea of getting easy money and an easy life, living with you. You didn't even see it coming."

"Of course I didn't," she said, "because he wasn't for real."

"Oh, he was for real all right," he snapped. "At least he would have been, if I'd let it happen."

"You should have let it happen then," she yelled. "It would have been nice to have somebody out there who gave a hoot about me." She looked at him in horror. "How could you do that, knowing that I was so alone?"

"Hang on a minute," he said. "Aren't you the one who just took out a life insurance policy on my head?"

"Sure." Then she stopped and added slowly, "But that was also Alan's idea."

He stared at his ma in shock. "Oh my God." They both turned and looked at Doreen.

Her eyebrows shot up. "Wow. I guess when they say, birds of a feather, they really mean it, don't they? I wonder how long before Alan suggested that you kill your own son?"

Peggy shook her head. "I wouldn't have." But she slid her gaze sideways and looked at him.

"Yeah, you would have," her son stated, staring at her. "Good Lord, I can't believe it."

He looked at the gun in his hand, turned toward Doreen, and held it out to her.

"Don't give it to her," Peggy cried out lunging for it.

"It's not real anyway," he said in disgust. "I'm outta here." And, with that, he turned and raced out into the night.

Peggy stared after him, the fake gun held loosely in her hand. "I can't believe he's even mine."

"He's yours all right," she noted quietly. "But the cops

will pick him up, so that'd be one less problem for you."

She shook her head. "Yeah, well, and then there's you. You're a big problem. I wasn't sure what you were up to at the visit today. Your grandmother's never once invited me in for tea."

"Ah." Doreen nodded. "Normally you just stop by to see certain people, is that it?"

"Yes," she confirmed. "I like to keep an eye on what everybody is doing, keep up-to-date, find out who's potentially got something to hand off, and who doesn't."

"Have you killed anybody else at Rosemoor?" Doreen asked curiously.

She shrugged. "No, but now that I managed to do it once, I was thinking that might not be a bad way to get a little bit of extra funding. Of course you'll kibosh that, won't you?"

"I will," she gave a clipped nod. "I have this thing about people treating each other nice," she murmured. "It's just, you know, one of those oddities of my personality."

The woman glared at her. "Now you're just mocking me. I'm not a bad person."

"No, of course not," Doreen agreed immediately hoping to keep her talking. Surely Mack was on his way, "but, if you were a good person still, you'd turn around and go to the cops and tell them exactly what you did."

"That'll never happen." And she took a couple steps forward, her hands fisting.

Doreen warned Peggy, "I really wouldn't attack me, if I were you." And then she remembered Nan's attack, and she got angry. "You're the one who attacked Nan too, aren't you?"

Peggy nodded. "I was looking for that stupid sugar bowl.

I never found it in that cupboard where she had it hidden. She told me later when I asked her about it that she'd given it to you."

"That's because she was planning on giving it to me," Doreen explained, "but she just never got that far."

"And now she did, so you have it."

"*Had* it. I've since given it to the cops," Doreen stated cheerfully. "So, even if you do manage to hit me too, it won't make a bit of difference. Because, boy, oh boy, we've already got your number."

"Says you," she sneered. And, with that, she jumped on Doreen.

But Thaddeus had finally come awake, and he flew into the kitchen and landed on her gray curly hair, pecking away and pulling at it. She screeched and grabbed him by the leg, throwing him off. Mugs launched himself at her, and he must have hit Peggy in the kneecap. She cried out and her knee buckled, going down to the floor.

By now Goliath jumped on her back and dug his claws into her back. Doreen just stood by and watched as the chaos ensued.

Finally Peggy burst into tears and called out, "Get them off me! Get them off me!"

Hearing a noise at her side, Doreen looked up to see both Darren and Mack standing in her kitchen, glaring at Doreen, before Darren jumped into action, cuffing Peggy.

Doreen pointed at Mack. "Don't glare at me. This woman attacked me. Besides, she killed Chrissy and was now looking at other women to kill in Rosemoor. She also attacked Nan, to get Chrissy's sugar bowl back. And her son killed your Alan guy up in Rutland because Alan was making a move on Peggy and her house. Believe me. We heard it all."

Mack asked, "Heard it all?"

"Yes." She pointed to her phone.

He looked at it and asked her, "Did you record it?"

She gave him a fat smile. "Of course I did." She turned to Darren. "Hi, Darren." And then she got closer to Mack. "I really need a hug." He opened his arms; she stepped into them, and, when they closed around her, she thought she'd never had such a great feeling as that sense of being home. She looked up at him. "We really need to find some nice people in this town."

He burst out laughing. "They do exist," he stated. "Whether you believe it or not, they do exist."

She nodded. "Well, maybe, just maybe, you should help me try to find them."

"And you know something? Maybe, just maybe, I can do that." And he pulled her closer into his arms and just held her tight. "I'm really glad you didn't get attacked this time," he muttered against her hair.

She chuckled. "You and me both."

Epilogue

Saturday

MACK REACHED OUT several times to Doreen to update her, to check up on her, then took her over to his mom's for midmorning tea. During which, Doreen hopped up, wandered around the garden, and made a mental list of things to fix.

As she returned to them, Doreen looked over at his mother. "I'll come by tomorrow and take care of those weeds," she promised, knowing how the ones right in front of the older woman's view bothered her terribly.

Millicent smiled gratefully. "Thank you. I know you've been busy with other things. Still, it does feel like I'm wasting your time, but I'd appreciate it, if you could come by."

Doreen laughed. "Actually, you're saving me," she said, chuckling. "I keep getting into trouble, when I'm not working."

Millicent shook her head. "What you do is very important," she said, "and it helps my son."

"Well, I try," she said quietly, "but I work in a much different way."

At that, the older woman nodded in full understanding. "You two make a good pair."

Doreen flushed and refused to look at Mack. "Well, we certainly make a pair," she finally muttered. "One who gets into trouble and one who tries to keep the other out of trouble."

At that, Mack laughed. "Isn't that the truth, but, even when you're supposedly out of trouble, you're in trouble."

"And yet I don't try to be," she said, looking over at him. "But sometimes people tell me things, and I guess my brain works in a weird way."

"A weird and wonderful way," Millicent said firmly. She chuckled. "And I'm really glad. It's shaken Mack's life up, and that's good. He was getting a little too set in his ways."

He stared at his mother in surprise.

She shrugged. "You and your brother both." She leaned forward and whispered, "Did you hear that Nick's looking at coming back to town?"

At that, Mack smiled and nodded. "That would be nice, wouldn't it?"

"It'd be really nice," she said. And then she looked at the gardens and sighed. "I sure hope he can make it happen soon."

Doreen looked over at her, frowning. "Did he give you a time frame?"

"No, he didn't. He did say that he'd make another trip here. He has to see somebody who's been avoiding him."

Mack raised an eyebrow and turned slowly to look at Doreen.

She flushed and slunk lower in her chair. "I wonder who that could be?" she asked in an innocent tone.

Mack sighed heavily. "Does he need to talk to you?"

"I don't know," she said. "There has been a phone message or two, but, over the last couple days, honestly, I just haven't wanted to talk to anybody."

He nodded. "And I get that, but you know if he needs you …"

She sniffed. "I don't want to deal with that."

He burst out laughing. "Yet you contacted Nick. And you know what he does for a living."

She winced.

"And he is doing this for free."

She sighed. "Fine," she said. "If he doesn't come soon, I'll give him a call."

"I'm hoping he'll come this weekend," Millicent said. "But I can't count on that. He is a busy man." She looked at Mack, at Doreen, and then again at Mack, back to Doreen. "Is Nick helping you out with something, dear?"

"Ever since my lovely lawyer died and left my divorce in a mess, your son Nick's been helping me clear it up."

"Oh, that's lovely," she beamed. "He's such a good boy. He's always willing to help."

At that, even Mack rolled his eyes. "Now, if you're coming back here tomorrow to work in Mom's garden, and you already have a worklist of what you need to do here, can we head to the beach today?" he asked Doreen.

"Sure," she said, bouncing to her feet. "You didn't mention that lately."

"Nope, I didn't," he said. "I figured, if I mentioned paddleboards, you'd run screaming in the opposite direction."

She turned and glared at him. "Please tell me that we're not trying that again." He just raised an eyebrow, and she sighed. "Fine. As long as we're going to the beach today, but I wanted to stop and talk to Wendy today too."

He looked at her in surprise. "Is she open on Saturdays?"

She nodded. "But you're right. It's probably a busy day for her, isn't it?"

"If it's money you're after, why don't you wait until Monday morning?"

"Fine. Let's go to the beach, get soaking wet, and … have some food," she said, looking at him hopefully.

He nodded. "I have a picnic packed."

She beamed. "Why didn't you say so?" she cried out. She leaned over, gave the older woman a hug, and said, "I'll see you tomorrow."

"Good enough," she said, with a smile. "You young people go have a nice day."

And, with that, the two of them headed out. Settled in Mack's truck, Doreen said, "I do still worry about Wendy." She felt more than saw his glance in her direction.

"Has she contacted you since?"

"No."

"If she's not ready to talk, … there's nothing you or I can do. It might be nothing at all to worry about."

"Yet, it felt … off. Wrong somehow." She pondered the little she'd seen and Wendy's disturbing reaction.

Mack pointed. "Behind Wendy's shop is Esther's famous quince trees," he said suddenly, taking his eyes off the road for a moment. "Esther makes the best quince jam and sold it for years at the Kelowna market. I have to tell you, her jam was 'the' product everyone bought back then. Even now, the market was and still is a lively place, and her jam? … That's the jam." And he burst out laughing at his joke.

"Quince?" Immediately an image of the fragrant pear-looking fruit popped into her head. "I thought they didn't taste great."

"They need to be cooked first, I believe. Honestly, I've never tried to cook them. The only quince I've ever eaten was Esther's jam. I've bought dozens of jars over the years. And those suckers trade like hot commodities." He shook his head at that. "I wish I could get her recipe, but she was crotchety back in the day. I can't imagine how she is now." He turned a corner and drove toward the beach. "Her place backs onto the alley at the back of Wendy's shop."

She looked at him in surprise, then giggled.

He shot a glance at her, a big smile on his face. "What's so funny?"

"We just finished *Poison in the Pansies*," she said, her laughter rolling out louder and louder. "Now we have *quince* in the picture. And *Q* follows *P* in the alphabet. So what kind of case works with the letter *Q*?" In between giggles, and Mugs woofing, and now Thaddeus cawing at the noise, she finally got out, "*Quarry*. That works. *Quarry in the Quince*."

And she went off in gales of laughter.

Indeed, it was a glorious day.

This concludes Book 16 of Lovely Lethal Gardens:
Poison in the Pansies.
Read about Quarry in the Quince:
Lovely Lethal Gardens, Book 17

Lovely Lethal Gardens: Quarry in the Quince (Book #17)

A new cozy mystery series from *USA Today* best-selling author Dale Mayer. Follow gardener and amateur sleuth Doreen Montgomery—and her amusing and mostly lovable cat, dog, and parrot—as they catch murderers and solve crimes in lovely Kelowna, British Columbia.

Riches to rags ... Chaos is down ... Everyone loves sparkly rings ... Some more than others!

Who knew a simple trip to the consignment store would find Wendy being strong-armed by two strangers? *So* not allowed—especially as it could affect Doreen getting her month-end check! Trying to get to the bottom of this is one convoluted story to sort out. It involves Bernard—an eccentric and handsome older man, who had a very young fiancée in his life—the breakup, and the resulting theft.

Corporal Mack Moreau is not at all happy with Doreen's new male friend, Bernard, who has the money to keep her in the style she was accustomed to. However, Mack is happy Doreen is staying out of his cases, if only she could stay out of trouble! Then again, Doreen can find trouble like this without any effort on her part. At least this time she also befriends another Kelowna icon, who lives behind Wendy's store and who is well-known for her quince jams and jellies.

Yet a big shiny reward from Bernard awaits someone who solves the theft and how it involves Wendy and the jam icon. Maybe—just maybe—that someone could be Doreen.

Find Book 17 here!
To find out more visit Dale Mayer's website.
https://smarturl.it/DMSQuarry

Get Your Free Book Now!

Have you met Charmin Marvin?

If you're ready for a new world to explore, and love ill-mannered cats, I have a series that might be your next binge read. It's called Broken Protocols, and it's a series that takes you through time-travel, mysteries, romance… and a talking cat named Charmin Marvin.

Go here and tell me where to send it!
http://smarturl.it/ArsenicBofB

Author's Note

Thank you for reading Poison in the Pansies: Lovely Lethal
Gardens, Book 16! If you enjoyed the book, please take a
moment and leave a short review.

Dear reader,

I love to hear from readers, and you can contact me at my
website: www.dalemayer.com or at my Facebook author
page. To be informed of new releases and special offers, sign
up for my newsletter or follow me on BookBub. And if you
are interested in joining Dale Mayer's Reader Group, here is
the Facebook sign up page.
https://smarturl.it/DaleMayerFBGroup

Cheers,
Dale Mayer

About the Author

Dale Mayer is a *USA Today* best-selling author, best known for her SEALs military romances, her Psychic Visions series, and her Lovely Lethal Garden cozy series. Her contemporary romances are raw and full of passion and emotion (Broken But ... Mending series). Her thrillers will keep you guessing (By Death series), and her romantic comedies will keep you giggling (*It's a Dog's Life*, a stand-alone novella; and the Broken Protocols series, starring Charming Marvin, the cat).

Dale honors the stories that come to her—and some of them are crazy and break all the rules and cross multiple genres!

To go with her fiction, she also writes nonfiction in many different fields, with books available on résumé writing, companion gardening, and the US mortgage system. She has recently published her Career Essentials series. All her books are available in print and ebook format.

Connect with Dale Mayer Online

Dale's Website – www.dalemayer.com
Twitter – @DaleMayer
Facebook – facebook.com/DaleMayer.author
BookBub – bookbub.com/authors/dale-mayer

Also by Dale Mayer

Published Adult Books:

Bullard's Battle
Ryland's Reach, Book 1
Cain's Cross, Book 2
Eton's Escape, Book 3
Garret's Gambit, Book 4
Kano's Keep, Book 5
Fallon's Flaw, Book 6
Quinn's Quest, Book 7
Bullard's Beauty, Book 8
Bullard's Best, Book 9

Terkel's Team
Damon's Deal, Book 1
Wade's War, Book 2
Gage's Goal, Book 3
Calum's Contact, Book 4

Kate Morgan
Simon Says... Hide, Book 1
Simon Says... Jump, Book 2
Simon Says... Ride, Book 3
Simon Says... Scream, Book 4

Hathaway House

The K9 Files

Lovely Lethal Gardens

Psychic Vision Series

By Death Series
Touched by Death
Haunted by Death
Chilled by Death
By Death Books 1–3

Broken Protocols – Romantic Comedy Series
Cat's Meow
Cat's Pajamas
Cat's Cradle
Cat's Claus
Broken Protocols 1-4

Broken and... Mending
Skin
Scars
Scales (of Justice)
Broken but... Mending 1-3

Glory
Genesis
Tori
Celeste
Glory Trilogy

Biker Blues
Morgan: Biker Blues, Volume 1
Cash: Biker Blues, Volume 2

SEALs of Honor
Mason: SEALs of Honor, Book 1
Hawk: SEALs of Honor, Book 2

Heroes for Hire, Books 7–9
Heroes for Hire, Books 10–12
Heroes for Hire, Books 13–15
Heroes for Hire, Books 16–18
Heroes for Hire, Books 19–21
Heroes for Hire, Books 22–24

SEALs of Steel
Badger: SEALs of Steel, Book 1
Erick: SEALs of Steel, Book 2
Cade: SEALs of Steel, Book 3
Talon: SEALs of Steel, Book 4
Laszlo: SEALs of Steel, Book 5
Geir: SEALs of Steel, Book 6
Jager: SEALs of Steel, Book 7
The Final Reveal: SEALs of Steel, Book 8
SEALs of Steel, Books 1–4
SEALs of Steel, Books 5–8
SEALs of Steel, Books 1–8

The Mavericks
Kerrick, Book 1
Griffin, Book 2
Jax, Book 3
Beau, Book 4
Asher, Book 5
Ryker, Book 6
Miles, Book 7
Nico, Book 8
Keane, Book 9
Lennox, Book 10
Gavin, Book 11

Shane, Book 12
Diesel, Book 13
Jerricho, Book 14
Killian, Book 15
Hatch, Book 16
Corbin, Book 17
The Mavericks, Books 1–2
The Mavericks, Books 3–4
The Mavericks, Books 5–6
The Mavericks, Books 7–8
The Mavericks, Books 9–10
The Mavericks, Books 11–12

Collections
Dare to Be You…
Dare to Love…
Dare to be Strong…
RomanceX3

Standalone Novellas
It's a Dog's Life
Riana's Revenge
Second Chances

Published Young Adult Books:

Family Blood Ties Series
Vampire in Denial
Vampire in Distress
Vampire in Design
Vampire in Deceit
Vampire in Defiance

Vampire in Conflict
Vampire in Chaos
Vampire in Crisis
Vampire in Control
Vampire in Charge
Family Blood Ties Set 1–3
Family Blood Ties Set 1–5
Family Blood Ties Set 4–6
Family Blood Ties Set 7–9
Sian's Solution, A Family Blood Ties Series Prequel
    Novelette

Design series
Dangerous Designs
Deadly Designs
Darkest Designs
Design Series Trilogy

Standalone
In Cassie's Corner
Gem Stone (a Gemma Stone Mystery)
Time Thieves

Published Non-Fiction Books:

Career Essentials
Career Essentials: The Résumé
Career Essentials: The Cover Letter
Career Essentials: The Interview
Career Essentials: 3 in 1

Printed in Great Britain
by Amazon

76095280R00169